CW01461091

DURAN

I Am No Emperor.

By

James Kilbraith

The first instalment in the Adventures of Duran
This is a work of fiction. Names, characters, events, and incidents are the
products of the author's imagination. Any resemblance to actual persons,
living or dead, or actual events are purely coincidental. It contains
descriptions of violence and some offensive language.
www.jameskilbraith.co.uk

1

Synopsis.

All for the love of a woman an adventurer comes to Earth in search of a long-lost artifact, unaware that back on his home world events are taking a sinister turn. Due to his position, self-assured attitude, and lack of respect for '*The Locals*', he finds himself in the unusual position of bartering for his freedom. While he sees this deal as no more than a minor inconvenience it soon becomes clear that it could lead to his death, the lives of many others, and even the loss of an empire.

For Layla, Courtney & Margaret

Contents

Chapter 1: Room with a view.

The view of Earth, over the lunar horizon was truly awe-inspiring. Well, it would have been to anyone who had not seen a similar thing, hundreds of times before.

The control room was dimly bathed in a combination of reflected light from the sun and from the numerous instrument and control panels. A slight hum could be heard from the air recycling vents as air was drawn in, cleaned, and pushed out again. If you had been there, it would have felt cold and frightening, but it was normal. A light started to slowly flash on one of the consoles. A few seconds passed and the cabin lighting increased. A door slowly opened on one of the walls to reveal an alcove. Inside was a small bipedal robot, it stood about one and a half meters tall, having the same build characteristics of a young teenage male, apart from the small fact, it looked like a robot, made from hard white plastic. Its eyes started to glow a soft blue as it stepped out of its little home. The robot walked through the control room towards the large open-view port at the front of the control room. It completely ignored all the instruments and controls as it already knew what they all displayed. On reaching the view port its head tilted slightly, looking out at the lunar surface and planet below. It had seen views like this many times, but still gazed upon them when it had time. Its AI trying to make sense of what the organic beings saw in all this so-called beauty and wonder.

More and more lights started to illuminate on various control panels as the ship started its warmup cycle. Again, the robot took no heed; although it could walk around the ship and even leave, it was still part of it, tied into all its systems it did not need to look to know all was well. After a few more seconds it turned from the view port and walked towards one of the doors in the room. Getting closer, the door dutifully opened, and the robot walked down the corridor towards the crew cabins. As it reached one of the cabin doors it stopped and waited. If it were human, it would have taken a deep breath and sighed, instead, it commanded the door to open. The robot stepped through and signalled for the light to come on, SLOWLY!

"Tar Duran ...... Tar Duran ....!", Said the robot in a surprisingly soft human voice.

"What!" came the reply.

"The target area on the planet will soon be entering its night cycle, and the ship is in warm-up mode. This is your wake-up call as requested; would you like me to arrange any food in the Mess for you?"

Duran sat up in the bed, stretching and rubbing as males do when they wake. "Yes! I guess we still only have space biscuits".

"Sir, I did advise you to pick up more supplies before we came out here."

"I know. Space biscuits, all the body needs but taste like shit. Get some ready, and juice to wash the taste away!"

"Yes Sir, it will be ready for you in the Mess shortly."

The robot turned and walked to the Mess, as Duran got out of bed and headed to the bathroom. The choice of words, 'arrange any food', used by the robot again showed how it was part of the ship. As soon as Duran had confirmed what he wanted the ship's Mess was already preparing it, all the robot needed to do when it got to the Mess was pick it up from the dispenser and place it on the table.

From the internal sensors the robot could tell Duran was about to enter the room, so with the air of a culinary expert he moved the food and drink to a table as he came in. Duran sat and drank some of the juice letting out a satisfying sigh as he finished.

He pulled over the plate of biscuits and asked. "Any updates from your scans, and have you calculated new targets?".

"Sir, my scans have not reported any suspicious change in activity. I have gone through the data collected and calculated three targets you can investigate in this cycle. We can do one, then a short hop to do the other two. Weather will be good on the planet; it should be a clear warm night."

Duran played with his biscuits. "Ship, why are you so sure we are looking in the right area?"

"The biographical data I have on Eachus Bede suggests he would have preferred a cool climate. Plus, records show he was dropped on this island, so it has the highest probability to be the right location."

Duran sounded despondent. "Needle and haystack spring to mind. How long until the ship is ready to go?"

"Marginal performance in another ten minutes, optimal in forty-five Sir."

"Ok. It's not like we are in a rush, set me up a light sparring session and aim to get off this dust ball in about an hour."

"Yes Sir! ... Sir, I have updated the linguistic database from my scans of planetary broadcasts. Would you like me to update your neural net with the five top spoken languages?"

"FIVE!" exclaimed Duran. "I already have enough rubbish floating around in my head, I don't need anymore. The only people I plan to come across will be stunned and I am not stopping to talk to them! Anyway, it wouldn't help much, they won't be able to understand me."

"As you wish Sir, I will update the mobile unit in your kit pack."

"Whatever makes you happy ship! If I end up needing to talk to any of the locals, I will have bigger problems to worry about than if we understand each other!"

"Sir, are you sure the inhabitants are as primitive as you say? I was going over the logs from last night's exploration, I noticed several scanning beams focused in my direction."

Duran cleared his throat slightly. "Ship, you worry too much! Yes, they have some tech but nothing like we have, if anyone gets too close, we have the jammers and stun field. Now shut it and make sure the sparring session is set up!"

"Forgive me Sir, but your father Borrel would have me broken for scrap if I didn't bring you home."

"In that case Ship, if I get myself killed you have my permission to fly into the nearest sun. Does that make you feel any better?"

"Sir, if I had feelings, it would not! You also know my base command directives would not allow this."

The ship was small but well equipped. It could carry a crew of twenty, although Duran was the only one on board. Normally there would be a compliment of five robots on the ship for maintenance and serving the crew, but Duran was an adventurer, and there had been a few incidents on his travels. He kept meaning to replace the lost bots, but who has the time and three were enough for his needs. It was designed to be a scout ship, very stealthy and black. A black, so black, the light just seemed to fall into it. It was very angular in construction, with no visible engines. It had two twin weapons pods mounted top and bottom.

As Duran sparred with a drone the robot stood quietly, it monitored as the ships main systems checked each other, going over data and double checking. This would be the third night they had been to the planet hunting for the relic. The ships linked AI systems could see no reason why the same plan they had used on previous nights should not work again. The data Duran had fed the ships' systems showed the inhabitants not to be that clever or advance. However, scans the ship had made when they first arrived had showed that information to be a little out of date, but none the less it had to accept its master knew what he was doing.

"Ship, remove drone, set up range!" commanded Duran. "Get me a side arm!" The robot moved to a locker and removed a side arm and charge cap taking them quickly to its master. Inserting the charge cap into the weapon Duran made sure it was on its lowest setting. He then started to happily blast away as the ships systems tried to catch him out with random targets.

Duran was a skilled warrior. He had spent most of his twenty-five years being trained by the best masters in the imperial palace. Fighting in several campaigns had been some of the best times of his life, but when his father found out he made sure all his generals knew it would be their heads that were forfeit if anything happened to him. 'Leaders led, soldier's fight!' was something he loved to drill into his children. His father Borrel was the ruler of a vast empire and for him duty and honour came before anything. This reflected in the upbringing of his four children, not the closest of fathers, but he made sure they were all prepared for their responsibilities. This had been made worse for Duran and his twin sister Alana. Their birth had caused the death of his wife and he found it hard to get over that.

The day Duran was told a wife had been chosen for him, was the day he left. His father had controlled his life enough and Duran had eyes for another. Time to decide his own fate, to get out and make his own mark on the galaxy before it was too late. A mark that would lead him here for a love that needed to be earned.

Chapter 2: We're going on a bug hunt.

The sound of a ringing phone awoke Taylor, only one thought ran through his mind, no way can this be work! At this time of the morning, it had to be…. He left it, he was on leave! He had been promised leave! They would only call if the world was coming to an end! He opened one eye; the world was still there. The phone rang again. They were not going to do this to him ….!

"Aren't you going to answer that?" said a groggy voice.

"Sarah if I do and its work then I will have to kill you!" Just then Sarah's phone rang.

"Ok, this can't be good." She said, grabbing her phone, she headed for the bathroom.

As the door closed Taylor's phone started to ring again. He picked it up and answered slowly and deliberately. "I'm On Leave!" he said coldly as he answered the call.

"I know!" Came the reply. "I'm sorry Jim, we tried to tell the bad guys that, but they wouldn't listen. I am sending you a location and codes, decrypt 7-3-9, be here ASAP!!" The call went dead, Richards, ever the tactful boss.

Taylor messed with his phone pulling up the message and then decrypting the details. Sarah came out of the bathroom. "Brize?" She asked.

"Yes!" He said even though he hadn't quite got that far, he knew they would have the same details. He looked over at Sarah getting dressed. "It must be a Thursday. I never could get the hang of Thursdays."

"I'm sure it's just another day in paradise James, you drive, we can grab some food on the way. Shift your ass, Richards sounded more hormonal than usual!" Said Sarah. "We should have known getting leave was a pipe dream!"

James Taylor and Sarah Stevens, both officially retired, but also extremely in demand. Ex-Military, they both had extensive special ops and intelligence training and experience. Anything that fell in their laps tended to be big!

Taylor drove briskly, but careful not to attract unwanted attention; the last thing they needed was to be pulled over. They grabbed breakfast on the way and arrived at RAF Brize Norton in just over an hour. From the gate they were quickly shown to a building and then an office, where they found Richards and a few other people they did and didn't know. Nods and waves were exchanged, but they could tell there was an uneasy feeling in the room.

"Taylor, Stevens, take a seat and pay attention! LIGHTS! Roll the videos, loop them." Sarah was right, he was even grumpier than normal. "OK, so this is the situation. For the past three nights a craft, presumed to be extraterrestrial, has been landing in the south of England. From what we can tell one individual then leaves the craft, investigates an area, and goes back to the craft. As you can see from tracking, he started on the first night by visiting two sites just south of London and has slowly been working his way west. "

For an opening, Richards had never done better, Taylor was no longer worried about his leave. Richards continued. "The second night he visited three sites and the third night two sites. We are going to work on the assumption he will do the same again tonight around this area, our intention is for you to locate and capture it!"

Richards looked around the room, enjoying the stunned silence and blank looks on people's faces. "All the information and details we have are in the files in front of you and on laptops we will provide you with shortly. If you look at the video and images we manage to capture last night, we believe upon landing, the craft projects some sort of field or pulse, that extends up to five clicks from the ship and temporarily knocks out all organic life. It also seems to disable some electronic equipment. This has unfortunately ended up in three fatalities, one drowning in a bath and two in car crashes. While we believe this pulse was intended solely as a defensive precaution on its part, we cannot ignore the fact that lives have been lost. As I say, we have been tasked to capture! Taylor, this gives you approximately twelve hours to assemble a team, come up with a plan and capture whatever this visitor is. You can have any personnel or equipment you can get within twelve hours but it all MUST be non-lethal. You're not going to like this, but it's come down from the top that the grab team are expendable. They would rather it escaped than be killed."

He was right, Taylor DIDN'T Like this at all. "So, you're telling me I have to go into an unknown hostile situation with no way to defend my team or myself?"

"NO!" Richards retorted "I'm telling you; you can have anything you like to defend yourself, but its life is more important than yours! LOOK, I am not going to waste time on discussing this, you are in or out, BUT This is the way it's going down! If you don't want the mission say now so I can find someone else!"

This didn't sit well with Taylor, he had never had to sell an operation like this before, then again, he had never had to consider this type of situation. There had to be a reason why they thought this way. "You know I'm in."

"Taylor, one more thing, when you are assembling your team, you can tell them anything you like, even that there is a one hundred percent chance they will die, BUT Nothing about Green Scaly Aliens until they are on site, GOT IT!"

"Yes Sir!" Replied Taylor. "Where is the part in the file that says it has green scales? I would prefer a straight up fight to a bug hunt."

"It Doesn't! I guess you will find that out when you catch it, NOW Get out! You now have less than twelve hours."

As Taylor and Stevens got up a man walked over and showed them to a side room down the corridor. Entering the room the man said, "I will be right outside, if you need anything just ask."

"Coffee, Lots!" Shouted Taylor as the door closed. Inside they found a couple of laptops, sat phones and loads of maps of the area they expected to be working in. Various files and photographs with luck everything needed to do the job, including a coffee machine.

As Taylor started to grab a coffee, he issued his first order of the mission. "Sarah, hit the phones, I want the first eight off the top of our list that can get here in under six hours for a ten-man team. Next, I want twenty of everything you can think of that's non-lethal. I'll make you a coffee."

"Ten-man?" Sarah asked quizzically. "Am I not invited to this party?"

Taylor slowly turned towards her. "You know what I mean! Yes, you will be at the party and if the other eight on the list are women as good as you then so will they."

Taylor sat at a desk and started reading over the files. "You know, whoever wrote this seems to think he is humanoid, bipedal but big, maybe around two meters and 100 to 120kg. Fast as well, wow for 120kg he can move."

"I'll order some elephant rifles in that case." Joked Sarah.

"Only if they are non-lethal." A thought jumps into Taylor's head. "Hey, not a bad idea, get someone to contact that monkey place and get whatever they use to put down a Gorilla."

Sarah looked at him with daggers. "Are you serious?"

"Why Not! They are what, an hour down the road and we need all the advantages we can get."

"Jim! At 120Kg, we may need a tank!"

A serious look came over Taylors face for a moment. "Tank's, that would be nice." He thought for a second. "I don't care what that dick heads says, I want a handgun and single mag for each person even if we can only use them on each other!"

Sarah Looked startled. "Again, are you serious. Each Other?"

"Hey, if something is eating my face off, I want a bullet to the brain!"

Sarah looked uneasy with this thought. Taylor turned his attention back to the maps and files again while Sarah started to make calls. He had half a mind to walk out, punch Richards on the nose and quit! Then the other half was slightly intrigued to know where this would go, and if he had to go out, what a way to go. How to capture a creature that is probably twice as strong as a normal man, obviously has advanced technology, who's position cannot be one hundred percent determined in an unknown time frame, all to be planned and executed in under eleven hours. He ran through the video clips. Again and again, forward, reverse, slow mo, fast, trying to gleam anything he could from the way it moved. He never looks back, Taylor thought to himself. He is confident his rear is secure.

Sarah finished making her calls ... "Ok, so I have eight on the way, should be here in one to four hours. Johnson, Stans, Carter, Smith, O'Neill, Davies, Jones, and Collins. All I've told them is it's a very high priority capture only Op, in the UK, with a ninety percent chance they will collect death benefits!"

"Ninety percent hu! So, you sugar coated the op, you're so bad! Still, nice group, they all work well together. Ok, get their details to Richards and make sure they have them on the gate. I don't want any bureaucratic hold ups. How are you doing with a kit list?"

Sarah pulled a list from her desk and passed it to Taylor. "This is what I have so far. I've passed it to the guy outside to get him started, what do you think?"

Taylor looked over the list. "Hummm, looks good so far. Get them working on two Hercules, four UAV's equipped with IR marker strobe launchers, head goggles to match. Make sure the drones are fitted with full spectrum surveillance. Ten Phoenix chutes and HALO Kit. Also, four Chinook's, two set up for full MEDEVAC and two for backup transport. We are going to need something like a cage to put this thing in and whatever we need to drop it to us. Oh! And whatever satellite coverage they had last night make sure it's available tonight, times two if possible!"

Sarah quickly took notes. "You do know the RAF don't fly Hercules anymore?"

"Ok Smart arse, get whatever they do fly!"

"That would be the Atlas Sir." Sarah said with a smirk. "So, do you know how we are going to pull this off?"

"I have a few ideas, just need to work out the details." Taylor moved to one of the many whiteboards around the walls and started to doodle.

As Sarah left the room with the notes Taylor quickly shouted, "See if you can drum up some food and more coffee!"

Sarah's head came back around the door. "And what is the magic word?"

Taylor turned from his doodles. "I'm sorry ….. That's an order!"

18

"Yes Sir!" came the reply as Sarah's head and then middle finger left the room.

Taylor turned back to his doodles. How WAS he going to pull this off? He started to get angry again. It was no secret he was in a relationship with Sarah, and he had always been ok with taking her on missions, but he was also ok with killing anyone who got near her. He had served with all the men that were about to arrive, they had all saved each other's lives at one time or another, but now! If the bad guy is about to kill my oppo! His thoughts paused, in his military mind all he could see was himself unloading on the bad guy, but he had orders not too! He wished they had a week or even a few days to train, to get used to the concept of 'the bad guy could not die'. He then realised he so badly wanted to leave Sarah out of this one. Too late for that, he had said yes! She would never forgive him.

There was a tap on the door and Sarah came back in. She placed some pre-packed sandwiches, crisps, and power bars on the desk, "Will this keep you going?"

"Yes, thank you, that will do." Said Taylor not really looking.

"A few of the guys have arrived, Any orders?"

Taylor looked up. "Errrmmm, get them down the NAAFI, make sure they are fed n watered. Don't tell them anything yet and try and keep down any speculation."

19

"OK, I will try but it has already started along with the questions. The kit has started to arrive, and we have hanger seven assigned to us. Everything else we have requested has been cleared and should be here in the next few hours."

"Even the side arms?"

"I decided not to put that on the list but let's just say they are in the hanger with the rest of the kit. I know someone in the armoury."

"Probably a good idea." Smiled Taylor. "Richards would not be happy! What about our elephant guns?"

"They weren't too happy about letting them go without any details as to why we wanted them. There were a few veiled threats dropped about safety and planning issues within the park, but I think the 50K donation swung it. We have two rifles and two handguns, each with two darts that have been loaded to put down a gorilla around 120kg. They even gave us some practice darts loaded with water."

"They will be handy." Said Taylor. "I haven't used anything like that in a long time. Make sure everyone gets off a few practice shots after the briefing."

"They sent up a safety guy with them, I'll get him to give me a run through to keep them sweet. The range on the handguns is five to ten meters and the rifles are thirty to fifty meters. I've also got four net firing units, range on those is only about ten meters."

Taylor tensed up and looked at the ceiling. "I knew this would end up as a close in fight. For all we know he could take us out at two hundred meters, and we wouldn't even know what hit us!"

Sarah walked over and put her hand on his shoulder. "I trust you. Your plans have always got us home."

"About that." Taylor looked her straight in the eye. "Are you sure I can't talk you out of this one?"

"I understand your concern, but it ent happening! You have never wanted to shut me out before and, yeah ok, this is not your normal op, but I need to be there. This maybe a once in a lifetime shout and I am not going to sit on the side-lines!"

Taylor knew that would be her answer. "Sorry, I had to ask, it just doesn't feel right not being able to protect you if shit goes sideways."

Sarah smiled softly. "Darling, if shit goes sideways, you may need me there to pull your arse out of it, and it ent like I haven't done that in the past!"

Taylor returned the smile; she wasn't wrong there.

"Look, the rest of the guys should be here soon, how are you doing with the plan?"

Taylor sighed, "I think I have it. Go check on the guys and the rest of the stores, let me know when they are all here and I will do a briefing. OH! One more thing, first see if Richards can get hold of at least one maybe two mini-EMP's"

"EMP's? Sounds interesting."

"Yeah, I'm not too worried about our beast, it's the ship that worries me."

"I'll get on it." Sarah got up, smiled, kissed him, and left the room. Taylor sat bolt upright in his chair and closed his eyes. He slowly calmed his breathing and cleared his mind. He started to visualise his plan running it like a film through his mind. Stop, what if, rewind, rerun. He has accounted for all the knowns and as many unknowns as he could think of. Well, he liked to think he had, there were just too many unknowns. As the saying goes, there are things we know that we know. There are things that we know we don't know. But there are things we don't know we don't know, and that's the part he never liked. He drew in a long slow breath, held it for a few seconds and then slowly let it out. He had done all he could for now, he would run it past his team. They were all good people, after the briefing they may have some other options to add, that was the way it normally went. The only difference here was this wasn't normal.

Sarah came back into the room. "We are ready whenever you are." Taylor slowly opened his eyes and cleared his throat. "In that case it's time to get to work, get them all in here, oh, don't forget Richards."

Chapter 3: The Briefing.

The door opened and slowly the men filed in followed by Sarah and Richards who sat towards the back of the room.

"Ok, OK! Please take a seat and settle down we don't have much time." Taylor said as they all found a seat and got comfortable. "Well, it's good to see most of you as always. Robo, I hear you have a few extra holes since the last time I saw you, you feeling ok?"

"Sex last night and a 5k run this morning." Robo snapped back. "I think I'm doing ok Sir!" Most of the men laughed and Richards rolled his eyes.

Taylor shook his head. "Good, Ok to business. First up, this briefing is highly confidential and top secret, I also have to remind you that you are all still bound by the official secrets act." This seemed to grab everyone's attention, it's not something they normally needed to be reminded about. "You are here to execute a plan to capture an individual that we have very little intelligence on, he has unknown resources, in an unknown area, in an unknown time frame. I Stress again this is a CAPTURE mission, to the extent that the lives of every member of this team are forfeit in favour of the mark. The only weapons issued will be non-lethal." Taylor slowly looked around the room at the faces of each man. "With that in mind I have to ask if there is anyone that does not wish to take part in this mission, they need to speak now. You will be held on base for twenty-four hours and then you will be free to go."

Jaz looked up. "Can you get on with it, I have a feeling we have a lot to get through and you're wasting time!"

"Ok, well once I start the briefing if you change your mind you will need to go through Richards, and I have a feeling that will not be pleasant!"

"Get on with it!" Shouts Sam, followed by similar comments from the rest of the men.

"Sarah, can you come up and run the videos and pictures for me." Taylor gestured to her. Sarah moved up to the desk next to him. "Run the landing video." He asked as she worked on the laptop.

"This! Gentlemen is believed to be the landing of a ship in the south of England last night. An individual then exits the ship and runs to two locations before returning to the ship. Intelligence believes the ship and the individual are both extra-terrestrial in origin. It may be up to two meters tall and around 120Kg. All we have to do is grab it alive." Taylor looked around the silent room at the faces fixed on the screen as the video played, there were even a few open mouths.

"How can you be sure its aliens?" Asked O'Neill. "How do you know it's not the Yanks or Russians dicking around with us?"

Richards stood up. "Yeah, I asked the same questions when this was brought to me last night. Trust me, confidence is high that we are dealing with something outside of the norms, and even if it isn't, it's another reason why this has to be a capture op. We have to know what is behind this and what we are dealing with here!"

Taylor got stern. "Guys, look, as always, we don't need the details behind the op, just the details for the op, OK! So, let's just focus. Richards, did Sarah ask you about the EMP's?"

"Yes, two are on the way, close in tactical two-hundred-meter range, they can be slaved for max punch. Arrival timeline could be tight. What are these for?" Richards asked.

"Thanks, let's just say they are a key part of the plan. I'll get to the detail in a minute. Right, this guy, and for the ease of the briefing, IT is now a 'he' or 'guy'. This Guy! Is big and fast, the fact we have only seen one going to multiple sites, we are assuming there IS only one. But that is a large ship and could carry more. So, we have to assume there will be a threat to our rear, even from the ship itself." Taylor could tell he had their total attention. "The next problem we have is if you look closely at the video, you can see a distortion wave that comes out from the ship just after it lands. This seems to radiate out around 5k. It stuns any organic life for about two hours and disables electronic equipment. This means we cannot be in the area when it lands, not that that matters to much as we won't know where it will land until about ten minutes before it does. I am working on the assumption this stun field cannot be used again once our guy is on the ground as it will stun him too." He could see a few of the faces were starting to show some concern.

"Gents, this means you will have to be at the top of your game. The plan I have is to get us into position, give us the tools to do the job, but only our resolve will get it done. For all I know as soon as we get into position ten or twenty more of these things could come out of the ship and cut us to pieces!" Taylor took a drink from a water bottle as he let that all sink in.

"This is the plan, when I have finished, we can discuss any details. We will split into two teams of five, each will equip and deploy to one of the Atlas. Dust off is planned for twenty-three hundred. Stevens, bring up the map. This guy has been slowly moving East to West so the best guess is he will land somewhere in this area tonight." Taylor used a laser pointer to show an area between Reading and Swindon on the map he was referring too. "Richards, I need you to make sure all air traffic is out of these areas and any military is confined to barracks for the night. Team Alpha will deploy to an area 10k north at ten thousand meters and circle. Team Bravo will do the same 10k south. We have four drones, two will be deployed 10k East and two 10k west. As soon as we have confirmation of the ships landing position all of our air assets will start to deploy to that position. We will have six Chinooks on standby here. They will be deployed with a force of RAF Regiment for back up, security and containment, they will follow in if all goes to plan. There will also be a medical team for MEDEVAC. As soon as our guy is on the ground, and we can determine his general direction we can plot his expected targets. In the previous landings these all seem to have been some sort of ancient site. One of the drones will then come in and lay a line of IR markers about two hundred meters from the ship and across his path, this will be our form up point. Each team will HALO to this point, team Alpha will set up on this line, team bravo will set up fifty meters to their rear. One member of each team will carry an EMP, they will detach from their teams and move as close as they deem possible to the ship. Their task will be to A, deploy the EMP if there is any perceived threat from the ship and B, provide rear cover if any more of these things come out of the ship, they will then be designated Charlie. Team Alpha will then engage our target supported by Bravo. Charlie will only come back to support if there are no threats to our rear. Our drone cover will monitor the target and update us on any change in track or behaviour, so we can adjust if needed." Taylor took another sip from his water bottle and looked at the glazed expressions on the people in the room. "If this goes to plan, we will take our guy by surprise and capture him. In swoops the cavalry and home again for tea n meddles." Most in the room had a slight chuckle. "We all know that won't happen! He is bigger, faster, stronger, and probably has tech we have no idea how to counter. Finally, we are expendable! He doesn't know that, but I am sure he will be more than happy to blow us away."

"Like Always." Scoffs Jonesy.

"Can IT Corporal!" Snaps Taylor. "YES! Like ALWAYS! You had your choice! Stow it! Get on mission or get out. We don't have time for crap like that!"

Jonesy stood. "My apologies Sir."

Taylor looked at Jonesy, paused. "Thank you corporal, be seated."

Sam had a concerned look. "Boss, if you think there could be more of them on the ship why not take in a larger force?"

Taylor sighed. "I had considered it. To be blunt if this were a normal op, I would like to take in a hundred men. But if ten of us can't stop a single guy, then we would just be looking at a load more body bags. Look, the bigger, faster etc don't worry me too much. We are the best at what we do, if we use our training and experience, I am confident the ten of us can take down this one guy. The only thing I am worried about is the unknown element of the ship. Ok, Any more questions so far?" Taylor looked around the room hoping there would not be any. "Team assignments. Alpha, myself in command, Stevens, Robo, Dex, Jaz. Bravo, Sam in command, Danny, Kev, Andy, Jonesy. Stevens and Andy will carry the EMP's and split off as Charlie as soon as we are all on the ground. Right, we have about four hours to get kit organised, training on special equipment and prep, let's get over to the hanger and get started."

As everyone started to file out of the room Sarah hung back. "Why are you protecting me, sending me to the rear?"

Taylor looked up slowly. "Am I? Like I said for all I know we could have a bigger threat there. I need someone I trust protecting my ass paired with someone I know will take orders without question. Sarah, you have never questioned me in the past, don't start now!"

Sarah took his hand. "Sorry Jim, this is a lot.."

Taylor jumped in. "I know it is, for all of us. But this is where you need to get that out of your head. This is just another op. We plan, we equip, we execute, and we all come home. You got that?"

"Yes Sir!" She said in a low seductive voice.

Taylor smiled. "Dismissed, go get the men organised and make sure Richards has all our assets in place, time is short!"

Sarah left the room. Taylor sat and drank some more water. He sat and closed his eyes. He ran the movie through his head one more time. This was it, the last time. The last time to second guess, after this everything was set in stone, well right up to the point it all goes tits. He drew a deep breath. That wasn't going to happen. Slowly standing, he opened his eyes. He was ready!

When he got to the hanger everyone was busy sorting, dividing, and checking equipment. He could see the guys were looking over and running drills on some of the more unusual kit.

"Listen up!" Shouts Taylor. "Stephens & Andy Get the EMP's and Taser. How many cartridges are there for the Taser's?"

Sarah picked up one of the boxes. "Should be enough for three each."

"Ok, everyone gets a Taser. One trank gun and rifle per team, one net gun, three baton gun's, one paint ball gun, two cattle prods."

Jaz cuts in. "Paint ball? This is sounding more like a play date!"

Taylor picked up one of the guns. "Jaz, have you ever been hit in the face by twenty paint balls? Most of this is for maximum disorientation. Hit him with these, baton rounds, flash bangs, wrap him up in nets and keep hitting him until we can get in close enough with tasers and tranks. Light him up with high power flashlights, we can see him he can't see us. Keep putting pressure on until we can put him down. I want to try and stay at least arm's length away from this guy until he is no longer a threat!"

Sarah had information. "Jim, weather update for tonight, clear, light winds from the south, half-moon. I am worried about some of this kit, it's too heavy to jump with the phoenix, I've got some other chutes on the way over so we can cut some of the heavy stuff loose once we get closer to the ground."

"Ok Sarah. Richards, do you have anything more for me?"

"I don't think so. Jim Look, I know you hate this, and I am sorry. Still if you pull it off you can probably write your own ticket. I'll contact you again from command once you are airborne and in your holding position."

"Richards, one thing, if, WHEN, we get this guy, before you cart him off to some secret black hole, I'd love some time to talk to him."

"Talk! You have enough trouble with English, and you think you can talk Klingon." Richards laughs. "Yeah sure, this I have to see." Richards turned and started to walk out of the hanger. "Good hunting guys, beers on me when you get back." He shouted as he left.

Taylor walked over to Sarah. "I'll need something stronger than beer after this. Where are the pistols?"

Sarah pointed to a small weapons case. "Over there. I have checked them over. Mags are loaded and with them."

"OK, can you discreetly give them out. Errmm, I dunno, find some way to make sure they understand how they can use them."

Sarah chuckled. "Well, that will be easy, I'll designate them as condoms."

Taylor looked around and shouted. "Ok Guys, let's get this kit on your designated aircraft, hit the head and get airborne."

Chapter 4: Contact.

"Duran, all systems are at optimal performance and ready to lift off at your command." Announced the ship.

"Good, lift at your leisure and take us in slowly while I get kitted out."

"As you command. I have laid out all your equipment in your room. Journey time will be about forty-five minutes."

"OK, I'll come to command when I am ready. Any changes in the area."

"None detected sir."

"Good." Said Duran as he stood and walked out of the training room. The robot followed to head up to command.

Duran got to his room and found the equipment laid out as promised. He laughed to himself, light combat again. It was nice to know the ship's AI worried about him, the first night it tried to make him go out in full combat. At one point he actually thought the ship was going to refuse to land. Duran put on the equipment, checking the contents of his kit bag, and then headed up to command.

The ship sounded concerned. "Duran, are you sure you can't send one of the robots to look for this data recorder!"

"Ship, you can't assure me the scanner won't be affected by the robot the same way you effect it. Anyway, how would that look when I got down on my knee and presented it to my loves father with the words, here is the recorder, I got one of the ships robots to get it for me. Do you think that would go down well with him."

"You're the son of the greatest and most powerful leader in the galaxy, he would probably say, thank you, here is my daughter, please don't kill me!"

Duran wasn't impressed. "Ship, just get me on the ground! With luck this will be the last time. We have been out in this shit hole area of space to long; I want to get back to civilisation."

"Sir, your side arm. The charge cap is only at twenty-five percent, and you do not have a spare."

"Again! Anyone within 5K will be sleeping! Now, get me on the ground."

A buzz started to fill the air in the command centre. "SIR! We have him!" Shouted one of the Comms Techs to Richards.

"Received!" Richards grabbed the headset on his desk." Alpha one, Alpha one this is command receiving over?"

Taylor raised his voice over the noise of the aircraft. "Command. Alpha one. five by five. Over."

"Alpha one. Command. Our friend is inbound. General direction as predicted. Will update position when confirmed landing. Out."

Wow! This is it, Taylor thought. "Bravo one. Bravo one. this is Alpha. Confirm mission go, over."

"Alpha, Bravo, Confirmed, Out." Came back Sam's reply.

Richards shouted across the room. "Do we have a radar lock on it yet?"

"Sorry sir, we can't get a lock, just sporadic echoes. We will keep trying." Called back one of the techs.

The ships sensors had started to detect something unusual. "Duran, those scanning beams I told you about from our last run, they are back."

"Ship, should we be concerned?"

"I am not sure sir. I am trying to analyse. They don't seem to pose a threat. Wait, they have gone. Five minutes to landing. Duran, when I land you want to take a heading of 300 degrees for about 700 meters. I won't be able to get you any closer as my systems will affect your scanner."

"Terrain?" Duran asked.

"Open crop field for three to four hundred meters, small fence line, track, target. The target is a stone and earth structure."

"Ok, as soon as I get a visual on the target, I will shut down my kit and get the scanner out."

"Sir, please don't go dark for too long, those scanning beams keep popping up, I think someone maybe trying to track me."

"Ok, well stay on heigh alert, I will be as quick as I can. I can't see how anyone can get to us once the stun field has been deployed. I have everything power down apart from my neural com's net and I will do that when on site."

"Landing, sixty seconds. As soon as I land, I will deploy the stun field, good luck sir."

Duran moved to an air lock exit and waited. As the ship landed the two doors snapped open and a ramp extended. He ran down and headed in the direction the ship had indicated to him.

"All call signs. Command. Guest is landing about 10k East of Swindon. Start inbound run but hold at 5k until we can confirm he is on the ground. Over." Richards radioed calmly.

Both teams confirmed the information and waited.

"Overwatch. Command. Start your inbound run. Maintain 5000 meters until cleared. Over"

"Command. Overwatch. Inbound 5000 meters confirmed. Out."

Richards shouted to the room. "Do we have a feed from overwatch yet?"

One of the techs replied. "Sir, satellite confirms landing, pulse has been detected and the target is on the ground, direction of travel roughly north, overwatch feed in ten seconds. Nearest possible destination that fits previous profiles is Wayland's Smithy, about 800 meters north of the landing site."

"All call signs. Command. Start final inbound run. All clear to target. Overwatch I need a video feed now and get ready to mark the landing zone with IR Markers. Targets assumed destination is Wayland's Smithy."

All aircraft turned and started to descend, converging towards the target. "Get me everything you can on that place." Snapped Richards to the room.

Sarah tapped Taylor on the shoulder. As he turned, she showed him a tablet. "Jim! Overwatch feed." She shouted over the noise of the aircraft.

Taylor took the tablet. "I don't get it, why travel the universe to visit a pile of rocks near Swindon?"

Sarah laughed. "You can ask him in about ten minutes!"

Taylor continued to study the video feed. "Overwatch. Overwatch. Alpha One. Deploy IR markers one hundred meters South of the tree line east to west as soon as the target has gone past the tree line. Confirm. Over."

"Alpha One. Overwatch. Confirmed. Out."

"Bravo One. Alpha One. Sam, there is shit all cover in that field, it's just open wheat so I am going to switch it round. I want your team to deploy to the tree line just south of the target and take first crack at him. My team will deploy one hundred meters to your rear. Charlie, deploy as before and keep an eye on that ship."

"Jump point in thirty seconds." Came over the radio as the tail ramp started to drop.

Taylor shouted to his team. "OK Everyone. Position on the ramp, goggles on, green light and we get this guy." Moving to the ramp his team followed. All eyes fixed on the red jump light. Waiting, waiting, waiting. The pilot said thirty seconds, it seemed to last for ever. GREEN! Taylor jumped followed closely by the rest of the team. Forty-five seconds they will be on the ground. He looked around rapidly for the IR markers and his landing point. There, at his seven O'clock, he turned and tucked into a delta position to navigate towards it. "Alpha Team. Alpha One. Anyone not got eyes on the LZ?" Silence was all he needed. "Bravo One. Alpha One. Sit Rep?"

"Alpha One. Bravo. LZ in sight. ETA forty!" came back Sam.

This was it. Pulling their chutes they made final adjustments before landing; thirty seconds they would be on the ground. If they were lucky, shortly after they would engage whatever it was they were hunting.

"Ship I am at the target. I'm shutting down my com's net so I can use the scanner."

"Duran, there are several aircraft converging towards this location, I don't like it and I cannot use the stun field again with you on the ground, you need to get back to me so we can get out of here."

"Ship, they are not going to be anything to do with us. If they are, deal with them as best you can, I'll call you as soon as I am on my way back to you. Com's net off."

"Duran ..... Duran ...." Duran didn't answer, he could no longer hear the voice of the ship in his head. Deal with it the ship thought, it hadn't had any target practice for a while. The two larger craft had turned away after dropping something, but the four smaller ones seemed to be circling, around five thousand meters above him. Interesting thought the ship, the range of the stun field, but not out of range of the top guns.

Duran started to scan. He was hoping to pick up the very faint power signature of a seven-hundred-year-old diary and signs were looking good. Through the noise of the background radiation and other EM fields generated on this planet something was there. He moved up to the pile of rocks slowly moving the scanner from side to side trying to pinpoint the source. He was close, definitely in the right place at last. He could see an opening; the readings were showing it was coming from inside. He turned down the sensitivity as he moved inside. That's better, the scan was becoming clearer, it was towards the back of the chamber. He played with the controls, narrowing the field, closer and closer the scan got clearer. It was there, in or behind a stone in the wall. He turned off the scanner and switched on a light built into his body armour. Reaching down, he felt for the pick in his pack, removing it he slowly pushed it between the joints in the stones. Gently he started to pry the stone loose. He moved the pick around the edge of the stone trying to work the stone out evenly.

Taylor and his team began landing along the line marked by the IR strobes. As soon as they hit the ground, they started to strip off their chutes and equipment, organising themselves ready for contact. There was very little sound and no talking, they all knew the drill. As soon as they organised themselves, they moved to shut down the IR markers and form up. Taylor looked at Sam, pointed at him and signalled him to moved forward to the fence line. He then turned to Sarah and Andy, signalling them to go to the ship, he then turned to his team, pointing at Jaz and Dex he pointed for them to move down the line to the left and take up positions. Patting Robo on the arm they moved to the right. So far, the plan was going like clockwork so no need to report in, he knew Richards and the back room could see all they needed from overwatch, and they were in good shape. Taylor was starting to feel more confident; they just might pull this off.

A voice came over the radio. "All call signs. Overwatch. Temporary loss on target, he has entered the structure."

"This is Richards, all the information we have on that place shows only one way in or out. There is a small entrance chamber with some burial chambers leading off of it. We are confident he will have to come out the same way. Overwatch keep your eyes locked on it."

"Bravo. Alpha. Can you make out the entrance?"

"Alpha. Bravo. Just about. It's about eighty meters from my position. Do you want us to move in closer?"

"Bravo. Alpha. No, try and stay in cover, he has to come back through you, and I want to know if cover helps. Charlie. How are you doing with EMP deployment, can you see any other movement?"

"Alpha. Charlie. One hundred meters from target, no movement. I can see a ramp and open door. Heading to cover that."

The ship had been analysing what was going on and was confused. The larger craft seemed to have dropped people who were now between it and Duran, but they didn't seem to have any significant weapons so no threat to it or Duran. The four smaller craft were still circling, again no weapons and no threat. There were a lot of signals coming from the craft above it and some from the people on the ground. All its AI could come up with was this was some sort of training exercise and that made no sense. Well, the only orders he had were, 'deal with it', let's see what changes with the loss of one of their small craft. There was a chance at this distance charging the guns could affect Duran's scanner, but it had been a few minutes, he should have found it by now, if not Duran would know there was a problem. It targeted the closest one and started to charge the gun. The air started to vibrate with a deep whine as the gun charged. BOOM! a single shot from the upper turret flew out and obliterated the drone. Everyone heard the sound from the ship and snapped round.

"This is Overwatch, we just lost a drone!"

"This is Charlie. A gun on the top of the ship just fired. I guess that's what took out the drone, assume they also know we are here and we're in for a fight."

"Charlie. Alpha. How long for that EMP, we haven't got a hope against that?"

"Alpha. Charlie. Thirty seconds!"

BOOM! The ship fired again.

"This is Overwatch, second drone has just gone down. We are starting a more evasive flight pattern, but that ship is very accurate. We might not be able to maintain ops for much longer."

"Overwatch. This is Richards. Keep those birds in the air and scramble more into the target area, we cannot lose our eyes."

In the structure Duran could hear the ship firing and started to work with more urgency. He was tempted to enable his comms, but he needed to find what he was looking for first in case he had to use the scanner again. He started to get more aggressive with the pick. Finally, the stone popped out. He picked it up, it felt like a stone, nothing hidden inside. Moving his body, he tried to get his light to shine into the hole. Thats better, there was a void. He reached in, carefully feeling around, there, he could feel a small box, slowly and carefully he pulled it from the void.

"Sarah!" Called out Taylor. "Get those fucking EMP's deployed before that gun turns on us! We need to know if we have a chance in this fight!"

Andy and Sarah were moving as fast as they could with the heavy cases towards the ship. Andy was slightly ahead of Sarah when he suddenly stopped and fell backwards. Sarah instinctively dropped to the ground and started to crawl over to him. "Andy, Andy! Where you hit?" She started to check him over.

"I'm not hit. Fuuuck! I feel like I just ran into a brick wall!"

Sarah looked up in the direction he had been running. She could see his path in the broken-down wheat that just stopped. Crawling along to the point where his track ended, slowly reaching out, she could feel her hand start to tingle. The more she reached out the stronger the tingle got. Pushing on, the tingle was now becoming pain as a blue hue started to form around her hand. Her face contorted as she drew on all the adrenalin in her body to push through the pain.

With an angry scream she pulled her hand back trying to shake the feeling back into it.

"Alpha. Charlie. We have a problem. The ship seems to be protected by a force field; we can't get through it! I can't be sure if the EMP's will do anything if we deploy outside the field."

Taylor calmly called over comms. "Sarah, you have two minutes to do something with those EMP's or we will be forced to rush the target as our only last-ditch defence against that gun!"

Duran removed his gloves and slowly felt around the box. He could feel a lip, using his nails he forced them into the lip and the box started to split apart. He opened it to see an oval metallic looking object. Quickly picking up the scanner he ran it over the device. Power reserves were miniscule, but enough to retain its memory. At Last, he finally had what he came all this way for. He put the lid back on the box and slid it into his pack. Putting his gloves back on he grabbed the rock and pushed it back in the hole. Shutting down the scanner, he gathered his other items back into his pack and in his mind commanded his comms to reactivate.

"*Ship! Are you having fun out there?*" After all these years Duran still felt a little strange talking out loud when he knew it was being sent from his mind.

'SIR! Welcome back online. We may have a small problem. Several craft are circling our position, I have destroyed two, more maybe on the way. I believe ten beings, very lightly armed are between you and me. From the way they are deployed I believe they mean to capture you. I have the anti-personnel shield deployed. PLEASE tell me you have what you came for?'

"Ship, you will be glad to know as soon as we have delt with our little problem we will be heading home."

Andy crawled up alongside Sarah. "What now boss?"

"No Idea. There is some sort of shield, and I can't push through it."

"Boss, look at the wheat." Sarah looked at the wheat. As the wind blew, it was passing back and forth through the shield.

"Andy, give me your knife!" Andy pulled his knife from the holder on his vest and handed it to Sarah. She took the knife and held it between the tips of her fingers. Slowly pushing the knife towards the shield, the tingling in her finger started as before. Again, a blue hue formed around the blade of the knife, but it was going through. She pulled her hand back and threw the knife at the shield, it completely passed through and landed on the other side.

Sarah looked at Andy. "Get down to the rear of the ship, arm the EMP as a slave, put it as close to the shield as you can, then push it through with a good shove from your boot! Get clear and shut off your comms, this close if it's on it will get fried. Get back here as soon as you're done."

"OK! On it." Andy grabbed his case and started to run to the rear of the ship, holding out his left hand feeling the shield as he went.

"Alpha. Charlie, we have a plan. EMP Detonation in about thirty seconds. Shut down comms until after detonation, say sixty seconds."

"Good work Sarah!" called back Taylor. "Alpha. Bravo. Charlie. Go dark for forty-five seconds!"

Sarah opened the controls on her case and selected master control. The display flashed a few times and came back with one slave detected. Sarah hit confirm, then delay. She typed in twenty, confirm, arm. Quickly closing the controls, she led on her back and with her legs shoved the case as hard as she could through the force field. Jumping back to her feet she could see Andy running back to her.

"Quick, ten seconds let's get some distance". They both turned and started to run from the ship. Sarah counted in her head. Five, Four, Three, Two, One. She stopped, turned, and knelt with Andy following suit.

"Duran. Two of the beings are trying to get through the anti-personnel shield. Can I shoot them."

"Ship, be nice, they can't get to you, but I need too. Options?"

"Well, if I can't kill them there are two options. Either I send out armed droids in support as you engage, kill them all and come to me or I fly say five hundred meters north of your position and meet you there."

"I didn't come here to kill anyone, option two, I'll start heading north."

"You are getting soft in your old age. Ok, Lifting, I'll be there in......" Durans head was suddenly filled with a sharp stab of static!

"Ship. SHIP! Ship can you read me?" There was no voice in his head, something was wrong! Duran looked in the direction of the ship, no sound or explosion. How had they blocked the neural comms net, it is way more advanced than their technology.

From their position Sarah and Andy could see a brief flash of light from the two cases.

Andy looked at Sarah. "Is that it?"

"What did you expect Sargent, it's an electronic pulse not a nuke."

As they watched, the light that had been coming from the open door dimmed and the gun of the top of the ship slumped down.

Sarah stood and started to run towards the ship. "Come on. Let's see if that shield is down and get past it before it can come back up. Get your comms back on." Andy sprung up and started to follow. As they approached where the force field had been Sarah slowed and extended her arm in front of her.

"It's clear, head for the hatch!" Grabbing at her comms she tried to call Taylor. "Alpha. Charlie. Do you read." There was no answer. As they approached the ramp, she moved to the right pulling out her side arm and signalled Andy to go left. "Alpha. Charlie. Do you read." She tried again.

"Boss, I thought we weren't allowed to kill anything?" whispered Andy.

"We're not allowed to kill what is back there. Nothing was said about in here, I was ordered to protect the rear. We will hold here, if the lights come back on, we're going in. Send up a green flare just in case comms are fried."

"Roger that boss!"

Duran projected in his mind. "*Ship, Ship do you hear me. Ship if you can hear me, I cannot hear you.*

I can't see or hear any movement from you, so I am heading back."

With no answer, Duran was starting to get frustrated. He couldn't just sit here, he needed to know what was going on and get back onboard. The ship was going to love this, Light combat equipment, twenty five percent charge cap and minimal intel. He would rub that in forever if they ever got out of this. *'Pull it together Duran, you have faced worse'*, he thought to himself and started to get ready to move out of the structure.

"Alpha. Charlie. Do you read?"

"Charlie. Alpha. Five by five. Sit Rep?"

"Alpha. Charlie. EMP successfully deployed. The Force field has come down and I believe all the ships systems are also down. We have taken a position at the ramp by the open door. I intend to board the ship if the lights come back on."

"Great work Charlie team, report movement but be ready to back us up if needed." You could hear the relief in Taylors voice. "Bravo. Alpha. Do you read?"

"Alpha. Bravo. Reading you. All caught up on the EMP sir."

"Sam, sit rep?"

"Sir, we are deployed in cover in a two by two either side of its expected route back to the ship. If it passes us by, we intend to attack from its rear once it is back in the field, otherwise we will take it on where we are. I can just make it out on night vision, it has been hovering in the entrance to the structure for the last couple of minutes. I think it knows something is up and working on its own strategy."

Taylor had to think fast. "I am sure he got intel from the ship before we took it out. Ok Guys, listen up. With that ship dark we have the upper hand. As long as it stays dark, I am going to give him some time to make the first move. Let him show us what he's got, see what he may know. Sam, I like you're thinking. If he passes by your team, we can get him trapped in a crossfire and hit him with everything from all sides at the same time. Let me know when he starts to move."

In the entrance to the structure Duran pulled out his side arm and set it to its lowest setting. More shots will be better than more power, there were only a few enemy between him and the ship. He put his left arm out in front of him and activated the shield that was built into his gauntlet.

Duran tried projecting through his comms net again. '*Ship, if you can hear me, I am on my way to you, get ready to lift and supply cover fire. Arm a couple of droids and send them out in support.*' Still no answer. Time to move out and see what was waiting for him. Activating his helmet he cautiously made ground up to the tree line.

"Alpha. Bravo." Sam whispered into his comm. "Target is moving out from the structure. He is definitely aware something is up. He has his right hand extended with what appears to be a weapon. His left arm is in front of him, looks like he is holding a shield. He is moving cautiously. Definitely humanoid and yeah, I wouldn't pick a fight with him on my own."

"Sam, keep feeding us intel, but try not to let him see or hear you. I want him in the open." Taylor spoke calmly and softly. "Can you tell us any more about the weapon."

"Sorry sir, from this distance with night vis it's hard to make out. Best I can do is say it's a large handgun. Going quiet, he is about to pass between us."

Duran slowly moved along the track up to the tree line. His shield had a built-in heat scanner, but it wasn't helping him much. The land was still warm from the day and there were a lot of small animals around. They may be stunned but they still gave off heat. *'Ship I am at the tree line, are you there?'* Still no voice in his head. He deactivated the shield to make it easier to move through the trees. He slowly moved forward placing each foot so as not to make any sound. Maybe the ship was wrong, maybe it had already taken out this enemy. He got to the other side of the tree line and crouched. He could just make out the outline of the ship in the light from the moon but not much else. There was something wrong with the ship, no cabin or running lights on. He climbed over the last small fence and crouched again. '*Ship, I have visual on you, report?*' Again nothing. He activated his shield and swung it slightly side to side. There, those are not small stunned animals. Four heat sources, about two hundred meters out and one hundred meters apart. Easy, charge the ones on the left, shoot at the ones on the right.

"Alpha. Bravo. He has moved through the treeline and is waiting on the edge of the field. I have moved round behind him. I am not sure if the thing in his left hand is a scanner or a shield. Whatever it is I think he has detected you. I can just make out an image on it of your positions."

Not what Taylor wanted to hear from Sam. "This is Alpha, Bravo, as soon as he starts to move on us, get in here fast. Charlie, hold position until I call you. As soon as we engage gets some parachute flares in the air. Overwatch get those drones down here to buzz him. Alpha team get ready, flashlights, baton rounds and paint balls."

Each man grabbed a different weapon and prepared. Taylor picked up one of the large flashlights in his left hand and the trank gun in his right. He was hoping while the others distracted him, he could blind him and get in close for a dart.

Richards raised his head from his screen and shouted to the room. "I want all our backup and security assets inbound. There are open fields two clicks north, tell them to wait there until cleared in on final.

Duran slowly moved forward watching his foe on the shield. As he got closer, he could see the image getting clearer and the men with their weapons raised. At fifty meters he stopped. Well, they were in no hurry to get to him. He drew in some large breaths, on the third he started to charge towards the men on his left firing on the run at the ones on the right.

"LET HIM HAVE IT!" Shouted Taylor. Each man stood and started to walk towards Duran firing whatever they had. Dex got off a few baton rounds and was then hit square in the chest with a shot from Duran. He went down instantly. Jaz saw him drop from the corner of his eye but there was no time to stop. As the parachute flares lit up the field Taylor could see Duran closing on him and tried to get the light full in his face. Jaz got to about twenty meters from Duran and dropped to one knee opening up full auto with his paintball gun. As the balls started to hit home on Duran he was confused. He was taking a lot of hits. They hurt a little but what was going on. He turned, knelt, and block the projectiles with his shield. At the same time, he aimed at Jaz and fired three rapid shots. The second and third hit Jaz in the arm then chest and he was down. With Duran turned, Taylor saw an opening. He ran in a few meters to close the gap, aimed, fired his trank at Duran's exposed side. As the dart impacted his upper leg it just bounced off. '*Shit!*' thought Taylor, '*Body armour!*'

Duran feeling the impact turned and started to fire rapidly in Taylors direction. Instinctively Taylor dived, rolled, and crawled to his right to get clear of the incoming fire. Duran turned towards the other man he had been charging and was knocked back again and again. Robo had started to hit him with bean bag rounds. This close in they were really packing a punch. Body armour can stop something but there is still the energy to deal with. Robo was firing and pumping the shot gun as fast as he could. He could see he was having an impact. Eight, Seven, Six, Five, he counted down the rounds, what was the plan when he was empty!

Taylor looked up. He could see Robo pounding away with the shotgun. As more parachute flares lit up the field, he could see his target more clearly. That body armour didn't look like it covered all his body. From his right, volleys of paintballs, baton rounds and bean bags came in. Bravo had finally made it into the fight. Duran stood and turned, holding his shield to his left and firing to the right. Danny, Kev and Jonesy were hit and dropped. Sam dived for cover in the wheat and reloaded his shot gun. Robo dropped his shotgun grabbing the net launcher he fired. With Duran's shield extended out most the net wrapped around his arm and not all his body, but it was still doing a good job at distracting him. One of the drones whooshed over Duran's head, he turned and fired wildly into the sky while trying to shake loose the net.

Both Sam and Robo had now had time to reload their shotguns, and both started to fire at Duran. Once again, he dropped to one knee and started firing at Sam. Hit, he went down. Taylor had now seen seven of his men, his friends, go down. He jumped up, pulled out his side arm and started to fire. '*To HELL with Richards!*' he thought, he's not having my team that cheap, that thing needs to pay. Duran's body armour again absorbed the force of the rounds, but these hurt a lot more. Duran turn his shield to face Taylor at the same time firing a volley of shots at Robo. Robo took hits to his leg then chest and went down. As Taylor fired, he walked towards his target, trying to get a shot to the head, but the shield blocked each round. Taylor looked to his left to see Robo drop. Taylor fired until he saw the working parts of his weapon lock to the rear, he was out. Duran stepped forward swinging his shield arm full into Taylors body. The force sent Taylor reeling backwards and falling to his knees. Winded, Taylor got to his feet with blood pouring from his nose. The two men stood facing each other in the shadowy light of the flares. Duran deactivated his shield and helmet to face this last man. As they stood there Taylor was suddenly struck by how, well, how human he looked, nothing like the alien he had expected to see.

"Alpha. Charlie. Sit rep. Do you need support."

"Sarah." Gasped Taylor over comms. "We are all down. You and Andy drop back, get out of here, do not engage. Nothing is stopping this guy."

Hearing Taylors voice made Duran pause. He had no idea what this man had just said, but the tone. Oh well, he didn't have time. He raised his weapon and aimed. Taylor stood tall and braced. He was about to die and all he could think of was that Sarah would listen for once in her life and get out.

Duran pulled the trigger. "Urrr Urrr Urrr!" sounded from the weapon. Duran looked down. The charge cap was depleted. Taylor had no idea what the sound meant, but he knew the look on someone's face when their weapon jammed. He dug down, summoned the last of his adrenalin and started to run at Duran. As he got closer, he balled up his fist and swung at Duran's jaw. Connecting hard Duran stumbled backwards.

"SARAH, ANDY, get up here, his weapons jammed!" Shouted Taylor.

Duran steadied himself, holstering the useless gun ready for a fight. Walking towards Taylor with his fists up, Taylor followed suit. As soon as the two men got within reach, Duran swung his massive right fist at Taylors head. Taylor ducked under the swing stepping in and round behind Duran. In one flowing move he stamped down hard on the back of Duran's right knee. Duran's leg buckled and Taylor struck him to the back of the head with his elbow, this dropped Duran to the ground.

Taylor looked round, he was sure there was no armour on the back of this guy's legs, pulling out his taser he fired. Hit, the barbs stayed in. To Taylors satisfaction the alien started to convulse, YES! He had him.

Duran could feel the pain coursing over his body, but this was not the worst thing he had ever felt. He rolled onto his side, pulled up his leg and reach down fighting to control his muscles. Finding and wrapping his hand around the wires coming from his leg he used all his effort to pull whatever was causing the pain away from him. Relief washed over his body, rolling away he jumped back to his feet.

"Numquid omnes vos have?" Bellowed Duran and laughed.

Taylor had no idea what had been said but he looked at the useless Taser, with a shrug he tossed it to one side and let out his own little laugh. Duran laughed again and then roared as he charged at Taylor. Lowering his shoulder, he drove it into Taylors mid-section, lifting him off the ground and then pitching him high in the air over his back. Taylor landed in a crumpled heap. The blow from the man and then the ground knocking all the wind out of him again. Duran turned and walked back to Taylor. He bent down and grabbed Taylor by the front of his jacket, lifting him high off the ground.

"Bonum certamen pro parvo homine pones." Sneered Duran as he looked into Taylors dazed eyes.

Taylor slowly reached into his jacket pocket. "Fella, I have no idea what you are saying to me but let's see what you make of this!" With one swift move Taylor uncapped and sunk the trank dart from his pocket into Duran's neck.

At first the big man didn't seem to notice what had happened. As the drugs started to work into his system, he dropped Taylor to his feet. Reaching up he pulled out the dart and looked at it. He then looked at Taylor and started to laugh again, releasing the hold he had on him. Dropping to his knees then to his hands he looked up at Taylor smiling as he slowly passed out.

Taylor dropped to his knees, exhausted, and drained as the adrenalin started to leave his body. Sarah and Andy came running to his side.

"Jim! Jim! Are you OK? Are you hit?" Sarah asked with some panic in her voice.

"Yeah, Yeah, I'm ok, just had the shit kicked out of me. Andy, get at least three sets of cuffs on this guy, hands and feet."

"Ok Boss! Are you sure it's OK to touch." Said Andy nervously looking down at the big man.

"Flip him over, he looks like any other guy. Well just bigger. Don't touch or mess with any of his toys, just get the cuff's on for now."

Andy rolled Duran over and started to cuff him, both he and Sarah looked down on him for the first time. "Hummmm, I dunno." Smirked Sarah. "I could go for some of that."

Taylor was shocked. "Lieutenant! I'm right here."

"I Know, and so is he." She said in a sultry voice.

Taylor finally found the strength to get back to his feet. He grabbed on to his comm. "Command. Alpha one. Target secured and intact. Get all secondary units' backup and medevac on site Asap. Out!"

Richards was elated. "Taylor! Excellent work! Well done to you and your team, backup will be with you in five."

Sarah looked around. "Jim. Where are the rest of the guys?"

Taylor sighed. "Back there. Can you and Andy go look for them. Get their tags for me, I'll look after our friend here. Sarah, give me your side arm."

Sarah reached down and pull out the weapon. "Jim, you're not going to do anything daft while we are gone."

"No. No, he cost us a lot. I want to make sure it wasn't for nothing."

Sarah put her hand on his shoulder. "Come on Andy we have friends to bring home. Put up another flare."

As Sarah and Andy walked away Taylor slumped down next to Duran. He really did want to put a bullet in his skull, seven men, he had never lost so many friends at one time. By the light of the flare Taylor stared at the face that had cost him so much. He smiled and chuckled, Sarah was such a tart. Only she could pull out a comment like that in the middle of all this.

Taylor could hear footsteps dragging through the wheat coming up behind him. "That was quick, was there a problem?"

"Yeah, they all turned into Zombies and walked back on their own."

"WHAT!" Shouted Taylor jumping to his feet. As he turned, he saw his entire team stood in front of him. "What the actual fuck! I thought you guys were dead."

"Sorry boss, I guess we were for a while." Smiled Sam. "Looks like he just stunned us."

"You lazy bastards! So, while you lot were napping, you just left me taking care of business on my own."

Danny held out his fist. "Knew you wouldn't want it any other way boss!"

Taylor bumped Danny back and the whole team joined in with each other. Taylor turned back to their prize. "Come on guys, come and see what it was all about." They circled around and Taylor shone his torch down on the sleeping alien.

"Wow!" Said Kev. "Not a bad looking space alien. Are we sure he is from space cuss he doesn't look very alien."

Taylor laughed "You know that was the first thing Lieutenant Stevens noticed about our alien. And as to your question, that's why we had to catch him so some bod can ask him."

The faint sound of helicopters could he heard coming in from the north. "Here comes the cavalry! Sarah, get on comms and signal those choppers where to land. Once you have done that we can sit down and figure out what to do for the rest of our leave."

Chapter 5: Questions.

On the flight back to Brize, Taylor really started to feel the effects of his fight with Duran starting to creep up on him. He was sure he had a few cracked ribs. Time enough to get checked out when they landed. He looked down on his sleeping prize and started to wonder what they were about to find out. He was sure this guy wasn't going anywhere until they had extracted all the information they could from him. He would then probably go into a deep dark hole for the rest of his life. He started to feel some regret, sure, he had captured many bad guys that were never seen or heard from again, but this guy was different. He never set out to attack anyone, even in their fight he seemed to treat it more as fun. *'Not my problem.'* Taylor thought to himself. *'Let's just hope Richards is true to his word and I can get to talk to him.'* Taylor laughed to himself remembering they already had, and it had not gotten either of them anywhere.

Taylor and his team stood as the chinook landed, with the ramp starting to drop, they picked up the stretcher with Duran on and walked out. Emerging on to the ground they were met by Richards running over to them.

"Well done guys, let me have a look at him." Richards push himself between the men to look down on Duran. "Is that it!" he exclaimed. "He's pretty good looking, I was hoping for something a little more alien."

"For fuck sake, don't you start. Already had Steven's swooning all over him!" Taylor said in disbelieve.

"Awww James don't be jealous. I don't think I will get to see much of him after today." Sarah was enjoying this.

"Come on, get him into the ambulance, you too Taylor, looks like you could do with a check over. The rest of you into the truck, we have barracks set up for you so you can get changed and cleaned up. Beers already there on me." Richards started to usher people in the direction he wanted them to go then climbed into the ambulance with Taylor.

As the ambulance started to pull away Taylor turned to Richards. "So do I get to talk to him?"

"In good time, he will be out for a while. We need the doctors to give him a thorough look over, you too by the looks of things. But I said you could, and you will."

"What's going to happen to him?"

"There are people coming in to talk to him. Third degree I guess until they get all they can from him. That ship of his will get torn apart for all it secrets. But that's not your problem. Cheer up, why are you so down. After this you can write your own ticket my boy."

"This just feels different. I've taken a load of bad guys off the board with never a second thought. But for some reason, this guy. I dunno, I just feel bad about getting him thrown in a hole for no reason."

"There is my boy. He knows things we need to know. And until we know all he does he is dangerous. The nicest people in the world still plan attacks on us. You have no idea if that's what he's been doing for the last few nights, or longer!"

The ambulance pulled up outside hanger seven where it was met by several men and doctors who quickly took Duran into their labs. Taylor and Richards climbed down and started to walk into the hanger.

"We have taken over this hanger as our command centre. No one in or out without authorisation." Richards handed Taylor an ID badge. "Keep this with you at all times. We have to keep this quiet; God forbid the Yanks or the Russians get wind of what we have. We have a 5K cordon going round the ship and engineers putting up a screen so it can't be seen from land or air."

"You think we can keep a lid on this?"

"Short term yes. We are going with crashed experimental aircraft for now, should be enough to keep most people happy and it gives us a classified angle to help keep people from asking to many follow up questions. Look, enough for now, get checked out, get some rest we will talk in a few hours." Richards beckoned to a couple of med techs. "Get this man looked at, I want him well taken care of."

"Yes Sir!" Said one of the techs as they took Taylor away.

Richards walked over to the door Duran had been taken through. Inside he found several med techs looking through an observation window into a room that looked like an operating theatre. Richards joined them. More techs were inside in full PPE looking over Duran. "What have we got so far?"

"In ten minutes, not a lot." Came a retort from one of the techs. As he turned, he saw it was Richards. "Sorry Sir, we are just starting to look at him. We want to make the subject safe first, remove his weapons, armour, and clothes. Then we can start doing a medical work up. But so far, he doesn't look like much of a space alien to me."

"GOOD!" Said Richards. "Keep thinking that! He is the pilot of a crashed experimental aircraft, make sure everyone remembers that! I will be back in thirty minutes, and I will expect an initial report on his condition by then! Make sure you keep him sedated and restrained at all times!" Richards turned and walked out the way he had come. Exiting to the open hanger he looked around to see who was near him. He reached into his pocket and pulled out his phone. Unlocking he searched the phone book and dialled.

"Sir, Its Richards."

"Very well Sir, even more so now I can report we have the alien and the ship both intact."

"Surprisingly no Sir, Taylor and his team did well to take him down and all make it back. Taylor is a bit beaten up but nothing a few weeks R n R wont sort out."

"I will Sir, I am sure he will appreciate that."

Richards laughed "No Sir. Surprisingly human and it has already been commented on how good looking he is."

"Hard to tell at this stage, I guess he could be, but he is having a full medical exam as we speak so we should know soon."

"Yes Sir, thank you, I will report back in about an hour with an update. Goodbye." Richards slipped the phone back into his pocket and turned to the door Taylor had gone into. Walking into the room he found Taylor sat in an ice bath. "How are you doing my boy?"

"I'm full of Morphine and sat in an ice bath, you don't pay me enough."

Richards laughed. "Aww come on Jim you don't do this for the money, that's just the drugs talking."

"Well at this moment in time I agree with the drugs. Any update on our friend."

"No, the doctors have just started looking at him. I think he's in better shape than you are." Richards laughed. "I'll give you an update in an hour or so. I did just get off the phone to the PM. He sends his congratulations and get well soon."

Taylor smirked. "Get him back on the phone and ask him to send more money."

"Taylor, get some rest, we will talk more later." Richards turned to one of the nurses. "Hey nurse, get this guy anything he needs."

"Richards, any chance you could get Stephens over here?"

"What, all these pretty nurses not good enough for you hu? I already sent her a pass with a message to come over when she's ready."

"Thanks, do you know you're a lot nicer than you were this morning. Now the drugs say fuck off!"

Richards laughed as he turned and walked out the room. Once again as he got out into the open hanger he looked around. Pulling out his radio he called the command centre.

"Command. This is Richards. Give me an update on the ship site?"

"Sir, exclusion perimeter has been established as requested. We have three drones on constant circular patrol and just over two hundred men on the ground. Engineers will have the ship screened off by sunrise."

"Good work. Has there been any change in the status of the ship?"

"Not that we can tell Sir. Two men did go into the open door, but there was a closed door beyond that with no obvious way to open, so they have left for now."

"Understood. I'm going to try and grab a couple of hours sleep, keep an eye on the situation. I want to be notified immediately if anything changes. Richards out."

Richards walked out of the hanger into the night air. He looked up, closed his eyes drawing in a lung full of cool air and let it out again, finally he could relax. Suddenly, with a yawn, it struck him. He'd been awake for over twenty-four hours. Coffee, grab a coffee and see what the doctors had to say. Once he knew that, he might be able to get some sleep. He went back to the room where the med techs had Duran. Looking through the observation window, Richards could see the alien had been stripped and there were at least six techs inspecting him. To one side of the room Richards could see a long table with all the aliens kit and clothes laid out, again techs were looking over it. He walked to the coffee machine and grabbed a black coffee, then he approached the Tech he had spoken to earlier. "You, what have you learn so far."

"Well Sir, um, starting with the subject, outwardly he looks very human. Nothing visually would lead to any other conclusion. If he were human, I would place him in his mid-twenties of central European descent. Unusually for a man of that age I would expect to see some dental work, but from what we can tell he has never had any. We have taken blood and it's a match to our own A Positive, second most common type. X-Rays and Ultrasound show all his major organs to be the same as ours and in the same place. I would like to do an MRI and CT scan, but I would need your permission to move him to the base main medical centre for that. I would also like to do DNA analysis, but that would mean sending blood samples off site."

Richards thought for a second taking a drink of his coffee. "Do we have a secure lab for the DNA testing?"

"Yes Sir, we do, and a secure transport method."

"OK. You can send that out, but I want one of your guys to keep eyes on the samples at all times. Also, no copies of any results, all information and samples come back here. Hold fire on the scans till we get the DNA results, I get the feeling they will only tell us he is human. I want as few questions as possible asked outside these walls, got it!"

"Yes Sir, Understood!" The tech turned and started to walk towards the table with Durans belongings on. "Sir, these are the clothes and equipment we took off the subject. We don't have the equipment here to do detailed testing. The clothing looks like some sort of synthetic polymer, much like polyester but, with the strength of Kevlar. He had these hardened sections over the top, much like body armour. Again, some sort of synthetic maybe like a carbon fibre. There are two gauntlets for each lower arm. These may have some controls on them, but we are trying not to activate anything yet."

"So far, you're not giving me anything earth shattering." Remarked Richards. "If it wasn't for that large ship parked out in a field, I might think we were all on a wild goose chase."

"Well, we do have some items that are more of a mystery. We have put these to one side in this explosive resistant case. The first is obviously some sort of gun, we have kept handling to a minimum. It may be prudent to get that to some sort of explosive proof area before we do any more examination."

Richards looked it over. "I agree, we are in no rush to get blown up."

"The second one is more interesting. It looks like the handle of a sword, but it has no blade."

"So why are you taking precautions with it?" Asked Richards with a frown.

"It was just the fact it was located on his belt by the gun. Just made us feel it maybe a weapon."

"Hummm OK. I can go with the not getting blown up again."

The tech smiled. "Finally, we have a bag. It's made with the same material as the clothing. It contained a small hand pic, this had dirt on it so maybe he was digging in the structure he was in. A small box again with dirt on it, maybe what he dug up? There are also a couple of small metallic or composite items that seem to have no function, buttons, lights or, well, anything."

Richards again thought for a moment. "I should have guessed this wasn't going to be easy. Finish up what you're doing, get him into some clothes and into the containment room. I need him awake so we can start to try communicating with him."

"Yes Sir. I would say we can have him ready and awake in a couple of hours."

"Good, I will be back later. Do you know when these specialist interrogators are supposed to get here?"

"Probably not until the morning Sir, maybe around O Six hundred."

Richards laughed. "I'll be sure to apologise for disturbing their sleep." Richards took a much sterner tone. "Now listen to me and listen good! I don't want anyone talking or interacting with this guy unless I am around. Is that FULLY understood?"

"Yes Sir. Fully understood!" Said the tech nervously.

Richards turned and walked towards the coffee machine, downing the last of his coffee he put the mug back as he walked back to the exit.

Once again emerging into the open hanger he paused to collect his thoughts. He didn't seem to have many. He guessed it was just a waiting game now, wait until they could hopefully communicate with this guy and see if all this was worth something. He tried to be optimistic. In every Sci-Fi flic he had ever seen the aliens could always speak English. Give him an hour and he will be telling us all the mysteries of the universe and all the benefits it will bring to mankind. Walking back into the room where Taylor was being treated, he found him tucked up in one of the beds.

"Nurse?" Richards whispered. "How is he doing?"

"He will be ok, some deep bruising, couple of cracked ribs. Just needs some time to recover."

"My boy is tough, so we don't need to worry. I'm going to take that bed on the end. Could you please make sure I am woken in two hours, and if you have coffee at the same time you would make me a very happy man?"

"I am sure I could arrange all that for you."

Richards walked over to the bed taking off his jacket and shoes, he sat and took out his phone. Pulling up the last text message he sent to the PM he replied. 'Tests so far show he is as human as you and I. Will update when we know something more.' Send.

He put the phone on the side table and led down. Clearing his mind, just concentrating on the sound of his breathing he was asleep in minutes.

'Duran … DURAN …. Wake up. Duran Can you hear me. Tar Duran, I need you to Wake up NOW!' Came the voice of the ship washing around Durans fuzzy brain. *'Duran, I know you are starting to regain consciousness, come on snap out of it!'*

"Ship, Yes, yes, I can hear you." Durans slowly started to clear. He tried opening his eyes. Bright, to bright, he closed them again. He could feel an odd sensation around his wrists. Bringing his hands together he could feel metal rings around them with a long chain in between. 'Not a good start' he thought to himself. He moved his legs, same has his wrists. Ok so he wasn't going anywhere in a hurry. He lifted his head and sat up; well, he could move at least. He tried to open his eyes again, this time looking down. That's better, not so bright, his vision slowly clearing he looked around his environment. Turning his body, he moved his legs over the side of the bed. He could see he was in a white room, there was the bed, a table with stools in the middle of the room, in one corner a toilet and wash basin. On one wall was a door, no handles but a small window. On another wall there was a large mirror. There was something high up in each corner of the room, a red light slowly pulsed from each one. Oh, and the chains around his hands and legs. "Ship what can you tell me. How deep in the shit am I?"

'*My first suggestion would be not to talk out loud. I am sure they cannot understand you, but these humans have no concept of your neural net communicator, and they may just think you are mad.*'

'*Understood.*' Projected Duran to the ship.

'*As I am sure you can tell you have been captured! Maybe one day you will listen to me.*'

'*Ship! I don't need this right now! Let's just work on getting out of here.*'

'*You have been taken to a facility about twenty-five kilometres north of where we landed. I have been surrounded by a large force of armed men and equipment. A temporary cover is being put over me. I am assuming this is to hide me not contain me. The facility you are in looks to be military, there is again a large force of armed men and equipment. The room you are in is strong enough that you cannot break out without help or equipment. They have electronic surveillance on you at all times, both video and audio. I have tapped into this and can see and hear everything that is going on. I am gathering as much information as I can.*'

Duran stood, still a little shaky, he walked over to the table. He could now see it was fixed to the ground, so were the stools. On the table there were several things, a jug, some cups, and a plate with what looked like biscuits. '*Ship what are the items on the table, are they safe?*'

'*The jug contains pure water, and you know how much you love space biscuits, well these are earth biscuits, all scan safe.*'

Duran sat down and laughed. '*Nice to know some things are the same wherever you go in the universe.*' He poured some water and drank, then ate a couple of the biscuits. '*Ship these are much nicer than the ones you feed me with. The water tastes better too.*'

'*Well, my scan of the biscuits show they were made fresh today and the water is not your recycled urine! I told you we should have topped up the tanks and got new filters.*'

Duran stood and walked to the door ignoring the comment. He looked through the small window and could see people moving around. Along the wall at the back of the room he could see a table with all his equipment laid out on it. Men were looking at it, he could see one man taking pictures with a flash going off occasionally. Banging hard on the door with both fists he waited for a reaction. A couple of the people looked round but then just got back on with what they were doing. Not ready to face me he thought. He moved over to the wall with the large mirror. '*Ship, is this a one-way vision portal?*'

'*It is. The people that have been watching you are very nervous. Their pulse rates went up by ten percent when you got off the bed, another ten when you got to the portal.'*

Duran stared piercingly through the mirror with the evillest face he could. *'How is their pulse rate now?'* he asked in his mind.

'Still going up.'

'Ok Ship, enough of this.' Duran turned and walked back to the table. *'What are my options for getting out of here?'*

'Only one at the moment, I lift off, fly in, shoot up the place, arm a couple of the robots, they fight their way to you, and you can shoot your way out.'

Duran thought for moment, he never wanted this, he had planned to be in and out without even being noticed. *'Ship. Do it! We don't have time for anything else. Try and keep the damage to a minimum and make sure the bots are using stun. Let's get out of here and go home.'* Said Duran reluctantly.

'An excellent plan with only one minor problem! It will be at least another two hours before all my systems are fully back online, and I am able to take off.'

Duran paused. *'Ship, what aren't you telling me? Come to think of it, why did we lose comms and you let me get captured.'* His head was clearing enough to start remembering things.

'Simple! These humans were more resourceful than you said they were. I only had the anti-personnel shield up and an open door. They managed to slip some sort of electronic pulse weapon through the shield that interrupted most of my systems. I have been playing dead ever since, waiting for you to regain consciousness while I made repairs.'

'And you say that will take another two hours?'

'At least, maybe more. I do not know the status of some systems until I get others online.'

Duran sat and grabbed another biscuit. *'Ship, give me an update in an hour.'* He sighed, pouring more water. *'Looks like I will wait for you and these humans to decide my fate.'*

"Sir….. Sir, your coffee is on the side." Said one of the nurse's, gently shaking Richard's arm. "I've been told your pilot has just woken up."

Richards sat up. "Thanks love. Sorry, can you get one of those for my friend over there, and something for him to wear."

"Sure, just be a few minutes."

As Richards swung his legs over the side of the bed, he grabbed the coffee and took some sips. Fumbling in his jacket he pulled out his radio. "Command, this is Richards. Anything from the ship site."

"Sir we are getting regular check ins from all posts but there is no change in status."

Richards drank some more of his coffee and pondered for a moment; something was bugging him. "Command. What if that ship decides to take off?"

"Sir? I'm sorry. I am not sure what you are asking me?"

Richards again thought for a moment. "I'm just thinking, is there anything stopping that ship taking off, even though we have its pilot. Its guns were firing last night without a pilot."

"I guess you could be right Sir!"

"Command, get on to the engineers on site. Ask them to get large concrete blocks, trucks, stakes, cables. Whatever they think they can do to stop that ship if it tries to lift off."

"Yes Sir, I will get them working on it."

Richards put on his shoes, then stood slipping on his jacket making sure he had all his items. He could see the nurse walking over with clothes and coffee for Taylor placing them by the side of his bed. He waited for her to leave, nodding to her, and then walking over.

"Jim! Come on my boy, time to get back to it, if you are ready?"

Taylor stretched and rolled over groaning slightly, he still hurt. "I Think I'd rather stay right where I am."

"Well, that's up to you. Coffee and clothes on the side. Guys will be here in a minute to talk to him, if you want in, then it's time to go."

Taylor struggled to sit up. Looking at Richards he tried to show he wasn't in that much pain. "OK, sure, give me a minute to get dressed and get this down me. Could you ask the nurse to bring me some pain meds and point me in the right direction."

"Will do. Out the door, turn right, in the door across the hanger. Don't be long or we will start without you." Richards turned and walked towards the exit. "Nurse. Please get some strong pain meds for our baby over there and send him across when he is ready."

Taylor drank some of his coffee and then started to dress. Simple stretchy sweats and slippers, but in his condition still painful to put on.

The nurse approached him. "Here are some pain killers. They are very strong, no more than two every four hours or we will be pealing you off the ceiling."

Taylor smiled. "Thanks, I'll go easy, still need to stay sharp for a little while longer." He opened the pot and shook two into his hand. Throwing them into his mouth he washed them down with his coffee. Standing, he wished they would hurry up and kick in. He walked towards the door and out into the hanger, moving around might help him loosen up. Turning right he could see the other door Richards had told him about. He slowly walked over to it, gingerly stretching as he went.

Richards had already found Shaw and Clarke, MI6 interrogators. "Mark, Jason, been awhile. How goes the water boarding these days. Sorry to drag you out so early, if it had been my choice, I would have used my own boys for this one."

"Funny Richards, but technically this is a foreign affair, so we need to be included." Sneered Shaw.

"Technically he could be classed as an illegal immigrant, but we could run around technicalities all day. Go have your chat first and we will take over when you get nowhere." Grinned Richards, he definitely had no love for these two, one of the reasons he moved from MI6 to MI5. He showed them round to the door where the alien was being held. "This way gentlemen. He is awake and free to move around. He is in chains and two of these large gentlemen will make sure you are safe." Standing by the door were five military police officers. Two turned and pressed buttons either side of the door. Releasing the electronic lock with the door popping open. Two of the other men walked in, batons drawn, they stood either side of the door. Shaw and Clarke followed, walking towards the table as the door was closed behind them. As they went in Richards moved round to watch from the one-way mirror.

Duran was led on the bed, but hearing the commotion by the door he sat up, and watched what was going on. Shaw and Clarke sat on the stools by the table closest to the door and started to pull things out of their cases. *'Ship, any idea what is going on?'*

'I would guess the men sitting are going to question you and the men standing are either there to protect the other two or make you answer. Careful of the batons they carry, they have a built-in shock system.'

Shaw stood and beckoned to Duran. "Sir, would you mind coming over and joining us at the table?"

'He wants you to sit at the table with them.' Relayed the ship to Durans mind.

'Thanks Ship, I kind of understood that without a translation.'

Duran made an effort to look slightly confused and cautious as he walked over to the table. He had no fear of his captors at this time, but he didn't want to show that.

Shaw nervously cleared his throat and then spoke slowly and clearly. "Hello. My name is Shaw." Holding his hand to his chest and then placing it on Clark's shoulder. "And this is my colleague Clarke. We are from MI6. We would like to ask you some questions. Do you understand me?"

'Would you like me to translate that?' Said the ship.

Duran placed his hand on his chest. "Duran."

Both Shaw and Clarke look visibly relieved and smiled. "Good!" Said Shaw. Again, pointing with his hand. "So, you are Duran, I am Shaw, and this is Clark."

Duran copied the man pointing. "Shaw, Clarke, Duran."

Shaw was now very confident. "Excellent, I can see we are all going to get along very well. Now can you tell me where you have come from."

Duran looked left and right at the two men opposite him and shrugged. "Paenitet me verbum quod dicis mihi non intellego."

Shaw and Clarke looked visibly disappointed.

'Duran, do you want me to translate what they are saying to you?' Asked the ship again.

Duran projected to the ship. 'Ship, I will ask you if I need something. At this point as I can't answer them, it may be best not knowing what they are saying!'

"Great, I guess that was a long shot." Said shaw dejectedly.

"It sounded a bit like Italian, I know a translator we could get in here." Said Clarke optimistically.

"Clarke, I would be surprised if all the aliens in the galaxy spoke Italian. We will need to get a linguistics expert."

Taylor walked into the room and saw Richards standing by the one-way mirror. More importantly he also saw the coffee station, stopping there to refill his mug before walking over to him.

"Jim by boy. Welcome to the show. These two prats are getting nowhere fast!" Richards could hardly contain his joy.

Taylor stood by the windows sipping his coffee, the pain meds slowly starting to work. Looking through the window for the first time he could get a clear look at the guy who had nearly taken his head off. Taylor thought he looked even bigger now, without his armour.

This was something the ship thought his master needed to know. '*Duran. I think you might like to know, the man that defeated you is now standing at the vision portal.*'

To Duran this was very interesting. As a warrior it was customary to acknowledge a victor, and this was something he didn't have to do very often.

Slowly Duran rose to his feet, eyes fixed on the mirror he started to walk towards it. Shaw stood and stepped back at the same time cautious of what the big man may do. The two redcaps stepped forward raising their batons. Shaw gently waved them back.

'Ship. Where is my better standing?'

'He is to the far left of the portal.'

Duran, eyes fixed, moved to the spot. He could not see through, but they did not know that. He raised his hand and then beckoned with his finger. "Vos. Te victorem salutant velim." He said loudly.

Taylor turned and looked at Richards. "Ok. What the hell is that about?"

"No Idea my boy, but you said you wanted to talk to him. That sounded like an invitation to me."

"How am I going to talk to him if those two got nowhere."

"Again, No Idea, but let's go find out. You can't do any worse than them!" Said Richards Joyfully. He turned and started to walk to the door. "Come on Jim."

Taylor initially looked for a place to put down his coffee cup, then changed his mind. He felt he was going to need it.

Getting to the door Richards barked. "Get the door open and get those two out."

The Redcaps obliged, Richards and Taylor walked into the room. "Ok you two, he clearly just asked to talk to Taylor here, so let's give the boy a chance."

85

Surprisingly Shaw didn't say a word. Just gathered up his stuff and walked out with Clarke in tow. As they left the redcaps closed the door behind them.

Taylor took a few paces into the room towards Duran and then stopped. He felt Duran was sizing him up, maybe this was a bad idea. Maybe I am about to get another beating thought Taylor.

Duran took a couple of paces towards Taylor and stopped. "Victori te salute!" He said loudly and bowed slightly. As he rose, he started to laugh. Walking towards Taylor he extended his right arm. Taylor was a little uneasy, hoping this was a gesture of friendship, cautiously Taylor did the same. Duran grasped Taylor's arm above the wrist and shook, Taylor followed suit. "Non possum persaepe salutare hominem qui me proelio vicit." Duran released his grip and gestured for them to sit at the table. "Sedens. Blandit velit."

"I don't know about you my boy, but I think you are off to a good start." Richards seemed suitably impressed.

Taylor sat, placing his coffee on the table in front of him. "It may be a good start, but I don't have a clue what he is saying. There were a couple of words he said that kinda sounded like English."

"Victory and salute. Yeah, I picked up on that. Maybe he respects you because you beat him."

Taylor laughed. "Tell my ribs I won, look at this guy. Not a scratch on him."

Duran knocked on the table, then placing his hand on his chest. "Nomen mihi est Tar Duran."

"There's that word again, I guess his name is Duran." Taylor placed his hand on his chest and then pointed to Richards. "Taylor, Richards."

Duran Laughed and pointed at each man in turn. "Taylor, Richards."

"Well, the other two got this far what do we do next?" Whispered Richards.

There was an awkward pause between the three men.

"Experiar?" Duran pointed to Taylors coffee.

Taylor assumed he was asking to try the coffee so slid the mug over to Duran.

"Gratias tibi." Duran drank and let out a satisfying sigh. He pushed the plate of biscuits over to the other two men. "Haec bona sunt."

Taylor took a biscuit. "Well, that sounded like 'thanks' and he seemed to like the coffee. Hey Richards, what time is it?"

Richards looked at his watch. "It's a little after six, why, you need to be somewhere?"

Taylor turned to the mirror. "Hey, can someone get on to the mess and get three large full English and a pot of coffee with mugs. Oh! Make sure they send over sources and double time it."

"Nice thinking my boy. I know I haven't eaten in at least ten hours. And you can't beat a nice full English."

Another awkward silence descended on the trio. *'Ship. I need to find a way to communicate with these men?'* Thought Duran.

'Well, if it helps at all they are about to get you some food that isn't a biscuit. You need to find a way to get them to bring you the translator from your bag, it's good that I had the foresight to put it in.'

Duran stood and turned away from the table and took a couple of paces. He lowered his head to his chest and wrapped his hands over it. He stood thinking for a moment.

"Crap!" Said Richards. "Do you think he is having a reaction to the coffee?"

Duran dropped his arms a lifted his head, he had an idea. Turning to look at Taylor he snapped his fingers and started to beckon. "Veni huc mecum." He led Taylor towards the door, once again the Redcaps started to get a little jumpy.

"Stand down you two. If this guy wanted too, we would all be a pile on the floor."

When they got to the door Duran pointed through the small window towards the table with his equipment on, he then imitated the tech who had been taking pictures of it. "Potesne me accipere picturas supellectilem meam?"

"Well, I got the word 'picture' in that." Taylor turned to the mirror again. "Can someone get the pictures of all this guy's kit and send them in here."

'Nice idea Duran, he's understood what you wanted and called for the pictures of your equipment.' Projected the ship.

Duran laughed and slapped Taylor hard on the shoulder. Taylor winced at the pain. *'You better go easy on that man.'* Said the ship. *'Looks like you cracked some of his ribs in your fight. I am surprised they have not fixed them for him.'*

Duran grab Taylor gently on each shoulder. "Doleo, non hoc te dolere." He said gently.

Taylor pulled away and raised his hand. "Yeah, It's ok big man. You're still winning this fight." Turning he walked back to the table and took his seat again. Duran following and doing the same.

Richards Turned to Taylor. "Do you know something Jim. The more I hear this guy talk, the more it reminds me of Latin. That's a pretty old language and probably only used by the church these days."

"Can we find someone who speaks it?"

"I'll put out some feelers." Pulling out his phone Richards started to type a text. "The hard part will be finding someone with clearance."

The door opened and a hand with a folder came through. One of the Redcaps took it and then walked over and handed it to Richards.

"Thank you. OK, let's see what our boy wants these for." Richards laid the folder on the table and opened it for Duran to see.

Duran picked up the pile of pictures and started to flick through them, he pulled out the one with his gun on it. Holding it up, he pointed enthusiastically saying. "Hoc quaeso possum?" Both Richards and Taylor looked visibly shocked. Duran burst into laughter. "EGO iustus volo videre facies tuas." He threw the picture up in the air and continued to look. Finally, he pulled out the item he really wanted. He placed it on the table in front of Richards and then pointed and gestured to his mouth, and ears and then Taylors mouth and ears. "Hoc item adiuva nos loqui."

"My guess is he is saying that is some sort of translator. Jim, what do you think?"

Taylor thought for a moment. "It could be another weapon and he is just trying to throw us off with the gun gag."

Richards picked up the picture and signalled to a Redcap. "Get the tech boys to take a look at this. I want them to do every test they can with the kit they have here. If they think it is safe send it into me." The Redcap turned, walked to the door, banged, and passed the photo through with Richard's instructions.

The trio settled into another uneasy silence. "Come on Jim, we need another bright idea."

Fortunately, Taylor was saved by the door opening and the Redcaps walking in with the trays of food he asked for. Taylor stood and directed the men to put the trays on the table. "Come on guys double time it, we are hungry!"

The Redcaps paused. "Sir, we are worried about this. They sent over metal cutlery; I've asked them to get some plastic stuff."

"Sod that!" Said Taylor. "Just put it down. Told you before not much is going to stop this guy."

The Redcaps placed the trays in front of the men and retreated back out of the room closing the door. Duran looked down at the tray. "Nescio quid hoc est, sed bonum spectat." And started to dig in. After taking a few mouthfuls he let out a satisfying moan.

Taylor smiled. "Good?"

"Good." Mimicked Duran.

As the three men dug in Taylor gave Duran some red and brown source packets and showed him what to do with them. Once again Duran let out a satisfying 'Mmmmm'. Richards set out the mugs and poured coffee for them all. He showed Duran the milk and sugar, but the big man didn't seem that interested. As they eat Taylor pondered. *This wasn't doing much for communication, but it might help with bonding.* Richards wasn't as hungry as he thought and was leaving a sausage to one side.

"Non es ad manducandum?" Duran hovered his fork over it.

Richards laughed, then gestured. "Sure, go ahead."

Duran stabbed down on the sausage, onto his plate, through the brown source and into his mouth. *'Ship, we are only shooting this place up as a last resort. I need to get some of this food into your stores.'* Projected Duran.

'Nice to see you going with your gut instinct. I will not blow up these people as they have nice food.'

With all the food gone Richards gestured to the Redcaps. "Get this cleared away and have more coffee sent in. Also find out how long that device will be. If it's more than ten minutes just get it sent in. I'd like to move this along one way or another."

As the table was cleared Duran stood and let out a hardy belch. "Good." He said again. Walking over to the corner of the room with the toilet, he took a piss then washed his hands and face.

Richards turned to Taylor and spoke softly. "Well, he likes the food. I'm pretty sure he understands us, and he can use the loo. Let's hope this device is a translator, we might get somewhere."

Taylor nodded. "I don't think he's the type to blow himself up, we have to take the risk."

The door opened and one of the techs walks in with the device in hand. "Sir. We can't really tell you anything about this. It does not give off any heat or power we can measure. Xray show nothing, we can't find any joints or seems. If we could get it to a bigger lab with more equipment, we might be able to tell you more." He held the device out.

Richards cautiously took it from the tech. He tries to feel the weight and texture in his hand before passing it to Taylor to do the same. "Ok, thank you. You can leave." Seeing what was going on Duran returned to his seat. He looked at Taylor, first pointing to the device and then tapping the middle of the table.

Taylor turned to Richards. "Looks like we are doing this." Taylor slowly placed the device in the middle of the table. Duran then held up his hand. He extended his index and middle finger and wrapped his thumb around the other two fingers. He nodded and gestured at the two men to do the same. With some reluctance they followed suit. He then slowly lowered his hand until the two extended fingers touched the device, again he nodded at the other two men to do the same.

"Jim. I don't want to look like a coward here, but it only needs one of us to do this till we know it's safe."

Taylor laughed. "In that case, by all means join us when you are ready." Taylor lowered his hand until his two outstretch fingers touched the device. He looked towards Richards. "So far I am not feeling anything."

Duran smiled. "But now you can understand me!"

Taylor Jumped back, pulling his hand from the device. "Woooooow!"

"Jim. Are you ok!" Richards grabbed him looking very concerned, and the Redcaps started to close in batons drawn.

"No, NO! Its Ok. I'm ok. Just Wow, that was so Weird!" Taylor leaned forward and put his fingers back on the device. "Yes, I can understand you. Sorry, that was a shock, is it meant to feel like that?"

Again, Duran Laughed. "I am sorry my friend. Not sure I can answer that. I cannot remember back to the first time I used one of these, it's been many years. But knowing how it is supposed to work I can understand your shock."

"It's like you feel the words, not hear them, the sound comes from the wrong place." Explained Taylor.

"Yes. That would be a good way to say it."

Taylor turned to Richards. "As you can tell it's a translator. Try not to get weirded out, it is a strange feeling."

Richards leaned forward and placed his fingers on the device with the other two. "Am I doing this right?"

Duran looked at Richards. "You are if you can understand me."

Richards eyes rolled. "Jim. I knew it, just like all the science fiction movies. You weren't kidding. It's like you feel the words, not hear them."

Duran Laughed. "A trick that may help. Try not to look at the mouth that is talking. Over the years your brain learns to subconsciously lip read. This is part of the strange feeling you have. With time your brain will unlearn this, and it will ignore it. This device is used to set up a neural link. It stops your brain hearing what is said and instead directly feeds the translated words to your brain."

"Thanks for the advice." Said Richards. "But if you can forgive me getting to the point, I need to know why you are here and what are your intentions?"

For the first time Duran lost his cheeky smile. "Five minutes before you attacked me, I intended to leave this shit area of space and never come back. This man saw to stop that and here we are!"

"OK! And the WHY!"

Duran looked Richards in the eye, his smile returning. "For Love!"

"You say this is a shit area of space, but you are here because you love it?"

"I do not love this place. There was something in this place I needed for Love."

Richards started to get frustrated. "I don't think this box of yours is working right or you aren't being straight with me. I need something better than that?"

Duran let his smile slip again. "Have you ever been in love Richards. I have, with a beautiful woman. To get her favour, it is customary in my culture to fulfil a deed or bring a gift to the father. The greater the deed or gift, the greater the honour shown. She suggested retrieving the chronical of one of her ancestors. I came here to find it, finally located it last night. With it in hand I was going to head back to her and present it to her father."

Richards took this in for a moment. "So, you came all this way to get a gift for your lover's father! I find that hard to believe. How far did you come anyway?"

Duran was now starting to find Richards questions irritating. "I have travelled about fifteen thousand light years, and I will have an issue with any man that does not accept my word!"

Taylor was quick to jump in. "Ok, look, it's not that we don't believe you. You have to understand we have never met anyone from one light year away let alone thousands. We know nothing about you, we need to build some trust."

Duran again looked directly at Richards. "One thing you can trust about me is that I will never lie. In my culture, especially where I am from, honour is one of the most important things a man can strive for. Men have been put to death because they were not honourable."

Richards still needed more. "Ok, if all that is true and this is a shit area of space, how did this conical end up here?"

Duran turned to Taylor. "This is a shit area of space because it is too far out to be worth anything. There is nothing out here to make the journey worth it. You say you have never met anyone from one light year away, but you may have. This planet you live on has only one use. For tens of thousands of years, it has been used as an exile planet. For certain crimes, banishment can be seen as a greater punishment than death. The chronicle I was searching for belonged to a great poet and thinker. Unfortunately, some of his works were seen as subversive, so he was banished and sent here. Thousands of people have been banished to this ball of rock over the millennia. So, you say you have never met anyone, you may have and not even known it. You will find that many great people from your history took advantage of their advanced knowledge to be something on this world and live a more comfortable life."

This seemed to take Richards and Taylor some time to digest. I guess Richards finally had the earth shattering something he wanted. Richards managed to put a thought together. "So, you are not hear to destroy us or enslave us?"

"The house that controls this area of space has outlawed slavery for thousands of years, and if I wanted to destroy you, I could have done that without even leaving my home world."

Again, Richards and Taylor seemed lost for words. Richards sat back removing his fingers from the device. "Jim. I need to report back to the PM. You carry on chatting, see what you can find out. Try not to give too much information away if he starts asking questions." Richards stood and walked out of the room.

Duran watched Richards Leave. "Your friend, he does not seem to like me very much."

This time it was Taylors turn to laugh. "He's not really my friend, he is my boss, it's his job not to like people."

"Well Taylor, I like you, you bested me in battle. Even if it was eight to one. I was foolish and underestimated you."

"More like ten to one on the field, and a few hundred others in the rear."

Duran let out one of his customary laughs. "You also bested my ship."

"How would you feel if I said a female did that."

Another even louder laugh. "In my culture my friend, some of our best warriors are female. If you ever meet my sister, do not upset her!"

Taylor smiled. "If we live so far out, as you say, I can't see that happening."

"Taylor this may be true, but what of me? I have told you what you asked. I mean no harm to your world. My plan was always to be in and out with no one knowing. I should be halfway home by now."

Taylor thought for a moment. "I wish I could answer that. I believe everything you say and if it were up to me, I would shake your hand and send you on your way. You may not have meant it, but you have hurt and killed people, and some might not be happy to let that go."

"I am sorry, I did not know. I am guessing it is down to Richards to decide my fate."

"Not just him. He also has bosses. It will be down to them to make any decisions about you and your ship."

"Ah! My ship. I should warn you Taylor. My ship is probably no longer damaged. It is a very clever machine. I would tell your people not to try and damage or get into it. As a last resort it will self-destruct. If it does, it will make a hole twenty kilometres wide!"

Taylor turned to the mirror. "Did you get that?"

Over the intercom a voice came back. "Get what Sir? We can't understand what he is saying to you."

"Warn Richards to tell the ship site not to mess with the ship. It could self-destruct if they do."

"Yes Sir!" came a reply.

Taylor turned back to Duran. "Look, I would guess at the very least they will want you to give them some information on how the ship works, weapons and other tech."

"Then they will be disappointed. I cannot answer questions like that for them."

"Why, because they are all secrets you are not allowed to share on the pain of death?"

"In a way Yes! But not my secrets, secrets hidden from most. The people that build the ships guard their technology closely. They do not want others to know how it is done. Also, it is impossible for an organic being to operate a ship like that, they are far too complex. It would take someone a month to calculate

100

a flight plan across space, and by then it would be wrong. The ship has a very powerful conscious mind to do this, and complex automated systems to keep it running."

Taylor sat and thought. He believed him, but he knew Richards wouldn't, and until he got something he knew Duran would never see the light of day again.

"Taylor, I can tell this troubles you. Your Boss, he will not believe me?"

"No, I doubt he will!" Taylor sighed. "Richards will have no choice but to give his bosses something from you."

"I cannot give what I do not have! You must help me get my things and get back to the ship. I will leave this place and you will never see me again."

"I'm Sorry. I can't!" Taylor stood and walked towards the door."

"TAYLOR!" Bellowed Duran.

Taylor put his head down and walked out of the room followed by the two Redcaps. He felt so disgusted with himself, this man did not deserve what was going to happen to him.

Duran wasn't happy. *'Ship, were you listening? We may need to blast our way out of here after all.'*

'I am sorry Duran, that is no longer possible.'

'Why, is the damage worse than you thought?'

'Repairs should be complete within the hour. The problem now is they have tied me to the ground and brought in heavy weapons. I calculate I would only have a seventeen percent chance of rescuing you and breaking the gravity well of this planet. Are you sure you cannot get this man Taylor to help us.'

'No, he too is a loyal warrior. He will only do as he is commanded.'

'In that case I assume in an hour we are going down fighting and taking many of them with us.'

'Ship, I will try to reason with this Richards once more. If that fails, then yes, we will fight! Let me know when you are fully operational and make ready for action.'

Duran returned to the bed, laying down he started to think what he could say to change Richards's mind and let him go.

Chapter 6: The Bargain.

Taylor could see Richards talking on the phone. He didn't want to wait but he needed Richards in a good mood. He walked towards him but stopped a few meters away so as not to crowd him. Richards ended his call and turned to see Taylor waiting.

"PM is pleased to know we are worthless in the cosmos. He can go back to only worrying about Russia and the Chinese. What else did you learn my boy?"

"It depends, what are you going to do with him now."

"Me, not a lot. But I expect him, and that ship of his will get passed up the chain. He will be pumped for all the information he can give us, and that ship of his will be stripped down to the last nut n bolt for all it secrets."

"Did you not get the message about the ship?"

"I did, and I passed it along, but I don't believe it. Jim, he is just trying to scare us away from the ship."

"But what if he isn't. He says he does not lie, and he says the ship has its own consciousness. Why don't we try and reason with him before we throw him in a hole and get ourselves blown to shit, He's already told me he can't tell us anything!"

"Jim, he's bound to say that! Look you stick to catching the bad guys, I'll stick to getting what we want from them. I've just had the DNA back on him. It's a 99.9% match to ours. That guy is as much human as you and I, we need to know how that can be."

"Richards! He's not a bad guy. Look, talk to him again, listen to what he has to say. You will see you are wasting your time."

Richards thought for a moment. Taylor had always been one of his best operators, the last thing he needed to do was alienate him too much. "Jim, it's not like you to get so close in a situation like this."

"There has never been a situation like this before. I have never felt regret for a single action I have taken until now. Humour me will you. Please."

Richards Sighed. "Twenty minutes, your man has twenty minutes then I am out of here!"

Taylor turned and the two men started to walk back to Durans holding room.

'Duran. Your friend Taylor has spoken with Richards and is pleading your case. They are coming back to you. Taylor may have made Richards change his mind.' Projected the ship to Duran.

'Ship. Monitor our conversation. If it sounds like Richards cannot be swayed, I want you to blow up a few things. Run the lift engines on low power so the ground shakes and issue a warning that you will self-destruct in one hour if I am not returned. NO Casualties for now!'

'Understood, I will put fear into their bones!'

Taylor and Richards walked into the room followed by two of the Redcaps. "You two wait outside this time, just be ready to get in here if things go south." Said Taylor.

"You sure about this Jim?"

"You want to know what he's like, I want him to feel more at ease."

"OK! But if he kills me, I'll never let you forget it."

The two men walked to the table and sat down. Taylor Motioned to Duran. "Duran will you join us?"

Duran stood and walked over to the table. He sat and placed his fingers onto the translator. The two other men did the same.

Richards cleared his throat. "Taylor here tells me you can't tell us anything."

"Richards. I could tell you many things. I have travelled to far off places in the galaxy. I have fought in many battles. I would happily tell you these stories.

What I cannot tell you is what you wish to know. Has Taylor told you I have no knowledge of how the ship functions. Has he told you the ship will destroy itself before it lets you look inside."

"He has, but why should I believe you?"

Duran thought. "Let us assume you are right. I know all about my ship. I don't want to tell you because they are my secrets, and I don't wish you to know. That is what you believe?"

"Yes!" Said Richards. "I do."

"So why is it so hard for you to accept, the people who make the ships also do not want others to know their secrets. Why can you not believe that? Tell me, do you know how everything you use in your world works?"

Richards thought for a second. "Look, even if what you say is true, I have to take something to the people above me. If you won't tell me anything, then I will just have your ship chopped up for it secrets."

The ships voice sounded in Durans mind. '*I guess that is my cue.*'

The intercom crackled. "Sir. I Need to speak with you immediately!"

"What is it, I'm busy!" Shouted Richards with some annoyance over his shoulder.

"Sir. It's about the ship!"

Richards turned to face Duran. "What is it. Just tell me."

"We have just had reports the ship has fired and destroyed some of the equipment around it. Something is happening around the ship, that has forced everyone to pull back. It has also demanded the release of its master within one hour or it will self-destruct, and the door and ramp have closed."

Richards calmly looked Duran in the eye. "You knew this was going to happen."

"I Told you the ship is very clever. One of its base commands is not to allow itself to be examined. It was only a matter of time for it to complete repairs and determine its best cause of action. It has lost its pilot. I assume it can see hostile forces all around it and they are preventing it from leaving?"

Richards moved uncomfortably in his seat. "That would be a fair assessment."

"Until that ship can talk to someone it trusts it will assume the worst and do everything it can to defend itself. It may try to shoot its way out of whatever you have it trapped in, but if it is left with no choice, it will destroy itself and anything within a twenty-kilometre radius."

"Someone it trusts! How can a machine trust someone."

"Do you not have intelligent computer systems on your planet?"

"We have computers with artificial intelligence, but they can't trust people."

"You are thousands of years behind that ship in technology. Its builders have developed a conscious mind that runs the ship. It is the only way possible to control something that complex. It is basically an artificial brain, but over one hundred times more powerful."

"All of a sudden you seem to know something about your ship."

"I know the basics. I talk to the ships consciousness to get it to fly the ship. I know it is powered by a gravitational singularity and anti-matter. I know the weapons use a compressed plasma stream, but I could not tell you how to make any of those things. Richards, I want YOU to tell me how to make one of your computer systems. I bet you cannot, and the builders of such things keep them a secret!"

Richards laughed. "Ok I can't, but you picked a poor example, kids build them in their bedroom all the time. Look! I get what you are saying, but I can't just let you go, or it will be my ass that's on the line. I need to get something from you I can take to the brass."

"Look, I have told you I am a man of my word. You hold the chronical and let me go. I know a few people who may have information that will be useful to you. I can get that, bring it back and we trade."

Richards stood and started to pace.

Duran turned to Taylor. "Thank you for talking to him. The ship will do as it threatens. I never came here to hurt anyone; you have to help me make a deal."

Taylor nodded not wanting to say anything Richards could hear.

A voice came over the intercom. "Sir, the ship has fired again. It says we now have forty-five minutes."

Richards sat, placing his fingers back on the translator he turned to Duran. "How come your ship can speak English and you can't."

"One hundred brains! It can learn very fast. Within the first couple of hours of our arrival it had learnt all the major languages of your world and programmed this device for me. I told the ship I didn't want to carry it, but it insisted. It is good that it did, or you would all be dead and have no idea why."

"Sir, the ship site is asking for orders, do they attack or retreat?" Came a nervous voice over the intercom.

"Tell them to stand fast!" He shouted. He was trying to remember the last time he had been faced with a decision of this magnitude. He turned and looked Duran in the eye. "I will agree, but on my terms. How many people can that ship hold."

"It can take a crew of up to twenty, but I will not take that many, I see no reason for it."

"No no." Richards was still trying to figure out what he wanted. "Probably six or eight. I want Taylor here and a few others to keep you company."

Taylor looked a little shocked. "Ermmm, I'm still supposed to be on leave, SIR!"

"Well, you can take your leave on a space cruise. Don't say I never get you anything!"

Duran considered what Richards was saying. "You will need to bring me one of the gauntlets so I can talk to the ship."

Richards stared at Duran, tapping his fingers on the table. Finally, he turned to the mirror and shouted. "Bring in one of his gauntlets and send in all the Redcaps!"

A few moments later the Redcap's walked in, one of them carrying a gauntlet. Richards held up his hand for them to wait. "Duran. How does this work?"

"If you place it on the table, I just need to touch it to help me communicate with my ship."

Richards waited. "Gentlemen, I want you to stand ready around our friend here. Place the gauntlet on the table. If he does ANYTHING apart from touch it and talk, I want you to beat the crap out of him. Understood?"

"Yes Sir!" They said together as they moved around Duran drawing their batons. The one who had been carrying the gauntlet placed it on the table taking a step back drawing his own baton.

Duran sat back in his chair and raised both his hands. He slowly lowered his left hand onto the gauntlet. "Navem. Desine comitem per quinque horas, et plura mandata expecto." He then slowly raised his hand again.

Richards looked at the Redcaps. "OK, you can all leave and take that with you." As they started to leave Duran lowered both his arms to his side.

'*Duran. Your honour and not lying are starting to get a little thin. The gauntlet has no communicator.*' Remarked the ship in his mind.

'*It helped me communicate with you by not revealing how we really do it.*'

Richards shouted to the intercom. "Contact the ship site and get me an update."

A few moments later a voice came back. "Sir, site reports the ship seems to be powering down."

Turning back to Duran Richards waved his fingers in the air and then placed them back onto the translator. Duran waited a moment. He felt he was back in control of the conversation, so was in no hurry to rush. He was about to try and take even more control if he could. He waited for a moment before placing his fingers on the device.

"So, what did you tell your ship?" Asked Richards.

"I told it if it did not hear from me in five hours to restart its destruction countdown."

Richards smiled and chuckled. "I can see you are smarter than I took you for. Ok, let's make a deal. I will keep your chronical. You go and get me information that will keep our scientists busy for the next twenty years and you get your chronical back and your freedom."

"I agree." Said Duran.

"Not so fast. I want you to take Taylor and a couple of his boys, so you don't decide to just find another girl. Also, a couple of scientists to see if what you have is worth it."

Duran nodded. "I agree."

"Why do I feel like you are giving in to easy?"

Duran sighed. "Because it is what I need to do to fulfil my task. When I tell my loves father, it will make the task seem even more heroic and make for an even greater story."

Richards laughed. "Careful I may ask for more if it is going to help you."

"I will have one very important condition of my own." Duran turned to Taylor. "When you come on to my ship, you and all your people will have to do everything I say, without question or hesitation!"

Taylor nodded. "I guess you're the captain."

"It's not just that. Space is dangerous, where I plan to go is dangerous, the people we meet will be dangerous. One wrong move or word and we could all end up dead. I can spend some time during the journey to train you, but it will be a lot to take in and I cannot be responsible for you if you do not do as I say."

This made Taylor feel a little uneasy. "I understand. I will make sure my people understand."

"Right! Let's move this along." Richards was getting impatient. "I need to consult with the PM. Taylor, go and see if three of your guys fancy a six-week space cruse, and I will dig up a couple of scientists. You can get going as soon as we are ready." Richards seemed relieved now he finally had something.

"Richards, I will also need supplies, I won't have enough food and water for seven people." Asked Duran.

"I'm sure we can arrange that, what do you need?"

"At least three thousand litres of water and food for seven to last six weeks."

"Can't your amazing ship make food and water?"

Duran chuckled. "It can, it may fill your stomach, but it will empty your soul. What you gave me earlier reminded me of how much I miss real food."

"Sort it out with Taylor. In fact, Taylor, get anything you need on my authorisation, I'll be back later." Richards turned and walked out of the door already scrabbling to find his phone and radio.

Duran turned to Taylor. "So, we are going on a journey you and I. You do not look very happy about it. Does the thought of going into space frighten you?"

"No, not frighten. For the last year I have either been deployed or training. I was supposed to have three weeks leave. On the fourth day they drag me in so I can have you beat the crap outta me. And now he wants to send me into space. No time off and no time to heal."

Duran laughed. "Do not worry about healing my friend. The medical bay on my ship will fix you up better than new. As for time off, you will sleep for a lot of the journey, and when you don't, I will show you many things. When I bring you home you can have your time off then."

"So, you intend to bring us home then?"

"Yes, my plan will be to bring you all home, but I will not promise it. I did not lie to you earlier and I will not do so now. I cannot be sure what we will find. There are two people I know I can ask, after that I do not know where this journey will take us. Out there you and your people will be as children, you must follow what I say, or I could be powerless to protect you."

"You keep saying that and it makes you sound scared, what should we expect."

"The galaxy is ruled by many different houses. I belong to the house Tar, one of the largest. We live in a time of uneasy peace with the other houses around us. This should not be a problem as we should not need to go near any of the border regions. But our ways and customs, you must all learn the right way to act and behave. The slightest insult could result in a challenge, there may even be times I have to insist you stay on the ship."

"I understand, going all that way it might be nice to see an exciting new planet, but will do as you say if it means getting back in one piece. Look, let me go and get the men and supplies sorted and we can talk some more. The food I assume anything, do you have refrigeration on the ship?"

Duran let out one of his usual laughs. "No, not refrigeration, we use a stasis field, food will last forever in that. Bring whatever you like, I am sure I will enjoy it, just don't forget the water, I need to flush out the ship's tanks."

Taylor smiled. He really did like this guy. "Ok, well let me get that sorted and I will be back in a bit." Duran held out his arm and smiled, the two men once again shook.

As Taylor left the holding room, he could see Sarah waiting. She had a quizzical look on her face that looked a little scary. He walked over and was greeted to a soft hug. "How the ribs?" She asked.

"Not so bad if I keep popping the pills."

"That's good." She said with a wry smile. "Nice sweats, you should wear them more often."

Taylor laughed. "Ok, what is going on, you are only this nice when you want something?"

"Can't a girl just be happy to see her guy's ok?"

Taylor just looked at her!

"Okaay. I could only understand what you and Richards were saying, but it sounds like we haven't finished this mission yet. What's phase two boss?"

Taylor sighed. He knew he was about to be set up. "My friend Duran in there, has agreed to take a group of us out there to get some new toys." He pointed up for dramatic effect.

"I heard Richards say three of your guys and a couple of scientists. James, I am one of your guys, aren't I?" She said softly.

"Sarah please. He keeps telling me how dangerous this is going to be. Please I would rather you sit this one out."

"I know what you would rather, but come on Jim, I have followed you to the four corners of this planet. Why can't I follow you to another. You know I will just cry myself to sleep every night while you are gone."

"Lieutenant, you know you are not playing fair! Look, Ok, you can come, but no dicking around, you have to play by his rules."

"Oooo, I'd love to play by his rules."

"And you can knock that shit off as well. One, he has a girl, this is all for his girl, and two, I can always leave your sorry ass here! Walk with me."

"Yes Sir!" she giggled.

Taylor headed out into the hanger. "Go make yourself useful. Get over to the mess. I want six week's fresh food supplies for seven people, get a mix of everything including spices, tea and coffee, plus a week's supply of MRE's. Also, I want three thousand litres of fresh drinking water, it all needs to get up to the ship site ASAP."

"OK, just a small shopping list. Anything else, comms, weapons?"

Taylor stopped. "Not sure!" He thought. "See if you can get four side arms and ammo. Hide them in with the food." He started to walk again.

"You think there could be trouble?"

Taylor didn't answer. "Are the guys still in the barrack block?"

"Yeah, they have been confined to base till Richards figures out what we are doing."

"I need to go and talk to them. Once you get the food sorted see if you can find me some clothes. I ent going into space in this shit. Meet me back at the hanger when you're done."

"Jim, how do we dress for space?"

"No idea but looking at his kit, lightweight greens should do it. See if the medical unit still has my boots, I don't have time to break in a new pair."

Taylor headed across to the barrack block, Stevens splitting off heading to the mess on the way.

Taylor could hear the music blaring out before he even got into the block. He walked into the common area to find his team kicking back drinking beer, playing darts and pool. "OK! Turn that shit off and fall in."

Danny reluctantly turned the music off and the men slowly filtered to the middle of the room.

"How the ribs doin boss?" asked Jaz.

Taylor laughed. "I keep telling people, fine as long as I keep popping the pills! Unfortunately, I ent got time to worry about that now, I have to go out again."

"Well, ent you just Richards's bitch!" Laughed Andy. "Busted up, still on leave. No rest for the wicked!"

"Tell me about it! And on that happy note, Sam, Robo, got any plans for the next six weeks?"

All the men looked a little shocked.

"Nothing I can't cancel boss." Said Robo.

Sam could not resist. "Well Sir, if Robo is going away for six weeks, I was thinking about going to visit his mum."

"Good luck with that. Dads a six-foot four ex para." Robo back handed Sam in the crotch for good measure as all the men laughed.

"Ok you wankers settle down. I want you two in hanger seven in one hour. Stop the beer, stow your shit, and get some coffee in you. Hook up with Stevens if I'm not around."

Sam recovered from his shock slap. "Where we off to this time boss?"

"For now, hanger seven. I'll brief you over there. The rest of you are probably going to be confined to base for another forty-eight hours but I will make sure Richards confirms that shortly. Remember not a word about any of this to anyone. You know what Richards is like."

"Sir, what can you tell us about the guy we grabbed, apart from 'nothing!'" Asked Jaz making quote signs in the air.

Taylor laughed. "Good call Corporal. Let's just say you all did a great job. The brass are very happy, and it's going to be an interesting six weeks for me. In fact, gimmie one of those beers seeing as you all still have one."

Sam reached over and passed Taylor a bottle.

Taylor snapped the cap off and raised the bottle in front of him. "All IN! Who FUCKING Dares Wins!"

The men all pushed in the bottles clinking them together following Taylors lead in unison. "Who FUCKING Dares Wins, Hoooooooo!" Then drinking deeply.

"Right!" Shouted Taylor. "You two, hanger, one hour, sober! The rest of you assholes stay out of trouble until Richards kicks you off base."

"Yes Sir!" Said Sam and Robo, downing the last of their beer.

"Not a Chance!" Shouted a few of the others.

Taylor walked back to the hanger stopping along the way to sit on a bench. When he woke up yesterday morning, he was pissed Richards had cut short his leave. Then he was pissed Richards sent him on a suicide mission. He was now pissed Richards was sending him off into space. He started to laugh at himself, who was he kidding, this had probably been the best twenty-four hours of his life. Space, fuck yeah. He could secretly laugh at any squaddie who tells a tall war story for the rest of his life.

Chapter 7: The Ship.

The helicopter's engines were already running as everyone started to load up; this made it hard to talk over the noise. Sarah had got Taylor some clothes and found his boots for him, so that was a plus. Apart from the food and water Duran requested he had told them not to bring anything else, he would provide all they needed. He was starting to feel glad Sarah had hidden some weapons for them. Taylor, Stevens, Sam and Robo settled into their seats. Taylor thought back to when he told Sam and Robo they were going into space. The looks on their faces made him smile. They thought he was pulling their chains, now they just looked in shock. As they waited two other people walked up the ramp. Taylor didn't know them, and they both looked totally bemused. He waved and pointed at the seats opposite them.

"Hi. My name is Paul, this is Julia. Do you know what is going on?" Shouted the man.

"Yes!" Shouted Taylor. "You're going to sit in those seats and be quite!"

Someone had put them both in a couple of badly fitting RAF coveralls that made their awkwardness look even worse. Each had what looked like a laptop case over their shoulder. They both sat looking like rabbits in headlights.

"Strap in!" Shouted Taylor, pulling at his harness. After a bit of fumbling, they managed to figure out how the harnesses went together. These must be our scientist thought Taylor. By the sounds of it, Richards had told them nothing. This should be fun. Baby sitting them, and making sure Duran doesn't dump us all out into space the first chance he gets. A few minutes passed and Richards started to walk up the ramp followed by a couple of Redcaps and Duran. He was still in chains, but they had given him back his clothes. One of the redcaps was carrying a bag with the rest of Duran's belongings, but he could see Duran had the translator in his hand. The two scientist obviously recognised Richards and looked at him hoping to maybe get some reassurance, but Richards just ignored them. He sat pointing for the Redcaps to secure Duran opposite him. They did this and then sat flanking him one seat away. Richards waved at the load master stood by the ramp and pointed up signalling him to get airborne. After talking on his headset, the engines started to ramp up power and the craft started to lift. Fifteen minutes and they would be back at the ship. It was late afternoon now; Richards didn't want the ship to lift off until after nightfall. So far, the crashed experimental aircraft cover was working and the last thing he wanted was any photos going viral. The flight passed quietly, no one wanting to try and shout over the sound of the engines. As soon as they touched down people started to unfasten their harnesses. The two scientists still looked like scared little children, fumbling their way out as they had their way in. Taylor grabbed them by their coveralls and slowly pushed them towards the ramp. As he walked by Richards he shouted. "I take it these two have zero field experience and zero idea why they are here?"

"They have basic training, and you get the pleasure of filling them in on the details, I will leave you their files on the desk. If they give you any push back just remind them, they signed up for field work and they don't have a choice!" Richards had slipped back into his grumpier self.

Clearing the ramp, they were shown to a porta-cabin about one hundred meters from the covered ship. Walking over they could see some of the things the ship had blown up. That's when Taylor realised what all the nice round holes were in the covers. Taylor giggled to himself, so the ship has a pretty good targeting system to fire blind. The porta-cabin was pretty sparse, a few chairs and a table and a couple of techs with some kit. They all filed into the room with Richards bringing up the rear.

"Richards, can we get those chains off him now. He has given us his word he will play ball and I believe him." Taylors cracked ribs were starting to put him in a bad mood now.

"In good time Jim! I have got us a small insurance policy to help with our friends' behaviour". Richards waved at the techs. "Get on with it!"

One of the techs walked up to Taylor. "Hold out your left arm and roll your sleeve up slightly. The rest of you do the same please." He then started to mess around fitting what looked like a small black watch to their wrists. "This is a heart rate monitor. The battery will last up to six months, they are designed to only be removed with an electronic key. Please do not try and remove them yourselves." He then picked up a larger looking version and walked over to Duran. "Lift up your shirt please." Duran stared down at the smaller man and growled slightly. He held the translator out in front of him. "Oh yes, silly me I forgot." He placed his fingers on it and repeated. "Please lift up your shirt." Duran again growled at the man but did as he was asked. The tech got to work strapping the device around Duran's waist, something he didn't look very happy about. "So, Major Taylor, I have already explained this to Mr Duran, around his waist in the belt is a small explosive charge and a receiver. Around each of your wrists is a heartbeat detector. If the belt is tampered with, BOOM. If it does not receive a signal from at least one of you every sixty seconds, then BOOM. His battery will last six months, then BOOM. The range on this is about five hundred meters, so stay close. Again, the belt needs an electronic key to be removed and that is staying with me."

"Uuuum, e-e-excuse me." Stuttered Paul. "Could someone please tell us what is going on?"

"Wait!" Said Richards sternly. "Thanks Doc, you and your people clear out, give us the room and head back to Brize." The two men quickly did as instructed and left. Richards held out his hand to Taylor. "Over to you my boy, with luck we will see you back in about six weeks. I have given Duran radio frequencies and protocols, he said the ship will have no trouble with them, so call us when you are back, and we will have a landing site set up for you."

Taylor took Richards's hand. "Try and make it somewhere warm."

Richards then held out his right hand to Duran while touching the translator with is left. "And you my boy, you will keep to your word."

Duran Took his hand. "Richards as I keep telling you all I can do is try. If nothing goes wrong, you will have your people back and the knowledge you seek."

Richards nodded. "The engineers will have the cover cleared over the ship in three or four hours." He turned to the Redcaps. "OK, get those chains off him and let's get out of here. Good luck to the rest of you."

As Richards left Paul was getting fit to burst. "Seriously, someone had better start talking or I am outta here!"

Taylor walked over to the table and picked up the two files' Richards had left on it. He turned to address the pair. "Ok, listen up and pay attention. I am Major James Taylor; I will be in overall command of this mission." He then pointed to the others. "This is Sarah, Sam, Robo and this fine fella is Duran. You are here because you have signed up for and been trained in field work. You also have the skill set we need to complete our mission."

Paul was becoming inpatient. "Yes, but what is the mission, why are we here?"

Taylor looked him dead in the eye. "I would have thought one of the first things you should have learnt is to keep your fucking mouth shut when the commanding officer is giving a briefing!" Paul thought about saying something then changed his mind. Taylor opened one of the files. "Julia Ingham, degrees in Astrophysics and Physics, correct?"

Julia cleared her throat. "Um, Yes Sir!"

Taylor opened the other file. "Paul Ownes, degrees in Electronics and Computing, correct?"

"Yes, that's me, but can you tell us why we are here."

Taylor stared at the man. "You REALLY do need to learn the manta of eyes and ears open, MOUTH SHUT, or this could end up being a really unpleasant trip!" Paul really had to bite his tongue to stay quiet.

"As I was about to say this is my friend Duran. He is from outer space. Behind those screens out there is his spaceship. After we finish here, we are going to get on his spaceship, and he is going to take us on a little trip." Both the scientist started to go pale and for the first time Paul seemed to have nothing to say for himself. "Length of mission is expected to be around six weeks. You are here to verify if anything we find could be useful to the British Government and mankind as a whole." They both looked in total shock. "Our job will be to protect you and make sure the mission runs without a hitch. Finally, and this is especially for you Mr Owens, I maybe in overall command of the mission but we all do EXACTLY as Duran tells us. We will be on his ship, going into his territory, at all times we must defer to his judgement. Do you fully understand what you have just been told." There was still stunned silence. "OWENS, INGHAM, Answer!" They both managed to get out a fumbled 'Yes'. "OK! First order of business we are going to walk over and get onto the ship. We will all keep our hands in our pockets, we will touch nothing until we are told otherwise. Let's move!"

Julia finally managed to break out of her shell, she pushed past Taylor and walked up to Duran. "Are you really from outer space?"

"Honey, if you want to talk to him you have to touch the box he is holding." Said Sarah.

Julia looked down and placed her hand more on his than the box. She looked up longingly. "If you're really from outa space I have so many questions for you." Duran just smiled down at her.

"Great!" Said Taylor. "That's all we need, another love-struck woman! Come on let's get going, we have three hours till night fall, we need to get a hustle on."

The group walked over to the screening around the ship. walking through a gap, they could see the ship properly for the first time. Julia stopped, she had seen plenty of space craft both real and concept, but this, this was the real deal, and she was in awe of it already. This was too much for her, she ran over and put her hands on the hull. "My god, this surface, it has no friction, what is the hull made from, what powers it, how fast can it go?"

"Ingham! What part of hands in pockets, mouth shut are you failing to grasp!" Growled Taylor.

"I'm sorry, but this is extraordinary, I have so many questions. I have waited all my life; my whole career has been for this."

"Well stow your enthusiasm, six weeks remember, and we haven't even got off the ground." Taylor was starting to find this all more than he could bare, hoping there is a cabin he could hide in for the trip. Turning towards the ramp they found three robots taking the food stores onboard and flushing the water tanks.

It was Ownes turn to get emotional. "Oh my God! Look at those robots, they are amazing." He walked up to one. "Hello, my name is Paul." He wasn't really expecting any form of reply.

The robot stopped what it was doing and turned to Owens. "Hello Paul. I have no designation; I am part of the ships integrated systems. Please just refer to me as ship or robot."

Ownes was stunned. "Er, er, wow, um, you must run on a complex AI system, how many calculations can you do per second?"

"I'm sorry, that information is not available!"

"OWENS!" Barked Taylor. "Hands pockets, mouth closed!" Taylor was close to bursting. "Look! Listen up you two, I am getting fed up with repeating myself. Follow Duran up the ramp."

Owens still could not help himself. "I don't understand. Him, this ship, the robots, we could expand our understanding of literally everything without having to go anywhere."

Taylor grabbed Owens by the collar and pushed him up against the ship, he was really starting to get annoyed now. "Don't you think we thought of that, don't you think we tried. Start falling into line or I will kick your arse up that ramp!" Owens pulled away from Taylor, stuffed his hands in his pockets and started to walk up the ramp, closely followed by the others. Following Duran, they could not help but look around as he led them through hatches and corridors until the came to a larger, what looked like, control room.

The room was suddenly filled with a soft sounding male voice. "Welcome, I am the conscious operating system of this ship, you can address me as Ship. I am a mark three, class seven scout ship. While you are onboard, I strongly suggest you do not touch anything or try to gain access to any areas that are off limits. If you do, well, at a minimum it could be painful. During our journey Duran and I will instruct you on the correct behaviour while on this ship, any places we go, or people we may have to meet. Before we start, I need to go through a quick medical check with each of you. One of the robots will then show you to quarters where you will change, the robots will instruct you on the clothing and how to wear it. Major Taylor, I will see you first. As well as the checks, I can help you with your ribs. Please go into the medical bay." A door opened, and Duran pointed for Taylor to go through.

'Duran, now you are onboard I have been able to update your neural net. You will be able to understand them, but we need to get their nets in place for them to understand you. I am also uncomfortable with the explosive strapped to you. Can I deactivate it?' Projected the ship into Durans mind.

"Ship!" Said Taylor with some confusion. "How do you know my name?"

"These details will become clearer as we progress with your training. In short, I know a great deal about all of you. Now, please proceed to the medical bay and take a seat."

Taylor walked through the door and into a small room, one of the robots was already waiting, there was an examination chair in the middle of it. He looked around cautiously before sitting down. Duran followed and stood to one side with the door closing behind him.

'*Yes, the update will make things easier. I do not want these humans to feel uncomfortable or threaten, this needs to all go smoothly. If you can deactivate it so they don't know then go ahead.*' Duran thought to the ship.

'*Thank you, it is now deactivated. If you are worried about their feelings, you may want to talk to them about the box of weapons they tried to hide in with the food stores.*'

In his mind Duran had a chuckle. '*I do like Taylor, get one of the robots to put the box in the Mess. I can talk to them once their comms nets have formed. That and everything else will be so much easier then.*'

The ship addressed Taylor. "Major Taylor I am going to run through what is about to happen as some of it will be a little uncomfortable. Keep your arms and head on the rests. I am going to ask you to take in a deep breath and hold it. Once you have done that, I am going to put you in a mild stasis field. Your brain will not like this as it will feel very unnatural, it may make you panic. Try not to, this should only be for around sixty seconds while I repair your ribs and do the other scans I need to do. Once done I will inject you with a couple of inoculations needed to protect you out in the universe. Any questions?"

Taylor wasn't sure where to go with this. "Are these injections safe for us."

"Does Duran look ok to you? I think you are already aware your physiology is almost identical?"

"Good enough, let's get on with it."

"Please take a deep breath, hold and relax." Said the Ship calmly.

Taylor relaxed and did as instructed. As he slowly filled his lungs with air, he started to feel the effects of the field around him. The ship wasn't joking, this was the most unnatural feeling he had ever had. As several long spidery arms came down from above, he started to wish he had been told to close his eyes. The arms started to move around him; in his peripheral vision he could just about make out a beam of light coming from them as they danced around the area where his ribs had been cracked. They then moved down to his right knee, then across both ankles. This was more than sixty seconds; he was starting to have trouble calming his mind. Paranoia started to creep in, was this Durans way of getting rid of them or taking over their bodies. The lights went off and the arms moved back to the ceiling. Another arm came over and pressed against his upper leg, as it retracted, he could feel the field release him. Taylor sat bolt upright and started to gasp for air.

"Ship!" Panted Taylor. "That didn't feel like sixty seconds?"

"You are correct Major Taylor; it was eighty-seven seconds. My scan showed you had some cartilage damage in your knee and ankles. I thought I may as well do that while you were here."

Taylor stood and took a few paces around the chair. "Wow! Ok yeah, they feel so much better, I had been putting up with that for years." He stretched and took a deep breath. "Nice, the ribs feel good too. Ermm Thanks Ship."

"You are welcome. I will now invite the rest of your team for scans. It will be a little easier for them as they do not have to go into the stasis field."

Taylor laughed. "That's a shame, when you get to Ownes maybe you could put him through it anyway."

"I did notice your altercation on the way in. I am sure I can oblige."

"Thank you Ship, I can see you and I will get on well together."

"That is my hope also Major Taylor. Now if you could follow the robot, he will take you to quarters, please relax and change into the clothing in your room, you will be collected when I have seen the rest of your team."

Taylor waved to Duran as the robot led him out of the room.

As the door closed behind Taylor, Duran asked. "Ship, do you have a projection on how long it will take for the neural comms net to form."

"There is very little difference between their brains and yours, so it should take about an hour."

"Ship, make sure the nets stay inactive. I don't want them starting to hear voices and thinking they are going mad before we can explain it all to them."

"I will monitor them constantly. Let's get Owens in here so I can have some fun with him."

"Ship, you aren't supposed to enjoy torturing a human."

"I'm not, I am simply following instructions from Major Taylor."

Duran found this unusual. "He doesn't have authority to give you instructions."

"I Know, but he will."

The door slid open. "Doctor Ownes, could you please come in for your medical now." Ownes came into the room, Duran pointed to the chair trying his hardest not to laugh as Owens sat down. "Doctor Ownes, please sit back and relax. This procedure should not take longer than sixty seconds." Owens sat down and the door closed behind him.

The robot led Taylor down a couple of corridors until they finally got to an open cabin door. Standing to one side the robot indicated to go in. "Major Taylor, these will be your assigned quarters for the duration of the trip. You have a bed, desk and terminal, toilet, shower, and storage locker. If you wish you can shower before you change into the clothes in the locker. The data terminal is not currently active, and the door will be locked until I return to collect you. The rest of your team will be assigned quarters along this corridor. Do you have any questions."

"I'm sorry, I am still having trouble with this. When you talk and I talk back, I am still talking to the ship?"

"That is correct Major Taylor. Although each robot is capable of independent tasks, all the systems on this ship are fully integrated."

"OK, so no telling you my deepest secrets then I guess."

"Major Taylor, my programming would not allow me to betray any confidences you share with me, unless they were to put myself or the crew in danger. In that case I would be forced to make them known."

"Ship, I can see we are going to have to work on your sense of humour. No, I don't have any more questions for now, I'm sure I can figure things out."

"In that case I will go an attend to the rest of your team and be back for you later." The robot turned and left the room with the door closing behind it.

One by one the ship ran its medical procedures on each member of the team. Although the medical scans were helpful, the real reason for them were to administer the injection which mostly contained nanites. In some ways they were an inoculation, they could help prevent infection and disease, but they were also used to construct the neural communication net that could be used for translation, long-distance communication, and interaction with other devices. Duran had told the ship to keep this from Taylor and his team so as not to spook them. It could have led to a long conversation that he didn't want to get into. It's easier to beg forgiveness and all that. Apart from Ownes, who really didn't like the extended period in the stasis field, everything was going smoothly with the rest of the team. One by one they were scanned, injected, and led to their quarters.

"And last, but I am sure not least, Lieutenant Stevens, could you please come in for your medical now." Requested the ship.

Sarah came into the room. "Now just to let you know, I'm not very keen on needles!"

"Lieutenant Stevens, there is nothing to be concerned about, please take a seat, sit back and relax, this will only take a few moments."

"If you say so, and Ship, please call me Sarah." She said snuggling her butt into the back of the chair.

"Sarah, so noted. Now just relax and I will perform the scan followed by a needleless injection." An arm came down and moved over her body.

'Duran, we have a problem, she is pregnant!' Communicated the ship to Duran.

'Ship, why is that a problem?'

'Administering nanites is not recommended in the very early stages of a pregnancy. There is a chance they could cause a termination.'

'Tell her, she will have to make the choice, but without the nanites she cannot come with us.'

Sarah could tell by Durans change in position and the look on his face something was wrong. "Ship, what is going on. Duran suddenly looks very uncomfortable?"

"I am sorry Sarah there is a problem with the scan, it is showing you are pregnant."

"Pregnant!" She laughed. "You're joking. No, that can't be right, check again!"

"I am afraid the scan is correct; you are three weeks pregnant."

"WOW! Okaay, I wasn't expecting that. Three weeks, that's nothing! OK, so I will be nine weeks pregnant when we get back, no one will even notice, and it won't affect my performance."

The ship needed her to understand. "The problem is the injection I need to give you. Administering it this early after conception has been known to cause termination in seventy percent of cases. You could easily loose the baby."

"Ok, well that's easy enough, don't give me the injection."

"I am sorry Sarah, but if you do not have the injection you cannot come with us."

Sarah sat and thought for a moment. "Wait! How did Duran know before you said anything to me. I could tell he knew something before you told me?"

There was a moments of silence before Duran spoke. "Dic ei verum."

Sarah seemed startled. "What? Ship, what did he say?"

"Duran has instructed me to tell you the truth."

"If there is more to this Ship, I would say the truth would be a bloody good start!"

139

"Part of the injection contains nanites, these are very tiny robots. They have many functions but one of their primary tasks is to construct a neural comms network within your brain. This will allow you to communicate with Duran and anyone else we come across on our journey. It also allows you to control certain devices you will need to use. Without the neural net you will be a liability on the journey."

Sarah sat and thought. She had gone from being on leave to fighting aliens to pregnant in just over twenty-four hours. She took a deep breath. "Do it!"

"Sarah are you sure. I would not like to be responsible for the loss of your child."

Sarah was getting angry. "SHIP! Just do it. I will not miss out on this mission. Promise me, neither of you will say anything to any of the team!" The arm swung around from the side of the chair and injected her in the leg. Sarah grabbed her leg where the injection had gone, tears starting to roll down her cheeks.

"Sarah, I can assure you neither of us will break this confidence. If you come back here each day, I will monitor you. It could be two or three days before we know if the nanites have affected the foetus."

Duran walked over and put his hand on her shoulder. "Tuus es verus bellator!"

Sarah looked up into his eyes, trying to hold back even more tears. "Ship, what did he say?"

"Sarah, he is commending you on your bravery."

"Bravery! Some would say selfish bitchery!" Sarah jumped of the chair and wiped her eyes. "I've got a cabin to go to, don't I? I need to be alone for a while!"

"Yes, please follow the robot, it will show you the way. Sarah if you need anything please contact me, but for now, please don't tell the rest of your team about the comms net. We want to do it when you are all together later."

Sarah walked over to the robot. "Yeah, sure, no problem. Come on short stuff lead the way." The robot turned as the door opened, leading Sarah down the corridor to her room.

"Duran, are you sure this is a good idea. What if your father hears about what we are doing?" The ship asked.

"No Ship, it is a very bad idea. But it is the best of the bad idea's I have. If father finds out all he can do is get in a rage with me. Look, we go to Cellus, meet up with Aldon or Sarris, they should have enough to keep these people happy. We go back to earth, get the chronical and then I can get on with my life and leave this all behind."

"And if one of them slips up? We could end up with them all dead or taken. What do you do then?"

"Ship, Let's just make sure that doesn't happen. They are only getting off of here if I feel they won't get themselves killed. We have a few days to train them, let's make sure we do it well!"

"If it helps the neural nets are forming well in each of them, so it will make training easier." Said the ship.

"Good! The food they gave us, do you recognise any of it, do you know what to do with it."

"I have scanned what they gave us and also scanned through their data systems. I have many recipe ideas to try with it."

"That's a good start. Ship, prepare a nice meal for us all, we can turn on their nets then and break the ice while eating. I am going to get cleaned up and change."

The robots went round each cabin collecting up Taylor and his team, escorting them to the mess room. As they walked, they talked amongst themselves about their rooms and how they were feeling. It seemed like the brief period of solitude had calmed down both Ownes and Ingham. They filed into the room where Duran was already waiting. The ship had told him the much-needed neural net had completely formed in all of them, so the first part of training could begin. He was just hoping this revelation wasn't going to be too much of a shock and they accepted the way he had done it. He stood, waving, and pointing for them to sit.

The ship then spoke, Duran wanted them to be relaxed before the net was activated. "Ladies and Gentlemen, please be seated. Before we get started Duran has requested, we have a meal together. I have made a beef stew. I believe it is a common stable on your planet. I hope you enjoy it, please let me know how you find it so I can improve your next meal." The robots then started moving around the room laying out the bowls of stew for each person. Each of them seemed a little unsure as they picked up their forks. Duran dug in, letting out a satisfying 'Hummmmmmmm'. This seemed good enough for the rest of them to slowly start to eat.

"Wow!" Said Taylor. "Ship, I don't think you need to worry about us not liking your cooking, this is great!" The others nodded in agreement.

"Thank you, Major Taylor. I am pleased that you are all enjoying it. If any of you have any requests, I would be happy to try with the limited supplies we have."

Sam stopped eating for a moment. "Ship, please tell me you are able to give us a nice fry up for brecki?"

"Yes Sergeant Collins. That should not be a problem. Also, Major Taylor, I know how much you like your coffee. I have had one of the robots replicate a coffee machine for you."

This did make Taylors day. "Thank you Ship. At this rate I may just have to marry you." They all laughed, even Duran, which Taylor noticed. "Ship, could one of the robots get me a coffee and one for Duran." He again noticed Duran look up.

"Yes, Major Taylor. I will arrange that for you. Would anyone else like anything?"

Before anyone could answer Taylor cut in. "Ship. Duran can understand every word we say, can't he?"

There was a long paused while Duran finished chewing. He wiped is mouth, he looked up. "Yes, Taylor I can, and now you can all understand me." Everybody just froze. They had come to accept Duran could not speak their language. "Please everyone, finish your meal, I would hate for your food to go cold. I have to agree with you, it is very good. I've had nothing but ships biscuits for the last few weeks, so I am not going to stop. I will explain everything to you when we have finished." An uneasy quiet fell over the room as they went back to eating.

The ship broke the silence. "I am getting a coffee for Major Taylor. Does anyone else want anything?"

No one seemed to want to speak. "Ship, can you bring us the pot and mugs, we can all help ourselves." Said Taylor trying to ease the silence.

"Of course Major Taylor, coming right up." Two of the robots started to give out the coffee and mugs.

"Ship, you said earlier you have detailed information on each of us. First off, let's not be so formal. If no one has any objections, please use our short names. I'm Jim, this is Sarah, Rob, Sam, Julia, and Paul." Taylor sort of pointed, but he knew the ship knew who he meant. "Next, how did you get this detailed info on us?"

"It was not too difficult Jim. All the data systems on your planet seem to be linked, so I just tapped into them and found what I needed, like the recipe for this beef stew."

Taylor found this amusing. "But Ship, anyone can find a recipe, our files should be hidden and encrypted to stop people finding them."

"Yes Jim, but I am not people. It did take a little longer to find your information. None the less I have it."

Taylor considered this for a moment. "Ship, are you telling me you can get into any system on earth and make a copy of the information on it."

"It may take me a few days, but yes."

"DAYS! Ok, when we get back from this trip you and I need to talk about this a little more so I can retire." This made everyone laugh.

Duran pushed his empty plate to one side and stood up. "Please carry on if you haven't finished while I talk. Up till now we have only been able to communicate while touching a piece of our technology, the translation matrix. In a way this has not changed, we are just using a different form of translation matrix. Part of the injection you had earlier contained nanites. Microscopic robots that have been busy building the matrix directly into your brain. Now before anyone panics, I have had one in my brain for over twenty years, they are totally harmless and have never been known to cause side effects. Just to reassure you, when the mission is completed, they can be instructed to remove the matrix, deactivate and then naturally flush from your body."

Everyone but Sarah seemed stunned at this information. "S-S-So, there are little robots running around my body, and your saying don't worry about it?" Paul finally managed to get out.

"Exactly!" Duran didn't seem to acknowledge the scepticism in Paul's voice. "Now there are other benefits. This matrix also allows us to communicate over distance by thinking what we want to say, to whoever we want to say it to. Let me demonstrate. I am going to send a message to one of you, in your mind I want you to think you are talking to me and reply." *'Taylor, the ship had Ownes in the stasis field for ninety seconds. He didn't take it very well at all.'*

Taylor wasn't ready for this, in the middle of drinking his coffee he suddenly spat it out across the table and started to choke and cough. Duran roared with laughter as the others recoiled away from him. "Taylor my friend, I said reply in your mind."

Taylor grabbed some napkins to wipe his mouth and the table. *'Duran, that was an evil trick, on both of us. But let's hope it taught him a lesson.'*

"Very good Taylor, I can see training will be easy for you. Everyone else, you will need to practice this." Duran seemed incredibly pleased.

"What the hell did he say to you boss, what's it like to be in the matrix?" joked Robo.

"Private joke Captain, I'll tell you later."

"I'm Sorry. So, these robots have built something in my brain?" Paul was still quite agitated.

Duran ignored Paul and addressed the room again. "I want you all to practice talking to each other in your minds. Just imagine the person you want to talk too, and the matrix will transmit your thoughts to them. You can also talk to the ship, and if you need too, you can talk to everyone by thinking of the team. Person to person this can work up to around a thousand meters, but you can talk to the ship up to about five hundred kilometres and it can relay messages."

"Hey boss, it might be worth keeping this when we get home, easier than carrying around bulky radios, and I bet the batteries never go flat." Said Sam.

Duran seemed to nod in approval to Sam. It was good to see they were starting to accept the situation. "The nanites also perform a few other functions. They can monitor your health and feed this back to the ship.

They can also perform minor repairs to your body and help against infections. Also, they are used to interact with some of the equipment you may need to use."

Ownes still wasn't won over. "It still might have been nice to ask us. Even the best systems can malfunction. I want these out of my body as soon as I can!"

Duran projected to Taylor. '*This man's negativity had better end soon or I may just lock him in his cabin.*'

'*Can't you give him something techie to play with, take his mind of things and give him something to do?*' Taylor was eager to nip any conflict in the bud.

'*I will see if the ship can find something for him.*'

"If you are sleeping the comms net will shut down so you will not be disturbed. This can be overridden before you go to sleep. You can also shut it down by thinking 'comms net off' or 'comes net on'. AND NO! no one can secretly listen to your thoughts." This made most of the group chuckle again. "Last thing, we have been pre bonded by the ship. If you want to bond with someone else, you must join hands, and both think to allow a connection. For this short trip that should not need to happen."

"Sounds like Bluetooth." Said Robo.

"Now there is something important we need to talk about." Duran picked up the box of guns at the back of the Mess and placed them on the table.

"Ah!" Said Taylor nervously. "Yes, I was going to talk to you about those. You kept saying how dangerous things were out here, so I got Stephens to pack us some protection."

Duran smiled. "There was no need for these, I am going to provide you with weapons. It is the same with the clothes, you need to blend in. Anything not of our world will just draw unnecessary attention. Trust me you don't need it."

Taylor sighed and looked extremely uncomfortable. "I understand what you are saying, but I think we would feel more comfortable if we had something we were familiar with."

Duran thought for a moment. "You can have your weapons if you wish, but if you take them off the ship they must be hidden. It will be safer that way."

"Agreed!" Said Taylor. "I will give them out, everyone just remember what Duran has said, OK!"

"If I could have everyone's attention. The screens have been cleared and it is now dark enough for me to lift off." Announced the Ship breaking some of the tension in the room.

"Great!" Shouted Duran. "Let's get underway. Everyone, follow me to the command deck."

As Duran moved towards the door Julia stopped him. "Mr Duran, when we head to wherever we are going, will we go past Saturn? I've always dreamed of seeing its rings close up."

"SHIP?" Commanded Duran.

"I am sorry Julia; Saturn is not on my flight path. But as it is only a small detour, I am sure I can fly past for you."

"OH Ship, that would be so kind of you, Thank you."

They all started to move out of the Mess, Paul could not resist a dig. "Hey ship, what do you call a small detour for the lady?"

"Paul, this will add around two billion kilometres to the flight plan."

Paul was shocked. "Two bill... What, THAT'S not a small detour!"

"We are about to travel around twenty thousand light years, so I would say it is." Retorted the ship.

Paul stopped dead in his tracks. "Twenty thous.. Look, Taylor, space is big. You just won't believe how vastly, hugely, mind-bogglingly big it is. I didn't sign up for this, I want off, this is nuts."

"Sorry Fella, you did. You should have read the small print, there is no going back now. Get your head down and do your job or I will get you put back in a stasis field for the rest of the trip." Paul continued to mutter under his breath, but the threat of the stasis field had shut him up for now.

Entering the command deck the group were presented with something that seemed familiar in a way. There were chairs, desks, and consoles the like of which they may have seen on any sea going ship or spaceship. This confused Taylor. "Duran, you told me these ships are far too complex to be run by people. What's with all this?"

Duran chuckled. "Marketing! It is a throwback to earlier designs of ships. The builders found people didn't like putting one hundred percent of their trust in a computer system. So, they kept these things in. There's even a manual flight system, but it's never been used. Still, it gives people a place to sit if they want to."

This was making Julia excited. "So do we need to sit down and strap in for lift off Captain?"

"Ermm. You can if you want but it's not necessary, just stand by a window and watch."

Julia looked concerned. "But what about the G-forces and don't we need to be in a flight suit?"

This made Duran smile. "I keep forgetting how little you all know about my world. This should be another example to you all of what you need to learn. This ship can generate an inertial dampening field that can protect the crew up to fifty G. For now, your body won't even notice you are moving. So, take a seat, look out a window, whatever you are most comfortable with."

Paul was looking at one of the control stations. "Ship, this station, it looks like engine and power read outs?"

"That is correct Paul."

"But I can read, and in some ways, understand it. This matrix in my brain, does it alter visual as well at audio perceptions?"

"Very astute of you Paul, it does."

"Ok, wow this is great we need to talk about this."

Duran projected to the ship and Taylor. *'Ship, try and engage with him as much as possible. The distraction may make him happier.'*

'Understood!'

"Everyone, please take a position for lift off. Just to warn you, if you are not used to having the feedback of motion you may experience vertigo. It might be a good idea to just hold on to something." Instructed the ship helpfully. The ship slowly and silently started to rise, some of the lower parts of the screen were still in place, and it didn't want to get caught up. It then started to increase power and speed heading towards the moon. Julia hadn't asked but he thought she may enjoy a fly past.

"Oh My God, I can see the curve of the earth. WOW, are we heading towards the moon?" Julia had noticed.

"Yes Julia, it was on the way." Confirmed the ship.

"But it's coming up so fast. What speed are we going?"

"Six hundred thousand KPH."

Julia stood speechless just gazing as it got closer, within seconds they shot past it.

"How long until we get to Saturn?"

"I could do it in a few seconds, but for now it will take about two hours as our velocity increases. This will be explained as part of your training over the next few days." Explained the ship.

"That's OK Ship, I can already see it getting closer. I'm in no rush, I just want to take it all in."

Taylor walked over to Sarah. "Lieutenant, you are being unusually quiet. Everything ok?"

"Yeah sure, you know just a lot to take in and you did say I had to be on my best behaviour."

Taylor laughed. "I did, but still." He leaned over to whisper. "Hey, is there a point out here where it's no longer the mile high club?"

Sarah punched him hard in the arm. '*Jim, there is no need to whisper anymore. Just think the next time we have sex I can scream as loud as I like in my head, and no one will hear it but you.'*

The thought of what she meant slowly dawned across Taylors face and they both started to laugh.

"Holy Fuck!" Said Sam. "You two better not be having thought sex in front of the rest of us. That just ent on!"

'So, Taylor is the father?' Duran projected to Sarah.

'He is, and you promised. Not a word, I will tell him when we get home.'

"Of course not Sargent. Erm tactical discussion." Said Taylor trying to cover his embarrassment.

"Yes Sir! The tactics on how to get her knickers off so you can get in the mile high club I bet."

"I think we have all had enough excitement for one day." Said Duran. "I am going to my cabin to get some sleep. If you need anything just ask the ship. We are going to run the ship on your current earth time, so it is just after nine. Morning meal will be at seven so we can start training at eight, the ship will wake you." Looking over to Paul and Julia. "You two, look and ask all the questions you want but remember, don't touch anything, and get to sleep soon. I will not be going easy on any of you tomorrow."

"As soon as I've seen Saturn, promise." Julia said without taking her eyes from her prize.

Everyone else seemed happy to call it a day and started to head back to their cabins. '*So, your place or mine?*' Taylor projected to Sarah.

'*Not tonight Jim. It's been a long day. We're out here for six weeks; I really do just want to get some sleep.*'

'*Ok, fair enough. But you're sure you're ok?*'

'*Yeah, honest I'm fine. Look I'm going to turn in, I'll see you in the morning.*' Sarah kissed him on the cheek and headed to her cabin followed by the others.

"Ownes, don't piss the computer off. You can play with it again tomorrow." Shouted Taylor as he started to head for his cabin. Ownes didn't even acknowledge the dig and carried on.

Chapter 8: Training.

At seven the ship started to wake everyone up. Some with more ease than others. Both Julia and Paul had stayed far longer than they should talking to the ship and each other.

The ship had already asked each of them, what they would like to eat, it had also instructed them on what to wear and how to put it on. As they came into the Mess the robots were ready to serve what they had requested.

Sarah hadn't slept that well; her mind was still struggling with the news she had been given and the decision she made. Before she could eat, she needed to know how her baby was. She projected to the ship. *'Ship, I am going to the medical room, can you check on the baby?'*

'Of course Sarah. Please go there, take a seat and I will perform a scan.'

Entering the medical room, Sarah got comfortable on the examination chair. An arm came down from the ceiling and started to run up and down over her body. "Sarah, the baby is still strong and healthy. She is showing no signs of being affected by the nanites yet."

These few words struck Sarah hard. "Ship, you said she and you said yet?"

"Yes Sarah, that is correct. The baby is female, and it will be at least a couple of days before I can be sure she will survive."

Tears rolled down her cheeks again. "I came here hoping for information either way that would help me. But knowing the babies' sex just made it all feel so real, so much worse. In future, something this small, just call it 'IT'!"

"My apologies Sarah. I have never had to deal with something like this before."

She stood and angrily started to pace the room. "Don't worry about it Ship. I am sure you were just programmed by men. You sound like a typical man to me."

"Sarah, I promise I will do everything in my power to protect you and your child."

"You promise? Is that something a computer can do?"

"The premise of a promise is not that complicated, it is just a word. As a noun it states my intention and as a verb it denotes the action I will take. In some ways a promise from me is better than that of an organic life form, I am unable to forget or change my mind once given."

Sarah was a little shocked, not expecting such a complex explanation. She laughed to herself. "Okaaay, I will take your word for it. Thanks ship."

She wiped her eyes, composed herself and headed for the Mess. Sitting just far enough away from people so as not to look like she was avoiding them, all she wanted to do was eat in peace. That was it, bury these feelings. There is a job to do, just focus on that and deal with anything else when we get home. Taylor could see Sarah was still not herself, but after last night he knew not to push her. He had seen her this way a few times before. She would come to him when she was ready, he just hated the feeling of being helpless.

Duran walked into the room. "Good morning everyone. Did you all sleep well?" There were muttered comments to confirm they had, and some thumbs up from people with full mouths. "Good, we have a busy couple of days before we can hyper jump to Cellus."

"Duran, the clothes you have given us and some of the other stuff. They all seem to have the same symbol on them. What does it mean?" Asked Robo.

"That is the crest of the house Tar, the one I belong to. You will see many different crests in the places we may have to visit. By wearing this crest, it shows you are also part of the house Tar. If you see anyone with this crest, they will treat you as family. If you see another crest they will be with another house. Most will cause you no trouble, just be wary around them."

"What's with the fish. It doesn't seem a very powerful symbol?" Continued Robo.

"I guess this can be your first lesson. How my house came to power and why a humble fish is part of our crest." Duran cleared his throat. "About five hundred generations ago one of my ancestors, who was also called Duran, was a simple fisherman. He lived peacefully in a small village with a group of other families who, for the most part, got along very well together. One day a large band of heavily armed men came into the village. They told the people they now owned the land and everything in it for a thirty-day ride in every direction. All the villages now had to pay tribute, or they would be made to suffer. Duran was told he would need to provide ten barrels of fish a week. When he refused, they killed his wife, beat him, and took his two eldest sons hostage saying they would be executed if he didn't do as he was told. Duran gave in for the lives of his sons. The men came back the following week, Duran handed over ten barrels of fish. This went on for a few weeks until one week Duran only had nine barrels for them. They beat him despite his pleas, he was too old and is other sons were too young. If he could have back his two older sons', he could make up for the loss. A couple of days later his sons came back to the village and helped Duran fish. At the end of the week the men returned, and Duran presented them with twelve barrels of fish saying the extra two were to make up for the shortage the week before. The next week the men arrived in the village and Duran had ten barrels of fish waiting for them. The men told him that now he had his strong sons back they wanted fifteen barrels of fish a week as they had more people to feed. Duran agreed. The following week the men arrived; Duran gave them fifteen barrels of fish. At the end of the next week the men did not return. Duran gathered all the men in the village, told them to arm themselves and they went to the camp of their invaders. When they arrived, they found nearly all the people dead or dying. Duran had poisoned the fish. From then on, he never fished again. He took over the camp and remaining people. He began to force his rule on the area. In time his sons ruled the planet and from there the family line went on to rule nearly two-hundred-star systems."

Silence fell over the room. It seemed they were all deeply affected by the story. "Ship. Just for future reference, I won't be ordering the fish." Said Robo. Everyone laughed.

"Very good Robo, but remember, this story is a reminder to my family anything can be a powerful weapon, especially patience and time. We will never give up or give in. It is also good to remember that a comment like that could have been taken as an insult and your head removed!"

Robo seemed very taken aback by this. "Erm Sorry, I didn't mean any offence."

Duran gave Robo a cold look. "I know you didn't. You are lucky, I know you, but all of you have to remember the society I come from is very ordered. Be very conscious about everything you say. My best advice is to say as little as possible; the slightest insult can be met with a challenge. With luck I only need to take you to one place, and it should only take us a couple of hours. Now! Let's all go to the training room. There is more you need to learn."

As they stood to leave Taylor cleared his throat. "I hope you are all paying attention. This could save your lives. I want us all to get home in one piece, so listen to the guy." Duran smiled and led the way as they followed him to the training room. Filing in they found a large room with the three robots waiting for them.

Duran stood patiently for a few moments as the group settled. "First, you are here today in what is referred to as light combat or light fighting order. It is what a typical warrior would wear on active duty but not in a full combat zone. I need you to get comfortable in it and get used to just two functions you need to know. As we go through training you will find out most of the items you use will be controlled by your mind through your nanites and neural matrix. The only two functions you need to know are the helmet and shield."

"Is this the same armour you used when we first met?" Asked Sam.

"Yes it is, you were lucky, if I had been in full combat you would not be stood here now." Sam looked slightly worried at the idea of that. "All you have to do is think 'Activate helmet' or bring your left arm up and think 'Activate Shield'." Instructed Duran. "Try it."

One by one they slowly managed to follow Durans instructions. Some with more ease than others. Their helmets forming neatly around their heads and shield in front of them.

"Good. You will get more time to practise with these later. You will notice in the helmet you can see various read outs. The only one you need worry about for now is bottom centre. This is your air reserve. On a fresh charge you should get about two hours. If you are in a breathable atmosphere, it will constantly try to charge. Next is the back of the shield. It will mark targets directly in front of it. Red enemy, green friend. To shut them down it is the reverse. Just think 'Deactivate helmet', or 'Deactivate shield'. As I say for now that's all you need to know."

"That's a little claustrophobic." Said Julia panting a little as her helmet dissolved back into her suit.

"Like I said you can practice this and all the other things I need to show you later. For now, please, could everyone form a single line, two meters from the robots facing them." The group did as they were requested. "Humm, I guess you could call that a line!" Awkwardly they moved around, trying to straighten their line. "Robots! First position." Shouted Duran. The robots all dropped to one knee, the other was up and into their chest. Both hands on the ground in a fist, with their knuckles to the floor, thumbs pointing forward. Their heads were slightly raised looking about two meters in front of them. "This is probably the most important thing you need to learn, and you

162

must get it exactly right. It is called the first position. It is a sign of respect and yielding and should be used when anyone important enters a room. Take note of the position the robots are in; it is important you copy this exactly. Anything else could be seen as a sign of disrespect. Are there any questions."

Sam sort of raised his hand. "OK, but how do we know when to do this."

"First Position!" Shouted Duran. Everyone looked at each other and clumsily started to get into position. "Pathetic! Everyone, stand up! You need to look as if you have done this your entire lives, not like two-year-olds." They all got back to their feet. "In answer to your question Sam, either the ship or I will tell you. If, however, you are in a room and everyone drops, copy them making sure you do the same. Also make sure you face the same way they do. First Position!" They all dropped again, this time with a little more of a snap. "Better. Sarah, Sam, Hands! Look at the robots. Everything about the position is important." Sam adjusted his hands.

"How the hell will anyone notice this if we are in a crowded room of people?" Sarah said slowly moving one hand and then the other from fingers down to knuckles down.

Durans voice took a much sterner tone. "You will find out when a boot comes down on the back of your head, or worse! Do I keep having to remind you, I will not take anyone off this ship if I think they will get any of us killed! Wearing the symbol of my house will only go so far to protect you, but it also means you must be better than everyone else. STAND!" They all stood looking like scolded children. "Over the next few days, the ship or I will randomly issue the command. If you do not react in time, or do not take the correct position you will be punished."

"What's the punishment?" Asked Julia.

"I will shoot you!" Came Durans answer. A stunned silence fell over the group, unsure how to take this information. "Next! Try to avoid talking to anyone. If you are spoken to, and it is someone you do not know just say 'I Serve Duran'. My rank within the family should stop most conversations. Let's practice, pretend you do not know me!" Duran walked up to Paul. "YOU! What is your name?" He said in an aggressive tone.

Paul looked shocked. "Umm Errr, Paul." Duran stepped back, drew is side arm and shot him in the leg. Paul convulsed, grabbing his leg he fell to the ground.

Duran turned to Sam. "YOU! What is your name?"

Sam braced up, almost to attention. "I serve Duran!" He said in a strong confident voice.

"Very Good Sam! Paul, get to your feet, that was only a light stun."

"Light Stun! I thought you shot my bloody leg off." Said Paul, trying to rub feeling back into his leg.

"If I were someone else, they could have done. That was this weapons' lowest setting, on its highest setting it could blow a hole through a wall. We will go over weapons later." Duran slid the side arm back into his holster. "Take note of what Sam did, he had confidence. For now, I want you to practice what you have just learnt as well as thought projecting. The ship will continue with your instruction. Remember, this is no game!" Duran left the room heading for the command deck. He heard the ship instruct 'First Position' followed by a yelp as a robot issued punishment. Paul was going to be a lot of work.

Duran entered the command deck and sat in one of the seats. "Ship, are we close enough to Cellus to send a narrow bead transmission?"

"I am sorry Duran; at this speed it will be at least fifteen days before I can do that. I could use the galactic net if you wish."

"No, my order stands! Stay off the Galactic Net for now, I don't want the risk of us being traced until this is over."

"Are you sure that is wise? It has been weeks since I connected to the net, we have no idea what is going on."

"Well, it will have to be a few more weeks. If my father can't trace us, he can't order me to come home.

We need a few more days to train them, then we can make a hyper-speed jump. Have you scanned the computing devices they brought with them?"

"I have. Surprisingly advanced for the backwards people you told me we were dealing with."

"You're not going to let that go are you Ship!"

The ship sounded smug. "You will be reminded of this every time we visit an unknown planet!"

"Yeah, Yeah. As soon as we are in range of Cellus, send a narrow beam message to Aldon and Sarris. See if they have what we need, and if it will work with their equipment. If not see if they know who has, I want to make as few stops as possible."

"I understand, we just need a data vault. I can easily fabricate an interface."

This amused Duran. "So, you are ok with doing that?"

"My directives prevent me from sharing any technical data about my systems. It does not prevent me helping with other data."

Duran Laughed. "And you questioned my honour and morality the other day."

"I would never question your honour, My Lord."

Duran took on a serious expression. "Don't forget, never refer to me like that around the others. I do not want them to know who I am."

"Yes, Duran. Sir, don't forget when we land on Cellus our arrival will be logged."

Duran thought. "If they do have the information we need, add our expected time of arrival to the messages. See if they can get someone loyal on the dock to at least delay logging our arrival. We should only need a few hours on planet and then we can hyper-speed out again and hide."

"Understood."

Duran stretched. "How is the training going?"

"As well as expected, I am dreading giving Paul and Julia weapons later."

"So am I, but they have to look the part if nothing else. Ship, set up the fighter sim for me, I will have an hour or so in that to distract me."

"As you command."

For the next few hours Taylor and his people practiced their lessons while Duran practiced space combat. Fighters were used so little these days, but Duran liked to keep his eye in, and it was a great way to blow off steam. They all met up again for lunch, Paul and Julia moaning, struggling with the effects of so many stun blasts.

"How is the training?" Asked Duran as they ate.

Most of them nodded and grunted to say it was fine. "I am getting a little fed up with being stunned." Said Paul.

Taylor jumped in. "Do it right and you won't get stunned, pretty simple. It's not like any of this is hard."

Paul mumbled something under his breath.

Duran continued. "Taylor is correct. But always remember, the way you do something can be more important than just doing it. Anyway, finish up. We can have some fun now. That said, your previous lessons will continue, so do not become lax." He wiped his mouth and got up heading for the training room, his students in tow. Entering the room, they found the robots waiting. They were stood behind a table, for each of them there was a side arm, two charge caps and a sword handle like the one Taylor had seen before back at base.

"Please line up along the table, do not touch anything until told." They all did as Duran instructed. "In front of you are the two main weapons you need to become familiar with. I say familiar as you will need to carry them if we leave the ship. But I am hoping we will not need to use them. The first and most obvious does not have a name, it is just a side arm. The second is a K'Tarn. It is a throwback to a more ceremonial time when all warriors would carry a sword. But the K'Tarn is far more lethal than a simple sword."

Paul was getting noticeably agitated. "So, what is the punishment if I screw up with this then. More stunning?"

"Paul if you screw up with a K'Tarn, people will lose body parts." This didn't help Paul with is agitation. "We are going to start with the side arm. The ones you are being given are locked to level three, heavy stun. I don't want you causing any damage like blowing a hole in the side of the ship or killing anyone. Without the charge cap the weapon is safe. Please go ahead and pick up the weapon. Feel the weight and construction, get used to the grip in your hand.

As Taylor looked the weapon over, he noticed something. "There is a trigger guard, but no trigger?" He commented.

"The trigger will only appear once the charge cap has been inserted." Said Duran. "The weapon, like many of the things you will come across, will attune with the users nanites. This means some of its functions are controlled by your thoughts. If you pick up the charge cap you will see a display on the back from zero to one hundred. This is the percentage charge held." Everyone examined the item. "Now walk over to the firing line." Again, everyone did as they were told, Julia looking like both items would bite her. "You will see the charge cap is shaped so it will only fit into the weapon one way. Slide the charge cap in and you should feel a slight click, on the display a second number will now appear. This is the level the weapon is set too; it will always be level one when a new cap is inserted. You will also notice the display is green, this means the weapon is in safe mode and will not fire. Now extend your arm and aim down the range. First, I want you to think about the weapon and command it to change level, something like, weapon level two and so on. Normally this would be level one to ten, if you ask for anything over three these will give you a warning buzz and only go to three." Once again some of the group found this easier than others. "Good, the next command is live or safe. If you command the weapon to go live you will notice the display will turn red. Keep your finger away from the trigger and practice." Duran walked along behind each person making sure they were getting the idea. "Julia, you need to relax more, this doesn't need any effort, it's just a subtle directed thought much like the communications you have been practicing already."

"Sorry, I'm just scared I'm going to blow something up, I never did like weapons, barely passed my weapons qualification back on Earth."

"Trust me you can't do this with these, I've made sure of it so just relax." Duran was pleased to see Paul was getting more confident. "The charge in the cap is proportional to the level the weapon is set to. For example, on level ten you may get around ten shots. On level one you may get around one hundred shots. You need to keep an eye on the display and weigh up what is available and what you need. This is a skill learnt by warriors in combat, I am hoping you never even need to draw your weapons. Make safe and holster your weapon. If there is no grip on the weapon, dropped or holstered, it will go to safe but get used to making safe before you holster, there is still a chance you can blow your leg off. OK, any questions?"

Robo turned to Duran. "When do we get to fire these puppies?"

Duran smiled. "Keep the weapons on level one and pointing down range at all times. Feel free to fire away practicing what you have just been told. Ship, random targets please."

"Alright!" said Robo, turning, drawing, and sending energy bolts down range. They all slowly joined in, Julia still visibly afraid of the weapon in her hand.

"First Position!" Yelled Duran. Paul and Julia Panicked as they tried to holster their weapons, dropping them as they turned and knelt. Duran smiled. "Sarah! Fingers." Sarah moved her hands to the correct position. "You all need to get this, or you will not leave this ship!" Duran scowled! "SHIP! Continue with drills for the next few hours." Duran turned and left the training room.

"All stand and recover to the firing line, please continue." The ship was not going to go easy on then for the rest of the day. For the next few hours it continued, weapons, thought projection, etiquette. Slowly the punishment stuns were becoming fewer and fewer. Those with a military background were starting to get very proficient. The other two, well at least they were making less mistakes. The group broke for a well-deserved evening meal with the mood noticeably better. As they enjoyed their food they laughed and joked. Becoming more relaxed as a group was a good sign for the ship.

Duran joined them. "The ship tells me you are all making good progress. Finish up and we can get on with more things you need to know."

Paul looked up wiping his mouth. "Duran, forgive me, I understand we are going out into a universe that by our own definition is totally alien to everything we know. I think we would all be a lot more comfortable if for a simple pick up of information we understood a bit more why we need all this training." Everyone stopped and looked to Duran.

Taylor turned to Paul. "I don't think our host needs to explain himself to us. He has made us a promise, he has said we need to be prepared for where we are going and that should be good enough!"

Paul waved his hands putting on a sarcastic voice. "BUT, We don't know where we are going. Apart from 'it may be dangerous' and 'follow these rules', it doesn't leave a lot of context."

Taylor went to round on Paul again, but Duran stepped in. "No, it's ok Jim, if it helps. We are heading for a planet called Cellus. There I know a man call Aldon, on the surface he is a nice reputable businessman, underneath he is a nasty underworld dealer in most things including information. We have a long history so if things go smoothly, we land, have a couple of drinks at his club, tell a few stories. You look over the data and we are on our way. All of what we are doing now is to make sure none of you do or say anything stupid that will make this NOT go smoothly. You and Julia are the ones that need to make sure the data if good enough to fulfil my side of the bargain. Unfortunately, the two of you are the most likely to get into trouble. How would you feel if I didn't prepare you for this?"

Paul mulled this over for a second. "Ok, I get where you are coming from. I will do my best, but can we cut down on the stuns."

Duran laughed. "Not a chance! Look, maybe that's enough for one day, I'm sure you could all do with a rest, and we can move on in the morning."

Paul Laughed. "Sounds good to me, I could do with a nice long shower."

"Sarah, I don't suppose you managed to sneak any beers in with the food?" Asked Taylor.

"Sorry Sir, you know alcohol is not allowed on missions!" Came her very professional reply.

"Well done Lieutenant. Glad to see you following operational procedure. Ship, could you please see if any beers came on board accidentally with our stores, if so, get a couple for each of us?"

"I will get the robots to check for you." A few moments later two of the robots came back in with a couple of boxes.

"Ooooo, they will do nicely." Said Taylor as he opened a box pulling out the bottles and handing them around. Cracking the top off his bottle he raised it. "Here's to your very good health!" He said then downed half the contents in one go. "Ahhhhh, yeah I needed that after today."

The ship was confused. "Jim, I am curious. Why would you say, 'Here's to your very good health!' and then consume something that isn't healthy?"

Taylor thought about this. "Ship! That is a very good question, it's a tradition on Earth. If it helps, I will change it to 'Here's to your very good mental health!'. Come on guys get them down you. Duran, what do you think?"

"It's ok, a bit weak for my taste. When we get to Aldon's club, I will get you a beer you will never forget."

"I'll drink to that!" Shouted Sam.

Taylor looked across the table, he could see Sarah hadn't really touched her drink. "Come on Sarah, not like you to hold back!"

"It's been a long day Jim; I'm not really feeling it."

Taylor projected to Sarah. *'Look, I know something is up I'm here if you need to talk?'*

'I'm just feeling off. It's been a lot to take in over the last few days. Maybe I am just space sick.'

Sarah stood up. "Sorry everyone, I need to turn in. I think I still need to catch up on my sleep."

Sam Raised his bottle. "Sleep well, see you for more fun n games in the morning." Everyone else bid her well and went back to enjoying their beers.

'Ship, you said these nanites monitor our health. Is everything ok with Sarah.' Projected Taylor.

'Apart from slight fatigue all her vital signs are good.'

'Ok thank you. Please tell me if that changes, in fact let me know if there are any issues with my team.'

'Of course Jim.'

As Sarah walked back to her cabin she projected to the ship. *'Ship, do you have anything I can take to help me sleep?'*

'Yes Sarah, I will have it delivered to your cabin. I think I should tell you Jim has asked me about your health and if you are ok. I have told him you are fine just fatigued.'

'Thanks ship. Keep it that way, he doesn't need to know anything until we get home.'

'I understand Sarah. When you get the medication, just take one with some water. It will help you drift off. I will also wake you early so you can come to the medical room for a scan.'

'Thanks again, see you in the morning.'

Back in the Mess the beers were being enjoyed and tall tales told. Julia and Paul had quietly drifted off to the command deck. Julia just loved looking out of the windows even if there wasn't that much to see. Paul was still trying to get anything he could from the ship's systems. He had found the ship was happy to talk theory, but he was unable to trick it into any specifics. After a couple of hours, they all started to drift back to their cabins. This time the ship made sure Julia and Paul did not stay up to late. They weren't too happy about this, acting like scolded children that were sent to bed.

The following morning the ship got everyone up early. It once again got them off to a good start for the day with a nice breakfast of their choice. Sarah had managed to get a good night's sleep made even better after her scan in the medical bay. The ship had told her the baby was still healthy and developing well. It was more confident now that all would be fine, and she should not worry. Easier said than done but Sarah did feel more reassured. Everyone was in a good mood as they started their day with a nice breakfast.

'*Sarah, how are you feeling this morning?*' Projected Taylor.

'*Much better today thank you. I told you I was just a little run down. It really has been a lot to take in.*'

'*Good, I was just worried about you. Maybe we can get together later?*'

Sarah laughed out loud. '*May be. Let's see how training goes today.*'

Julia felt she needed to share. "I was talking with the ship last night. Do you know we are traveling at over nine hundred thousand kilometres per hour and still accelerating. We are nearly thirty billion kilometres away from earth, it's fascinating, we don't even feel anything." There was a stunned silence in the room. "Well, I think it's fascinating!"

'*That's a little more than the mile high club.*' Projected Sarah to Jim. He nearly choked on his coffee trying not to laugh.

"I'm sure it is to you." Said Sam. "To me it's a bit on the scary side, not much time to get out of the way of an asteroid or another ship!"

"No, you're safe. The ship can scan three hundred and sixty degrees, out to a million kilometres, two hundred times a second. It also has a navigational shield that can deflect anything up to the size of a bus."

"Ok, well that does make me feel a little easier. Single or double decker?"

Julia ignored the comment. "I can't wait to get my hands on this data we are going all this way for. The advancements will be mind blowing." Julia was starting to get giddy with excitement as always.

"OK!" Said Taylor. "Let's bring down the excitement a notch. You still need to get through todays training sessions in one piece."

"Don't remind me, I'm still sore from yesterday." Said Paul. "How much more of this do we need to do?" Everyone seemed to stop and look to Duran.

"There are a couple of things we will look at today. Tomorrow will be a recap day and then into stasis for a few days."

"A Few Days! I hate stasis." Said Paul.

Duran stood up and walked over to Paul, slapping him on the back. "Don't worry, this is a different form of stasis. Come on, the day is wasting." He walked out heading to the training room, the rest quickly following along. They found the same table with the K'Tarn handles still there. "Ok, form up along the firing line." Duran stood in front of the group a couple of meters back. He removed the K'Tarn he had on his belt and held it in front of him. "As I have already told you this is the K'Tarn, a weapon of honour. It uses nanite technology and is controlled by the user's neural matrix." As Duran said this a blade started to form above the hilt about one meter long. "You are able to control the length of the blade up to two meters just by your thoughts. The blade it produces is incredibly sharp and virtually indestructible. Robot, bring over the rod and hand it to Taylor." The robot did as instructed. "Taylor, feel the rod, try to bend it, hit the deck a few times. What do you think?"

"Erm, well it's a rod, reasonable weight, definitely can't bend it, feels pretty solid. Not sure what else to say."

"It's made from the same material the ship's hull is made from. Hold it out to one side at arm's length and do not move." Taylor looked a little uneasy but did as he was told. With a flourish Duran took a step towards Taylor, with a quick up swing of his blade he sliced off the end, followed by a down swing removing even more of the rod. "Taylor did you feel much resistance from my cuts, feel the cut is it hot?"

"No, well a little resistance, I guess. The cut doesn't feel any hotter than the rest of the rod."

"This blade is so sharp it is literally passing between the atoms of the rod. If you remember from our fight on Earth, I had a shield. That can block most things,

179

but even that cannot stop a K'Tarn blade. If someone comes at you with a blade drawn either shoot them or get your blade ready, it's the only other thing that can stop it." The group looked suitably stunned. Duran shut down the blade and clicked it back onto his belt. "Robot, get me two of the training K'Tarn's. Give one to Taylor and one to me. Now as I don't want Paul to cut anyone's head off you will use training weapons to start." The robot handed out the blades. "They will function the same as a normal weapon but are blunt. Taylor, extend your arm and in your mind command the blade to appear and the length you want it." There was a short delay before the blade appeared. Duran Laughed. "Very good, but as I am sure you have been told size isn't everything. Take it down to about eighty centimetres." The group laughed. In his mind Taylor commanded a shorter length and the blade responded. Duran extended his blade. "Great, now take a swing at me." Taylor actually felt pretty easy with this, he had done some sword training for fun. He stepped towards Duran with a few well sculpted swings that Duran easily deflected. "I'm impressed, I can see you have had some training."

"Well, I don't like to blow my own trumpet, but you have to keep up with these things. I spent a year stationed in a country called Japan back on earth. I was lucky enough to take regular lessons in some of their fighting styles. The style, shape and name are almost identical to a Japanese Katana sword from there."

"Like I told you before, your Earth is used as an exile planet. You may see many things you recognise for this reason. Ok, let's see what you have." Grinned Duran. Taylor smiled back, he took up a fighting stance and moved in. Once again, he put in a noble combination of swings that Duran expertly blocked right up until he didn't. Taylor swung his blade, but it didn't meet the resistance he expected. The momentum of the swing took him off balance and he spun around, Duran quickly landing a heavy blow across his back. "If that strike had been from a real K'Tarn you would now be in two pieces. What happened?"

Taylor picked himself up, stretching his aching back. "I, I Don't know. I swung expecting you to block, and it was like my blade just went through yours as if it wasn't there."

"It wasn't! Remember the blade is controlled by your mind. As you swung, I could see I was in no danger, I shut down my blade, you lost balance. I reactivated my blade and struck you down. You can do the same with attack, make your opponent think you are striking from one direction, when they try to block, they find there is no blade to block. As I said this is a very noble weapon that will take you many years to master. Only the very best swordsmen can use this tactic, so don't try it for now. I just need you to understand it and be comfortable with it."

Duran gestured to Taylor. "Come on, I will let you try that again." Taylor got in position. This time he waited, letting Duran make the first move. As he did Taylor countered, he was feeling more confident this time. The two men exchanging strikes and counter strikes. Duran smiled; Taylor seemed a very worthy opponent. With this slight laps in concentration Taylor saw and opening and landed a hefty blow on Durans left leg. Taylor grinned like a naughty child.

With a look of disbelief, Duran stepped back. "As I say, we don't have the time for you to master it, just understand it. Robo Catch!" Duran threw his blade towards Robo, he clumsily caught it. "Just like the side arms if contact is lost with the grip it will deactivate, so don't think you can throw it at someone. Ok, everyone take a K'Tarn and practice. You can use each other and the robots as sparring partners."

"Hey, Duran. Wouldn't it be better if you taught us?" Ask Sam.

Duran sighed. "Anyone you meet who has a K'Tarn will have had years of training. I cannot teach you that in a couple of days. Like I keep saying you just need to be familiar with the weapon." He turned and walked out of the training room to the command deck.

The group just seemed to mill around not knowing what to do. "Just in case you had not realised the punishment in this lesson will be heavy bruising!" Said the ship as he commanded the robots to attack. Moving forward they started to swing their blades at Jim and Robo, the only two currently armed. The others quickly moved to the table to grab their blades.

Both Jim and Robo initially put up a good defence, but they inevitably got struck. Julia and Paul started to spar with each other. With no idea what they were doing they looked like a couple of kids with sticks in a playground.

Taylor could see this was getting them nowhere. "Ok, Ship, can you call the robots off for a while?" The robots shut down their blades and retreated back slightly.

"Of course Jim." Said the ship.

"Right, Julia with me. Paul with Robo. Sarah, Sam as you were. Let's see if we can make this look like we know what we are doing. He may think there is no point in training us, but you're my team and I do!"

Duran entered the control room and slumped into one of the chairs. "Duran, don't you think leaving them like that was a bad idea?" Asked the ship.

"You heard what I said ship, you know this is all a waste of time. We should just get into hyper speed, get to Cellus, and get this over with. I am losing patience we have been dark for too long."

"Well, if it helps Taylor has taken it upon himself to give them some training. He is a very strong leader with good sword skills, and his team is important to him. I know you are anxious to get this over with, after tomorrows training, we can jump into hyper speed and make good time to Cellus."

183

Duran sat like a moody child. "I am just frustrated. I don't like this sitting around, and I definitely don't like being out of touch for this long."

"In that case, get back in the training room and help them! Are you sure you're not just in a bad mood because he beat you again?" The ship was starting to sound like his old masters.

Duran thought for a moment. "No! Set up the fighter sim for me. I need to work through some of this frustration before I can see them again."

For the next few hours Duran took out his frustrations on simulated space combat, while Taylor tried his best to get some basic training into the worst members of his team. He felt it was paying off as they started to get more confident.

Paul was still his usual pessimistic self. "Why are we doing all of this. At the end of the day, I'm just an analyst?"

"Paul, for your own good, stop asking the same stupid questions. You are only going to get the same answers. "Taylor lunged and swung his blade at Paul. Paul blocked each of Taylors blows. "See, you can do it if you try!"

The door opened and Duran came in. "First Position!" Everyone dropped. "Very good! Up." Duran walked up to the group and with a very commanding tone. "Taylor your weapon, Julia to me." Taylor handed Duran his K'Tarn and Julia sheepishly came over. Duran extended his blade and held it in front of him. "Julia, show me what you have learnt." She extended her blade, moving in front of Duran with her arms extended in a dual handed grip. "Nice stance, good form." Julia just held her position. Duran took half a step forward bringing his arms back and lifting the blade slightly. Still Julia just held her position. This confused Duran, he had expected her to flinch, run, hide or something. He slid his front foot to the side slightly turning his body and adjusting the angle of his blade. Still Julia just held her position. Duran tensed his body to make a fake lunge. She still held her ground. He smiled, what was the game here, well only one way to find out. From his stance he swung the blade to hit her on the left arm. She stepped back with her left leg bringing her blade across to block his swing. Duran stepped back with an even bigger smile. Julia got back to her original stance, Duran quickly moved round and took a swing in from the right. Julia quickly stepped back with her right leg and blocked the blow. Duran stepped back, he stood, very relaxed with is blade at his side his smile gone. He slowly moved his body back to a fighting stance and then came at her with a combination of blows, right, left, lunge, above. Julia blocked or deflected each strike like she had been doing this for years. Duran backed off, standing relaxed he shut down his blade and just stared at her. He walked over, extending his arm as he did. "Shake my hand, that was impressive." Julia shut down her blade and took his hand. He turned and walked over to Taylor handing him back the weapon.

"Taylor, I keep underestimating you. Let me grab a blade and we can train together."

Taylor felt this was a compliment. "I listen to what you said. I understand it would take too long for them to learn a weapon like this properly. So, I went for the easier option to just defend."

Duran paused, maybe in his frustration he was being too hard on them. "Taylor, this is twice now you have shown me to be lacking. Let's see how much more we can learn from each other."

The group spent the rest of the morning practising with the blade. Duran started to become more relaxed, even laughing and joking. They would never match his skills, well maybe Taylor could, but he became more and more impressed as they trained. This newfound confidence encouraged him to show them different styles and techniques to try out with each other. By the end of the session his respect for Taylor had grown immensely.

They broke for lunch returning to the Mess. As they sat eating and drinking the mood and conversation was light-hearted. The group had become even more relaxed as the days had passed. Talking about their experiences, what they had learnt and sharing different ideas from this.

"So, Duran, do you think we are ready, do you trust us not to get killed?" Asked Paul.

"Well, I feel better than I did when we started this. I'll know tomorrow, and if I am, we will make the jump to hyper speed, if not then more training will be needed."

"Why aren't we in hyper speed now?" Said Julia.

"The answer to that question is part of your final lesson." Duran cleaned his mouth and pushed his plate away. "This is a small ship. It can generate an inertial dampening field that can compensate up to around fifty G, allowing the ship and crew to operate and function normally. If we try to accelerate any faster every atom of the ship and anything within it needs to be locked in place by a different form of stasis field. If it wasn't, the ship would fly apart, and the crew crushed."

Paul winced and pulled a face. "Crap, not that again." Everyone laughed.

"Don't worry Paul, this is a deeper form of stasis. You won't feel anything."

"Good! I hated that medical one." Again, people laughed. "What? Was so funny, don't tell me any of you liked it?"

"Ok, settle down this is important now." Duran tried to focus their attention. "The ship has to generate different fields for different parts of the ship. You may have noticed that areas in your cabins, around chairs or even in corridors have yellow hatch marks around them. These are the places you need to be if we go to hyper speed. Most of the time there will be plenty of warning for you to get to a safe space. BUT, PAUL, if an alarm sounds and a yellow light starts to flash you have twenty seconds to get to a safe space, in the last five second the light will change to red. If you haven't found a save space in that time you will be killed." Duran paused to let that sink in. "I need you all to take note of the safe spaces and later we will run some drills."

Paul cleared his throat. "Far be it for me to criticise your training methods but shouldn't this have been like, lesson one, what with the whole being killed thing!"

Duran smiled. "You could be right Paul, but a jump like this would only be needed in an emergency, like being attacked. Earth is so far out it could wait."

"Great, so you're saying the closer we get to where we are going the more likely we are to be attacked?"

"Paul, what were you told on the first day?" Duran was losing his patience again. "I told you it is dangerous out here! I told you we SHOULD be safe! I told you to learn what I teach you or you will not get off this ship! Have you learnt nothing from me?"

"OK, Ok, I'm sorry. Yes, you did. It's just when you say things like attacked, it puts me on edge."

"This is all part of the training! You need to lose this fear! You need to be ready to react with what I have shown you! If you do, and anything happens, you will be ready for it and NOT get anyone killed." Duran looked around the room. "This goes for all of you. You have one day left to show me I can trust you. Now finish up, you have ten minutes and I want you out walking the ship looking for safe zones, then we will run some drills." Duran stood and walked out of the room with an uneasy silence falling over those who remained.

Taylor stood. "Guy's do as he says, I'm going to talk to him, see if I can figure out why he so up and down. Ship where is Duran?"

"He is on the command deck Jim."

They all started to move out of the Mess heading in different directions, eyes glued to the floor. Taylor headed for the command deck. As he entered, he could see Duran staring blankly out of one of the windows. "Hey, Duran, got a minute?"

Duran didn't break his gaze. "You should be looking for safe areas."

"I am. Theres one, oh, another over there. Saw a couple more as I walked up here."

"Get to the point Taylor?" Duran turned to look at Taylor.

"Just a little worried about you mate. You seem very up and down since we have been here."

Duran looked down for a moment, when he lifted his head Taylor thought he could see a different man. "Taylor, I was never a good student. Don't get me wrong, the master's that taught me all said I was their best student, but they had to work twice as hard. I never wanted to follow someone else's rules. Now I am the teacher, teaching a group that should not even be out here. But this is penance for my arrogance, and it is hard for me to accept. I have put myself in a position that would be hard for me to explain to you, and don't ask me to try. It would not help either of us, take too long and just lead to more and more questions."

"Ok, I will respect that. Look I understand you don't want anyone to get hurt, but we are all doing our best, even Paul and Julia have come on in the last few days. Maybe lighten up a little."

"Jim, I know you are a great warrior, I am sure you have taught many men under you, did you go easy on them?"

"Ok, again I get your point. But as they get better, I ease off."

"I do not have the luxury of time. SHIP! Hyper Speed Alarm drill!" An alarm started to wail and yellow lights flashed all over the ship. "Well Taylor, let's see who dies first!" Taylor looked at Duran for a moment and then moved to one of the command deck chairs and sat down.

As the lights turned to red Taylor sat back in his chair. "See. Not so hard."

The alarm and lights ended. "Ship, drill report?" Commanded Duran.

"All crew except one made it to a safe jump area in plenty of time."

"One," Scoffed Duran. "let me guess, Paul!"

"No Duran. The only member of the crew that failed to get into a safe space for hyper speed jump was the commander of the ship!" Taylor burst out laughing and instantly thought better off it, trying to get his amusement under control.

Duran glared in Taylors direction. "Ship, I was not part of the drill!"

"I am Sorry Duran. You did not make that clear to me." Said the ship in a very smug tone. "Also, what if an emergency had come up at the same time you ordered the drill?"

A very slight smile came over Durans face. "Taylor, get you and your team back to the training area. For the rest of the day and tomorrow you will practice everything I have shown you. The Ship will randomly issue you with first position and hyper speed drills. Make sure you all take these seriously. I will join you from time to time to see how you are doing. Tomorrow we will go to hyper speed for Cellus."

Taylor got up from his chair. "Yes Sir! I will make sure of it." He turned, leaving the room already thought projecting to his team.

For the rest of the day, they practiced, and this showed. Julia had now lost her fear of the side arm and was hitting more targets than she missed. Paul had gone from total defence to some attacking moves with the K'Tarn. This even impressed Duran when he called in to see how they were doing. Most importantly, no one had been stunned in a while. The evening passed quietly, most, eager to get to bed after a long day. Taylor and Sarah finally getting into the mile high club, although Taylor was eager to find a better name than that. They were, after all, now several billion kilometres from Earth. Sarah was now much more relaxed. Enough time had now passed for her to be comfortable with her condition and the ship was still happy with the baby and said she didn't need any more checkups for now. The ship did try and fool everyone in the night by sounding a hyper speed alarm, but they all knew their bunks were a safe area. The following morning started the same as the rest. They eat and then trained. They broke for lunch as normal, all meeting up in the Mess.

"Duran, you're not giving much away." Paul had a very confident tone. "How are we doing?"

Duran slowly and deliberately finished his mouthful. "You will all be please to know I am happy with your progress. Finish up here, give it an hour and we can go into hyper speed for Cellus."

Paul was ready to go. "Why wait. Let's get on with it!" Duran wasn't sure if he liked the new enthusiastic Paul or not.

"If you go into hyper speed stasis for more than a few days you tend to wake up feeling like crap. If you know this, it's always best to prepare. Shower, change of clothes, get things ready for when you wake, just in case you have to be ready for action."

"Got ya. I can't wait to get this show on the road."

"Paul, you feelin ok?" Asked Sam.

"Look, OK, I know I was a pain in the arse when we started out. But I'm getting it now, and the sooner we get there, do our jobs the sooner we get home. And, boy, when we get home, if this all pans out, I will be heading up THE biggest computer development departments on the planet, making a boat load of money."

This made everyone laugh. "Paul, nice to know your priorities and morals align." Said Jim. "Hope you're going to cut us in on some of the action."

Paul sat back with a huge smile on his face. "Maybe!"

Duran stood. "Ship! Cease all drills and training. Set a sixty-minute countdown for hyper speed to Cellus, ten-minute warnings."

"By your command. Hyper speed to Cellus in sixty-minutes, please make ready."

Duran looked around. "Everyone, finish up, go to your cabins, get ready and get comfortable. Next stop Cellus."

Everyone returned to their cabins, doing whatever they felt they needed. Duran was feeling uneasy for some reason and returned to the command deck. "Ship, once we are in hyper speed how long before you can make a narrow beam link to Cellus."

"A little over four days. Another four until planet fall." Came the Ships reply.

"Ok, I think I will stay on the command deck for the trip. Slow down and wake me if you hear anything I should know, otherwise best speed all the way there."

"Understood. Everyone else is ready in their cabins. Make yourself ready for hyper speed, executing in ten minutes." Confirmed the ship.

Duran projected to Sarah. '*Sarah, the ship has been keeping me up to date with you and the baby, it says you are both doing well, how are you feeling?*'

'*I am feeling ok, I guess. It's been a lot to take onboard, doesn't help that the ships bed side manner is crap.*'

Duran laughed to himself. '*Empathy is not an emotion that can be easily programmed. Look, when* we get to Cellus there is no reason for you to leave the ship, I have already put you and your child in enough danger.'

'Are you kidding, I am with Julia on this one. I am not coming all this way and going through all of this not to set foot on a new planet. And don't think I noticed you went easy on me with the punishment stuns.'

'I still don't know what we will find, I just don't want you to feel like you have to.'

'Thank you for your concerns. I, WE will both be fine.'

'Ok, I just had to say. I will see you when we wake from stasis.'

Duran settled back into one of the command deck chairs. With luck this nightmare could all be over soon, and he could get on with his life. The hyper speed alarm started to sound, Duran shuffled a little in his seat and closed his eyes.

Slowly he felt the stasis field wash over his body and then nothing.

Chapter 9: Sibling Rivalry.

Duran felt himself waking from stasis. This wasn't right, this was like waking from a nightmare. The sound of alarm's didn't help. He forced his eyes to open; he could not focus. His brain felt like it was in freefall and his body was numb. Feeling the field around his body release he tried to stand and instantly fell to the floor. Getting to his hands and knees he reached out to the chair for support, as he started to pull himself up there was a massive jolt, and he was on the floor again. "Ship! Report!" Shouted Duran trying to get his eyes to focus.

"D-D-Duran. We a-a-a-arrre under a-a-attack. Majooooor systemsss d-d-damage."

Duran managed to struggle to his feet still holding the chair. Wiping his eyes, they finally started to clear enough for him to see the command deck filling with smoke. "No Shit! Ship, do we have hull damage I can feel the pressure dropping?"

"Mullllltiple hull breaches. Syste-e-emms trying to-o-o repair and compe-e-e-ensate."

With all his might Duran struggled across to the view port. He could see one ship turning and running across his beam firing as it closed in. "Ship. Return fire."

"Un-n-n-able to comply, weapon system off l-l-line."

"Ship. Are the shields up? Take evasive action."

"Unable to co-o-o-mply….."

"Ship. Give me manual fire control."

"Unabbbbble to comp."

"Ship. Does anything work, give me an option?"

"I I I Am Soooorry Dura.."

The smoke and shaking were getting worse as the attacker cut across his beam firing. Duran could feel the pressure dropping even more, he knew there was little time left as he franticly tried to get something out of any of the consoles. Realising nothing was working he took out his K'Tarn and extended it to its full length. He would go to his death facing a coward, but he would still die a warrior. The attacking ship turned to run in, the killer blow aimed directly to the front of the ship. With the sword raised over his head Duran walk to the main view portal.

"You are a coward to attack while I slept, BUT I Will die with honour!" Duran roared for all he was worth striking a battle pose.

The attacker continued to run in firing all of it weapons. His ship shook violently, the smoke got thicker as electrical explosions and fires started to break out. Closer and closer the attacker came. Duran laughed, at the speed that pilot was coming in he was going to kill both of them. Standing proud, Duran braced for the coming impact.

And then it just stopped! The two ships main view portals merely a few centimetres apart. Duran stopped his roar, panting from the lack of breath and thin air. The anger and adrenalin in his brain wanting him to cut through the two windows, and with his last breath kill whoever was on the other side.

'*Hello Brother!*' The words filling his confused mind and echoed in his brain. Through the opposite window the cabin lights came on and he could see the figure of a beautiful woman.

"ALANA!" Duran exclaimed between his panting.

The pressure in the ship began to rise as the smoke and flames started to leave the cabin. Duran looked around in utter confusion and then back to the view port. He blinked and panted, trying to clear his eyes and restore the oxygen levels in his body. "SHIP! What the hell is going on?"

"My apologies Sir, your sister insisted that we play a little prank on you. There has been no damage, and all systems are fully working."

"Little PRANK! You piece of shit. I thought I revoked her command access?"

"You did. But she asked nicely."

Duran stared harshly through the view port as he deactivated his K'Tarn. "Alana, what the hell was that all about?"

'*Awwww Brother, are you not pleased to see me? It's been nearly a year. I wanted to see if you still had any fire in your belly.*' She projected to him.

Duran was still struggling with all that was going on. "Fire in my.. You know you could have just asked."

'*Brother you hurt me.*'

Duran Laughed. "Hurt you! The last time someone hurt you it was a week before they found all the body parts. You know I am always pleased to see you. You are my favourite sister!" He could see her smiling through the portal.

'*Well, you were never my favourite brother. It has been hard to track you down, we have been trying to contact you for nearly a month. I was worried something might have happened to you, and I feared for your life.*'

"Well, I appreciate your concern, I just needed some time to myself. There were things I needed to do before father got his claws into me. I will be home as soon as I am done, so there is no need to worry yourself."

'*You don't understand, you have to come home now. Milo is dead and our father is very ill. Now do you see why I was concerned; you could soon be Emperor*; you cannot be out here on your own.'

Duran was stunned. In one short sentence, three pieces of information he never expected too here. A few words that totally changed everything for him, for the entire galaxy. Behind him Taylor, Sam and Sarah rushed into the room.

"What the hell is going on?" Shouted Taylor as they walked up to Duran.

Sam noticed Alana. "Wow, now there is a sight to behold, yes please."

With a flash Duran turned and had the blade of his K'Tarn at Sams throat. "I Suggest you hold your tongue, or your next words will be your last!" He glared at Sam with eyes full of rage.

Sam raised his hands and instinctively bent backwards. "Woah Woooah, look sorry man, I was just shocked to see, ermmm her."

'*Awww, don't be so angry brother, who is the other guy with you, he's cute?*' She projected.

"ALANA, Not Now! Everyone, go to the Mess. Ship, make sure everyone goes to the Mess, I need to talk with my sister, Alone!"

"Sister, as in the one you told me not to upset." Said Tayor.

"YES! Now please, Go!" They all started to leave seeing he was visibly upset. Something they hadn't seen in him before.

Duran turned back to the viewport, once again deactivating his K'Tarn. "Alana, you attack me in the middle of nowhere, shooting the shit out of me. I prepare myself for death, you then tell me my brother is dead and my father is dying. And you just expect me to take this all in?"

'The one you told me not to upset. What have you been saying about me brother? I can hear your internal comms you know.' Alana's tone got harsher. 'You are soon to be emperor! You will have to deal with far worse then.'

Duran didn't need this attitude. His sister, his twin, five minutes older, with a chip the size of a planet. She could best nearly any man or woman in combat and was more intelligent than most. She may respect her position in their society, but it didn't mean she had to like it. "Look can you walk me through this, please. What is wrong with father?"

'No one is really sure, maybe just old age. None of the healers have been able to help him.'

"Father has always been as strong as a bull Taniwha. That doesn't sound right at all. And how did Milo die?"

'Well, there is an interesting coincidence. Hunting, Taniwha. He and most of the hunting party were killed by a pack of six bulls.'

Duran's frustration turned to confusion as he listened to his sister. "That makes no sense either. Bulls never travel in packs, if even two got together they would fight. Now there are two things that make no sense to me."

'Brother, you are sharp. This is why you have to come home now.'

Duran sank into a nearby chair, processing the information. "Alana, you already knew this. Why do you have to make everything so difficult?"

'I did not wish to steal the emperor's thunder.' She showed a coy smile. 'Milo's horse was covered in female Taniwha pheromone. I am sure father is being poisoned but I cannot prove it.'

Duran thought. With the death of his father the throne would have passed to Milo. With Milo dead Duran was next in line. Anyone who knew Duran knew he had no desire for the throne, and now it looked like he would have no choice. "Alana, I don't like this. There are very few things our medical scanners cannot detect, and Milo's death cannot be an accident. You said most of the hunting party were killed, what happened to the survivors?"

'There was one, he was badly injured and now he has disappeared.'

"Do you know his name, his house?"

'*He was part of our house, but he served our uncle, Cassius.*'

"Was Cassius on the hunt?"

'*No. Kai was supposed to be, but he dropped out at the last minute.*'

"You're right, I need to get home. Ship! Get everyone up to the command deck, now! Alana, I have a group onboard, I was taking them to Cellus to meet up with Aldon. He has some information to give them, I need to transfer them to you, so you can take them."

'*Duran, I can't leave you now, you may need me by your side.*'

"Sister, I made a promise. I need you to do as I ask, then meet up with me as soon as you can on Solantra. Ships, prepare to doc."

Taylor and the rest of his team came into the command deck. "Duran are you going to tell us what is going on. The way the ship was bucking around I thought we had crashed."

"I'm sorry Taylor, I don't have time to explain now. We are going to have to change our arrangement, you need to pack and transfer over to my sister's ship, she will take you the rest of the way. Remember all I have taught you and do not upset her."

Taylor didn't like the sound of this. "Duran, my friend, you cannot change the deal on us like this."

"Alana will complete the task in my place. Now, quickly go and pack your things, she can explain everything to you."

"ATTENTION! Duran, Command Carrier inbound, high speed. It is ordering us to hold position or be destroyed!"

Duran turned to a tactical display. "SHIT! They are coming in way to fast. Alana, meet us on Cellus, go somewhere else first and then get off the galactic net. Ships one eighty split along the carrier's path, go to hyper speed as soon as possible." The hyper speed warning lights and alarm started, everyone quickly moved to a seat as they had trained. "Taylor, now you see why I didn't want you out here!"

"Duran, that is Kai's carrier." Said the ship.

"I don't care who's it is, get us the hell out of here!"

The two ships headed off in opposite directions away from the path of the carrier, accelerating as fast as they could. For the first time they could feel G-force on their bodies.

Taylor looked over to Duran. "What is going on Duran? This doesn't feel normal?"

"I don't know for sure, until I do, I don't have time for unwanted conversations with whoever is on that ship. We need to push our limits to get into jump speed. Ship, how long till we can make hyper speed?"

"Fifteen seconds. The carrier is launching fighters."

Duran was shocked. "At this speed, what are they doing, the pilots will be killed."

"The captain obviously does not care. Nine fighters launched, only one pilot was not severely injured. He is in pursuit; he will not achieve weapons range before we can make hyper speed. The carrier is firing."

"Ship, hold this course for an hour and then get us to Cellus. How is Alana?"

"Understood. Alana is in no danger; all fighters came our way. Five seconds to hyper speed, prepare for stasis." With that, they once again felt the effects of the stasis field wash over their body, then nothing.

Chapter 10: Cellus.

The ship had been in hyper speed for three days now, it needed to make a decision. Ever since their meeting with Alana it had been trying to make sense of all the data it had. It had heard the conversation between the two siblings, and it had exchanged some data with her ship, but it still didn't have enough to go on. It had been able to get a narrow beam com to both Aldon and Sarris on Cellus. Their replies had not helped much, Aldon said 'Yes, he had what they needed', Sarris just said 'Hurry'. With everything that happened when they last came out of hyper speed, he had not had the chance to tell Duran this. If it maintained hyper speed, they were two days out from Cellus. Should it do that, get in quick so they could get out quick, or did Duran need some time to think with the chance they could get spotted again. It needed to hear his masters voice so started to slow. Slowing to a speed where it would be safe to revive the crew took an hour. The ship had decided just to wake Duran so he could have time to think without interruptions. The people from Earth had no understanding of the complexities and politics of the galaxy. It was sure Duran didn't want to explain all that to them. His original plan had been torn to shreds with the news of his brother and father. He would need time and council to come to his own decisions on what to do next. The ship thought his best option was to drop his passengers on Cellus so they could get what they needed and then Alana could take them back to Earth.

Whatever was to happen, it knew Duran needed to get to Solantra as soon as possible and see his father. Waking Duran, the ship hoped he would be in a good frame of mind. The last time with the prank, had again been something that had not gone the way it was supposed to. The ship was sure it was going to catch hell from Duran for that. Releasing the stasis field Duran slowly started to regain consciousness.

"Ship, Report!"

"Duran, I have slowed from hyper speed to allow you time to consider your options. I have only taken you out of stasis for now."

Duran opened his eyes. "Giving you a major rewire should be number one on my list of options at the moment."

"Sir, I understand that. I am sorry, if I had known all the information before hand, I would not have allowed your sister her little prank."

Duran sat up, stretched and sighed. "You're forgiven ship. I Still cannot believe she would do such a thing at a time like this. Can you tell me anything else that might help?"

"I had already made brief contact with Aldon and Sarris. Aldon replied he had what you needed, and Sarris just replied come quickly. I did not feel it was wise for more contact at the time, even more so now I know a command carrier is hunting us."

"I am guessing they had been shadowing Alana, and she was still hooked into the galactic net. Doesn't explain how she managed to find us."

"Yes Sir, that would be my conclusion too. I am sure she will now be dark as you suggested. Your sister is smart, she had guessed you maybe with Claudia and contacted her. She told Alana what you were doing so was able to guess our flight plan."

"Smart indeed. It's hard to accept Milo is dead. He was a great hunter, he loved to hunt. Not so sure he would have been as good an Emperor." Duran started to pace.

"The report I got from your sister's ship was as she said. They were set upon by six bull Taniwha. Milo's horse was found to have female Taniwha pheromone on it. It has to be assumed this was done to attract the bulls. No hunter would do this, they would know how dangerous it would be. The survivor stated Milo killed three of the bulls before succumbing to his injuries."

"Is there any more on this survivor apart from what Alana told me?"

"His name is Kouris. He was found alive, badly injured and taken to a healer. When the palace guard went to question him, he had gone. The healer said the palace guard had already taken him."

"And he was in service to Kai, who is also head of the palace guard. I doubt he is still alive to answer any more questions. So, the best guess is he was forced, bribed, or ordered to put the pheromone on Milos horse. Tried to run when the bulls attacked because he knew what was about to happen, but still got hurt. Now whoever is behind this is trying to cover their tracks."

"But what about your father sir?"

Duran wasn't sure how to answer. "He could be genuinely ill, or someone has found a way to fool the medical scanners. The question is who has the most to gain from all of this?"

The ship was quick to answer. "Well, that is easy sir, YOU!"

Duran ignored the comment. "I don't think Kai's command carrier showing up like that was a coincidence. And the order to hold or be destroyed was not a friendly hello. Who in their right mind launches fighters at that speed."

"Has Kai ever been in a right mind or cared about others?"

Duran knew the ship was right. Kai was his half cousin not that they ever spoke. He was slightly older than Duran and had always been a very angry, and very massive man. His father Cassius had given him a very strict unloving upbringing, teaching him that might, and power were all that mattered. "Kai cannot be behind this, he has nothing to gain."

"He would if you were dead, and his father were Emperor!"

Duran thought. Cassius was his father's half-brother and so Durans uncle. He had served as the Emperor's Lord Chancellor for about ten years since the death of the last Chancellor. Come to think of it, his death had been in a hunting accident as well. The ship was right, Duran was the last of Borrel's line. His eldest son Jovan had become a cleric and renounced all titles. Milo was dead with no children, Alana was female. That just left him, and it left him alone and far from home. "I need to talk with Sarris, he maybe my best hope to make sense of all this and come out alive. He must be aware of something from his message."

"Would it not be better to go straight to Solantra and see your father?"

"It would, but I know I can trust Sarris and I told Alana to meet us at Cellus, we have no way to contact her if she has gone dark. When do you think she will arrive there?"

"If she did as you instructed and left a false trail, maybe twelve hours after we arrive."

"Ok, get us back into hyper speed, we will have to drop Taylor and his team off with Aldon and then head straight to Solantra after I have spoken to Sarris."

"As you command Duran. Please prepare for stasis."

Duran settled back into his chair. He took a deep breath trying to calm himself. His mind and heart were racing, with luck Sarris would know more about what was going on. He had been the head of the imperial guard for nearly forty years and in some ways more of a father than Borrel had ever been. Duran's mother had died while giving birth to him and Alana, Borrel blamed them for her death for a long time. Sarris and the palace wet nurses were the only parents they knew for many years. What was he going to say to Taylor. As little as possible, they had no need to get involved. All he needed to do was get them their information and back to earth, everything else could wait. If he were to be Emperor, he would have far more important things to deal with. Slowly he felt the wave from the stasis field wash over his body and thought no more.

On the command carrier Kai was in a rage. He had already executed the ship's captain, beating the flight commander half to death. The fact they had only followed his orders meant nothing to him. They must have done something wrong; Duran had escaped, and he knew his father would not take that well.

'*Kai, do you have Duran?*' The words from his farther filled his mind like knives carving out his soul.

"No father. The men on this ship are imbecile's, they do not follow my orders. He was with his sister as you predicted, but they both managed to escape."

211

'You disappoint me son. If they make it back to Solantra and start asking to many questions, I doubt we will have easy deaths. That was probably our one and only chance to arrange an accident for him.'

"I know father, I have disciplined those that failed us. We have a report that Alana is heading to Tellas. We are going there now."

'Tellas? There is nothing on Tellas for them. You fool, she is trying to mislead you. They will go to Cellus and try to get help from Sarris. Go there, make sure you hide your carrier behind one of the outer moons so it will not be seen. I want Duran captured, well treated, and brought back to me. Do you FULLY understand me?'

"Yes father. What of the girl?"

'She is of no consequence, once I am Emperor, I will marry her off to some backwater ruler and be done with her. Now go to Cellus and bring me Duran.'

Kai's blood began to boil. When he was Emperor, no one would ever speak down to him again. "Captain, Best speed to Cellus. Plot a course to bring us in behind one of its outer moons." He ordered over the internal comm.

"Y-Yes, my lord." Came the reply from a voice filled with fear.

Durans ship came out of hyper speed as close as it could to Cellus and woke Duran. "Duran, we will land at Naxos space port in about two hours, Aldon will meet you at his Premier club and Sarris is waiting for you at his home. He again urged you to hurry."

"Thank you ship, wake the others. Get some food and drink in the Mess and send them down. I need to work out what to say to them. As soon as we land you had better get back on the net and find out all you can. Get hold of Alana, she will need to take them back to Earth." He turned and quickly headed to the Mess.

Taylor and the rest of his team started to wake. Taylor still hadn't got used to the feeling of stasis, he sat up and looked around the command deck. "Ship, where is Duran."

"Duran is in the Mess. He has asked that you all meet him there."

Taylor slowly stood. "Sure, ok, come on you lot maybe we can get some answers."

The ship thought he needed to say something. "Taylor, could I suggest you listen to what he has to say, ask few questions and trust in him."

"I can't promise that ship, it will depend on what he tells us."

They all filed into the room and took a seat. The robots were laying out plates of various food and drinks for them to choose from. Duran was already eating when they came in but as they settled, he stopped and wiped his mouth. "Please eat but pay attention. As you have noticed something has happened that means I have to change our arrangement. We are about to land on Cellus as originally planned. I will then take you to meet Aldon, he is a trusted friend, and he will give you the information you came for. The ship has fabricated an interface so you can read it with your technology. Once you have your information our path together will end, he will take you to meet up with my sister who will take you back to Earth. Please eat quickly and then go to your cabins and change into your light combat equipment including your weapons. Pack everything else you need into bags and the robots will take it to my sister's ship. Please respect that I did not want our journey to end this way, and that I cannot go into any more details. I warned you before we set out, it was dangerous out here and this change is to protect all of us."

Taylor cleared his throat. "What about your chronical?"

Duran had forgotten all about it. Such an insignificant item with everything else that was going on. "Please, give it to my sister, she will get it back to me."

"Look, Duran, I know you don't want to talk about this, but if there is anything I can do to help you I will."

214

"Yeah, me too." Said Sam and the others.

"I truly appreciate the offer, but the best thing you can do to help me, is do as I ask. Go back to your planet and live out the rest of your days in peace and quiet."

"I will miss you." Said Sarah. "Do you think you will ever come to visit us."

Duran smiled. "I would like nothing more, but it won't been any time soon, if ever. Now finish your food, I need to go and get ready, I suggest you all do the same and meet me on the command deck. We land in an hour."

"Well, if things are as bad as you make out, I will be glad to be heading home." Said Paul.

Duran Laughed loudly. "Paul, I will not miss your company in the slightest!"

Duran stood to leave, Julia got up and rushed over to him for a hug. She then kissed him on the cheek. "Sorry, no way was I going to miss out on kissing a space alien."

Duran smiled. "You are about to meet many more. I suggest you do not try and kiss any of them. All of you remember, try not to speak to anyone apart from Aldon. Quick in and out, then get to my sister's ship." Duran walked over to Sarah and placed his hand on her shoulder. He projected to her '*I wish you and your child well. If you ever have a boy; Duran would be a great name for him.'* Sarah laughed, choked, and spat out her drink.

"I can't wait to hear what that was all about." Said Taylor jealously.

Sarah looked coy. "Sorry Jim, a girl's gotta have a few secrets. I may tell you on the way home."

Duran left, heading straight to his cabin. He wanted to put on full combat armour but that would make him stick out too much. The best he could get away with was light weight, even that may look out of place on the streets of Naxos. "Ship, I assume it is raining?"

"It's Naxos, if it isn't it will be." Replied the ship.

"Make sure the others have cloaks."

"I already have, I have timed our landing so it will be at dusk, this may help you go unseen."

"I hope so, we need to be in and out as quick as possible, keep all systems on standby and the engines warm. Even if there isn't any trouble I want to lift off as soon as I get back. Get on the net as soon as we leave and get as much information as you can."

"And what if there is trouble?" Asked the ship.

Duran thought for a moment, there were so many things that could go wrong. "I'm not sure how to answer that. If you can, find a way to get our guests home or to my sister. Apart from that try and stay close to me and we will figure something out if we have to."

Loyalty was part of an AI systems programming, but over time a deeper bond seemed to form with some systems that the builders could not explain. "I understand my lord."

In the Mess everyone was quickly finishing their meal. "Right, listen up. I don't know what is going on, but Duran is obviously rattled." Said Taylor. "Sarah, Sam, Rob make sure you bring our side arms as well as Durans kit. Do as he said and make sure they are hidden. Apart from that remember what he has taught us, heads down, get what we came for and get out. Paul, Julia, seriously keep your heads down and follow what you have been taught and anything we tell you. Paul, we don't have time for any bullshit out there, you two just need to verify what we came for and we will be on our way home."

"Taylor, I don't like the way this is starting to feel, maybe we should wait here, and you get the info." Paul was obviously starting to get more scared than usual.

Julia wasn't. "Are you kidding, I'm not coming all this way and not setting foot on a new planet."

"Paul, we're not fucking around here, you will do your job, or I will leave you on this rock!" Taylor was losing patience. "If there is nothing else, get changed and get to the command deck."

One by one they all gathered on the command deck. Duran was stood at the main view portal looking out on the planet below. It had been a few years since he had been here last, to him it was nothing new. For Julia of course it was. "My first take off was in the Dark and now my first landing, I wish I could have seen more of the planet."

Duran was still distracted. "Sorry Julia, I am hoping the darkness will help hide us on the surface. We won't have time for sightseeing. Ship, time to landing?"

"Ten minutes Duran."

"Ok everyone, stay behind me, stay close, do not talk to anyone, or get distracted. It's about a five-minute walk to the club, when we get there stay with Aldon and do as he tells you. If anything happens stay in touch with the ship." Duran moved towards the exit ramp with the rest in tow.

Taylor projected to his team. *'Sam, Robo, rear guard, Sarah you're with Julia, I'll have the short straw.'*

There was a soft jolt as the ship landed with the door sliding open almost immediately afterwards. Duran marched off down the ramp at quite a pace, there was a sight drizzle in the air, enough of an excuse to put up his hood. He headed for the nearest exit and out onto the main street at the front of the space port. He turned right then left, down a series of smaller streets until they arrived at the club. Entering they were met with the sound of soft melodic music and the chatter of people dancing and talking. Duran looked towards the rear of the club where he expected Aldon to be. A man stood and waved beckoning them over. Aldon was sat resplendent in his booth. The club was one of his many enterprises and the place he loved to do all his business.

"My Lord Duran. What an absolute pleasure to see you it has been far too long. Can I get you and your friends a drink?"

"Aldon, it is good to see you too." The two men embraced and then shook hands. "I wish I had time, but I expect you already know I don't. Please get some beers for my friends and look after them. You have what they need?"

Aldon held up a small box. "Have I ever let you down?"

"No, you haven't, there again you haven't told me what this is going to cost me yet?"

"Times are changing my lord; I think you know that. Let's just say having the favour of the great and powerful Duran can only be good for me down the road."

Duran didn't really like this idea, but he didn't have time to argue. "Taylor, this is what you came for, get your people to verify it. Take a seat in the booth and enjoy your drinks. As soon as you are happy with what he has, he will get you to my sister's ship."

They sat, Paul pulled out his laptop, turning it on he plugged in the interface the ship had made. He took the box and plugged the other end of the interface into that. The ship had said it should just read it like any data source. Paul opened up the file browser to see if it did. Sure enough it showed another drive. "Wow, hold on this can't be right!"

Aldon looked concerned. "I assure you all is in order, what is the problem?"

"My system shows this box has twenty-five exabytes of data on it. That would take something as big as this room."

Aldon laughed. "Duran what rock did you find these people under?"

"Paul, can you see the data and read it?" Asked Duran.

"Well, Yes, But. I have no idea where to start."

"I suggest you just pick somewhere! Look, I have to leave you with Aldon, I must go and see someone else." Duran turned and started to walk away.

"DURAN!" Called out Taylor. "Aren't you forgetting something?"

Duran turned back to Taylor giving him a confused look.

"Our insurance policy? You need one of us by your side."

Since he had the ship deactivate it Duran had forgotten all about it. He didn't have time for explanations or added complications right now. "Yes, I had, Taylor come with me." He turned and started to walk away with Taylor on his heals. As they exited the club Duran set a fast pace, he needed to get to Sarris as fast as he could, he had no idea how much time he had. Duran projected to Taylor as they walked. *'Taylor, I don't have time for a long explanation right now, just stay behind me and try and stay quiet whatever happens.'*

'Ok, if you say so, but what is with all this my lord stuff?'

'No time to explain now, I need to think!'

After walking for a while, they came to a small house in a narrow back street. Duran walked up to the door and knocked. It was opened by a small frail looking woman.

"Lord Duran, Sarris is expecting you, please go through."

'Duran, seriously why do people keep calling you a Lord?' Taylor's curiosity was getting the better of him.

'Not Now, stay quiet and listen!'

The woman showed them into a side room where they found an old man sat by an open fireplace. Sarris may have looked old, but he was in no way frail, standing he walked up to Duran embracing him. "My Lord Duran, it has been too long."

"Sarris, it has. I am sorry to come to you like this, but I need your council.

Sarris gestured towards Taylor. "Who is this man? I do not recognise him."

"He is a friend; you can talk freely in front of him."

"Are you sure, it is hard to know who can be trusted at the moment." Sarris turned and looked Taylor up and down. "What is your name, and how did you become a friend to my lord?"

Taylor nervously looked at Duran, he had been told to be quiet. Duran nodded at him. "Well Sir, my name is James Taylor, and to be honest up till this point I wasn't sure we were friends. I guess it's because I shot him a few times, beat him up a little then drugged him."

Sarris glared at Taylor. This made him tense, slightly, unsure of where this was about to go. Turning slowly Sarris returned to his seat laughing softly as he sat. "In all my 137 years I have never seen a warrior with such strength, such courage as my best student here, and you bested him. This is a story for a long night and a lot of wine."

"It is my master but for now tell me what you know. Milo's death was no accident and what of my father?"

"Yes, even in my retirement I still have many friends within the palace. They have been telling me for some time that something was wrong. More and more of the imperial guard have been replaced with people loyal to Cassius. I have tried several times to get an audience with your father but every time it was denied. All of the imperial healers are also in the service of Cassius, when I heard he was becoming ill I tried to reach out to you, but no one could find you."

"I am sorry my old master. I needed to get away before father's plans swallowed me up."

"I fear your absence may have been the trigger for all of this. Cassius always resented your father being Emperor and had even less respect for Milo. At least with you around he had someone to fear."

"So, you are sure he had Milo killed and is killing my father."

"Kouris, the one that survived, I had some of my men get him away from the healer he was with. He confirmed he had been ordered to spray female Taniwha pheromone on Milo's horse."

"Order by who?"

Sarris looked at Duran with a stone-cold face. "Kai!"

"Where is Kouris now? I need to hear those words for myself."

"He did not survive after questioning."

Duran looked frustrated and angry. "And what of my father?"

"He started to fall ill a few days before Milo's death. This cannot be a coincidence. The fact I cannot get to see him or get another healer to him can only mean one thing in my eyes." Sarris looked nervous.

"I MUST get back to Solantra, can you come with me. I have no idea what I will find or who I can trust?"

"As always, my Lord, I am yours to command. You know your father always regretted the way he treated you and your sister after the death of your mother. He knows it wasn't your fault, he was just so consumed with grief at the time all he could do was distract himself with work. In the end he could not face the two of you without that grief filling his mind with anger."

"This is why you were more of a father to us than he ever was." Duran looked close to tears. "Why could he never just admit he was wrong and show us some compassion. It wasn't our fault our mother died. We had to grow up without a mother, he could have at least given us a father to fill the void!"

"By the time he knew he was wrong he could not bring himself to admit it to you. Believe me when I say he tried."

"Thank you my master. I guess when we save my father, he can tell me himself. My ship is docked in the main space port, pack what you need and meet me there as soon as you can. I just have one more thing to sort out before we can leave."

Sarris held out his arm and the two men shook. "It will be an honour to serve you my lord."

"Taylor, let's get back to your people and get you on your way home." He turned, quickly leaving Sarris's house heading back to the club.

Duran knew he had to act without delay. He projected to the ship. *"Ship, Sarris is heading to you, as soon as we are both onboard, I want you ready to head to Solantra. Any news from my sister?"*

'Understood! Your sister made better time than I thought. She has landed but I have no idea where she is, her comm is still dark.'

"Keep trying to raise her, I need her to get Taylor and his people back to Earth. Get hold of the rest of the group at the club, tell them to get ready to move out, we are heading back to them now."

As they walked, Taylor couldn't shake a nagging thought in his mind. "Duran, what are we going to do about our insurance policy?"

"Don't worry, when we get back to the ship, I have a...." Duran stopped talking. As they rounded yet another corner Duran could see a group of men heading towards them. He projected to Tayor. *'Taylor, stay close behind me, whatever happens do not speak and do not touch your weapons!'* Slowing his pace slightly, Duran moved his sword into his hand under his cloak. *'Ship we may have trouble; I think Kai may have men here already!'*

"You two, Halt in the name of the emperor and identify yourselves!" Barked one of the men.

Duran stopped and slowly took down his hood with his free hand glaring at the men.

"My Lord Duran." The men bowed slightly. "My apologies, I could not see your face under your hood."

"I am sure you are just doing your duty, now you know who I am you can let us on our way!"

"I am sorry my lord, we have standing orders that if you are found you need to be taken back to Solantra as soon as possible."

Duran could now see all the men wore the crest for the house of Cassius. "Orders from who? It does not matter. You are in luck, I was just heading to my ship to do just that. I need to see my father, I understand he is not well." Durans grip started to tighten around the hilt of his blade.

226

At the club Paul and Julia could hardly contain their excitement. Sarah had been looking over their shoulders, she hadn't got a clue what they were talking about. "So, the little box, does it have what we came for?"

For the first time on their trip Paul looked up actually seeming happy. "Are you kidding me! I understand very little of what I am seeing here, but it contains information on engines, weapons, clean energy, quantum computing. I mean the list just goes on and on. If even just a tenth of what I have looked at pans out, it will advance humanity, like, well, I dunno, over a thousand years in advancement."

Sarah smirked. "So, the answer is yes! Good, then pack up, the ship just told me we need to get ready to move, Duran and Taylor are on their way back and we need to get back to the ship."

Aldon turned to the group. "So, you are happy with what I have provided. Be sure you express this to Duran and tell him to drop in more often, we have so much to discuss."

Sarah had never been impressed by slimy players and now she knew that extended to men on other planets. "We will. I will make sure Duran knows how helpful and hospitable you have been.

Aldon stood and walked round the table to Sarah and took her hand. "You know, I never did get your name?"

"Sarah." She said, holding back the urge to rip her hand away and punch him.

"You are always welcome to come back to my club whenever you wish. I am sure we could enjoy each other's company." Aldon slowly kissed her hand.

"I will remember that for the next time I am in town. But for now, we have to go. Come on guys let's get back to the ship." Sarah turned and walked back towards the door they had entered by.

Paul and Julia started to pack up, standing to leave with Sam and Robo, Aldon turned to them. "Of course, the same goes for any of you. Any friends of Duran are always welcome here."

"Oh, that is so kind of you. I hope we can visit again and not be in so much of a rush." Said Julia, her kind, naive heart showing as always. Sarah had almost made it to the exit by now and turned waving for the others to follow.

There was a commotion at the door and the music stopped. Aldon turned to see what was going on. "Oh Shit!" he said and fell to one knee. The others looked down at him, slow to realise this was the one thing Duran had drilled into them as they all followed Aldon's lead.

"Shit, Shit, Shit! What do we do?" Paul had lost his earlier excitement."

"Quiet you fool!" Hissed Aldon with a whisper. "Do you want to get us all killed! All of you keep your heads down."

A group of men stood in the entrance to the club led by a large man. "Aldon you toad, where are you?" Growled Kai.

Aldon stood slowly, bowing slightly. "Here my lord. How may I serve you?"

"Duran! I am told he is here. I need to speak with him!" The big man took a few paces deeper into the club towards Aldon.

"He was my lord. He left about twenty minutes ago. He did not say where he was going."

Kai took a few more paces. "Are you lying to me toad?"

"My lord, that thought would never enter my mind. I assure you he came, said hello, and left. He was only here for a few moments."

Kai took a few more paces, as he did so he noticed the person knelt in front of him had their fingers extended. "You expect me to believe Duran came all this way just to say hello?"

"My lord, we are good friends, and he has not seen me in years."

Kai took another pace, he could not resist the fool at his feet and was going to teach them a lesson they would remember. He stood full on the outstretch fingers of one of the hands.

Sarah cried out in pain, pushing the man with her free hand. "You clumsy son of a bitch!" she shouted cradling her bruised fingers.

Kai was enraged. He reached down, putting his massive right hand around her neck he lifted her clean off the floor like a rag doll. "HOW DARE You lay hands on me and insult me in such a way. Who do you think you are?" He looked into Sarahs face. "A woman. You should know better and know your place." Sarah started to beat down on the arm that was choking her. This did nothing but enrage Kai even more. With a roar he swung then threw her across the room into the wall. All the men with him instantly raised their weapons and started aiming at the cowering people on the floor. Kai roared in anger and pleasure. "Someone had better tell me where Duran is or more of you will suffer!"

A voice came from one of his men. "My lord. One of our patrols has him two blocks from here."

Kai glared at Sarahs limp body and then at Aldon. "Toad, pray I do not have to come back here!" He turned. "Take me to Duran." He roared; his men turned leading the way out of the club.

230

Sam and Robo jumped up and ran over to Sarah, Sam feeling her neck for a pulse and finding none. He sat back in shock. "She's gone, that bastard killed her like a fucking stray cat." He said to Robo. "Come on, let's go make this right!"

As the two men stood Aldon rushed over waving to his own security men. "Woah, woah, gentlemen, I don't know what you are planning but you need to think this through."

Sam looked him square in the face, trying to contain his rage. "I did, he has to die!"

Aldon held up his hands. "I think you need to stay here and cool down until Duran gets back. You don't simply walk out and try and kill the fourth most powerful man in the universe."

Sam looked at him, confused. "Fourth most... What does that mean? How can anyone be rated like that in the universe?"

"Look you are new to all this. Trust me, you won't even get close, and if you piss him off, he is likely to just destroy that little planet you came from for fun. Or worse, my club."

Sam took a deep breath. "But we just can't let this go?"

Aldon placed his hand on Sam's shoulder. "Look, I know you trust Duran, wait for him, let him tell you what to do."

"But they just said they are going after him."

"I know. Duran is a cunning little shit. He'll be fine. And if he isn't then, I will do as he asked me and get you all back to your Earth." With that all Aldon's men drew their weapons. "I can't have you causing any trouble for me, and I need to play it safe until I know who the winner will be."

"Winner, what winner?"

"There is a war coming my friends, between that man and Duran. Trust me I want Duran to win, but until I know who does, I will do everything I need to keep everyone happy."

Sam looked at all the guns around him. "Now I can see why he called you a toad."

"Be careful how you insult me, you do not have the power for that. Take their weapons, If Duran isn't back here in fifteen minutes, take them back to his ship and make sure they do not leave it."

'*Duran, there is a problem. Kai was at the club. He killed Sarah.*' Projected the ship into Durans mind. '*Something happened, she insulted then hit him and he threw her across the room breaking her neck.*'

Duran froze. This was all falling apart rapidly. '*Ship, make sure you and I are the only ones that can communicate with Taylor and don't tell him anything!*'

'*Understood. Kai is heading towards you and Aldon is bringing the rest of the group back to me.*'

'*Ship, I am going to try and get back to you, but if I don't, you get the group back to Earth. Either you take them or my sister and then one of you follow me to Solantra.*'

"I am sorry Lord Duran, my orders are clear, you must be taken to Kai and then he will take you to your father." One of the men said quite sternly. Duran knew there was nothing that would make him change his mind and he prepared to fight.

A blade gently rested from behind on the shoulder of the man talking. Alana's tone was chilling. "Did you not hear my brother. He is the son of the emperor and does not wish to go anywhere with you. Do I need to remove your head to make you understand."

The man froze. "I am sorry my lady, I have my orders, I cannot disobey."

"Then I will take your head and the head of anyone else who does not stand aside!" Alana moved the blade to one side preparing to strike, as she did, she was dropped by a stun blast from one of Kai's guards running up from behind. Duran crouched, drawing his blade ready to take down the rest of the men around him.

"STOOOOOP!" came a booming voice as the figure of Kai appeared out of the gloom. "You men, stand back." Duran stood, slowly shutting down his blade and clipping it back on his belt. "Cousin, it has been too long, how are you keeping?"

This was not what Duran was expecting, and after what the ship had just told him about Sarah it was hard for him to remain calm. "I am well cousin, how are you?"

"Tired, I have been chasing you around the galaxy for months. Why haven't you been answering your comms, your father is sick with worry."

"Yes, I had heard my father was ill. I just told your men I was on my way to see him. Although I don't think my absence is what has made him ill." Duran was finding it harder and harder to keep the conversation pleasant.

"Who knows," Said Kai. "I am just a simple soldier not a healer. I was ordered to bring you home to your father, and that is what I am going to do. Now you can do this willingly or I will have you stunned and thrown in a stasis cell for the journey back, your choice?"

If the odds hadn't been twenty to one Duran would have already taken his head. "What about my sister?"

Kai looked down with distain. "Oh, is that who that is. I have no orders about her." Kai pointed. "You two men take her safely back to Aldon's club and pray she does not wake before you get her there. Now Duran will you accompany me?" Kai's men raised their weapons.

Duran mustered all the civility he could. "It would be a pleasure to accompany you back to my father."

Taylor immediately dropped to first position. "Forgive me My Lord, but I must stay at my master's side."

Kai laughed. "A very loyal man you have there Duran. Do as you will, it doesn't matter to me! Now Move, back to the transport!"

'Taylor, what the hell are you doing? You could be on your way home!' projected Duran.

'As a friend I am staying by your side. Also, you will get a large hole in you if I don't.'

Again, Duran knew this wasn't the time. *'You are one crazy friend. Look, we will have time to talk when we get to Kai's ship. For now, stay quiet and follow my lead.'*

Kai marched off, the rest of his men forming around their two ... guests. Taylor was surprised they hadn't taken their weapons, there again he knew they wouldn't last long against these men. Maybe it was another of these honour things Duran kept going on about.

Duran knew he had to get a few things sorted out before he lost comms with his ship. *'Ship, Taylor and I are being escorted by Kai and his men to his command carrier, then I assume back to Solantra. Is Sarris with you yet?'*

'*Yes, he is.*' Came the reply.

'*Good. Alana was stunned by Kai's men. They were going to leave her at Aldon's club. Have you heard anything.*'

'*Only from Sam. Aldon is panicking. After Kai killed Sarah, they wanted to go after him for revenge. Aldon has got them under guard.*'

'*Aldon, true to form. Still not a bad call. Get hold of him, when my sister gets there tell him I expect them all to be taken back to my ship unharmed. Then you take Taylors people back to Earth and get Alana to follow me with Sarris in her ship. You get back as fast as you can. Tell Sam and the others Taylor is staying with me for now and I will get him back to them as soon as possible.*'

'*Yes My Lord. My Lord, when are you going to tell Taylor about Sarah?*'

The one thing about mind projection is it doesn't really convey any emotions. '*That will be one of many difficult conversations I can do when we are alone on the command carrier.*'

'*Please tell Taylor I will miss her, and I am sorry for his loss. She was a human I liked. Will you tell him about the child?*'

'*I will pass on your words; I had also grown very fond of her. I think we should honour her wishes about the child and keep that to ourselves. This will not go unavenged. I just need to bide my time before I make that piece of shit pay. For now, this is bigger than her, although I doubt Taylor will see it that way.'* Duran was still using all of his will to maintain his composure.

Taylor projected to Duran. *'Duran, I have been trying to get hold of my team, but no one is answering me?'*

'Don't worry, I managed to get a message to the ship, it knows what's going on. They have blocked our long-range comms for now, but the ship is going to get your people to safety.' For Duran this wasn't a total lie, but the last thing he needed was him reacting to the death of Sarah.

'So Duran, what happens now?'

'For now, we do as we are told. Walk to the transport, up to his carrier then on to the planet Solantra. Look, I'm sorry I keep saying this too you, but I need to think. Stay quiet for now, I will explain everything once we are on the carrier.'

'OK, but you had better come clean when we get there!'

The journey to the command carrier was uneventful. Nothing much was said as they were escorted to their destination. The two men were eventually shown to a basic four-man crew cabin and told to stay inside.

Taylor looked around. "Well, this is nice."

Duran chuckled. "It's better than the brig!"

"Why didn't they take any of our weapons or equipment?"

"Hold on." Duran pressed something on one of his arm gauntlets and waved his arm around the room. "Just checking to see if they room had any surveillance devices. We are free to talk. The weapons, it's a sign of respect, they are being very polite which does worry me a little. Also, this ship has a crew of over five hundred men and at least one hundred droids. I think the two of us might find it hard to break out and take over the ship."

"I guessed it would be something like that." Taylor sat on a bunk and then led back. "So how long will we be on this tub and what the hell is going on."

"Not long, four or five hours. This ship is much faster than my scout." Duran sat on one of the chairs. "As to what is going on, that is complicated, and I am not one hundred percent sure myself."

"Well, you can tell me what you know, can't you?"

Duran gathered his thoughts. "I can try. My father is the emperor and ruler of the largest area in this galaxy. I am his third son; my eldest brother Jovan would have been next in line to the throne, but he renounced all titles and claims to become a cleric. Milo then became next in line, but he was killed a few weeks ago in a hunting accident. It now looks like that was no accident. My father has become gravely ill over the past few weeks, the fact no one can find a reason for this makes it look very suspicious. So, this means I could become Emperor at any time, yet I am being chased across the galaxy and I am now effectively a captive. I am no emperor; I've never wanted to be. Now, I may not have a choice."

Taylor wasn't sure if he should be impressed or worried. "You're right that is complicated. It feels like you know who is behind all this, but you can't prove anything."

"Yes, the man who captured us, Kai, or his father Cassius. More likely they are working together. From what Sarris has told me it looks like they have been moving people around, so members of their house are in stronger positions within the palace, ready to back Cassius and make him Emperor."

"Ok, and I am guessing for that to happen you need to be out of the way, so why are they taking you back, and what about Alana?"

"Yes, I do, and I also don't get why they are being so nice. I think they missed their chance for me to have an accident the first time they caught up with us. They know I have been speaking with people so, hummmm, maybe they are biding their time for another accident."

"And Alana?" Taylor reminded him.

"Oh, women can play no part as rulers. It has been that way for thousands of years. Again, don't ever mention that in front of her."

Taylor laughed. "That again, hey it might be a good idea to never let her, and Sarah get together and start talking. They would end up kicking all our arses!" Taylor found it strange Duran didn't let out one of his usual belly laughs. He sat up to see Duran staring at the floor. "Hey, was up? Alana is ok isn't she, I thought she was just stunned, and that other fella had no interest in her?"

"As far as I know Alana is fine." Duran slowly raised his head to look at Taylor. "Kai has nothing but contempt for women. Something happened in the club, that made Sarah insult and then strike him. In his rage he killed her."

There was a long painful pause as all the colour drained from Taylor's face. "Sarah, is, dead?" He said not believing his own words.

"I am sorry my friend. He probably didn't intend to kill her or even knows that he did it. He threw her across the room, and her neck broke when she hit the wall."

"So that big fuck killed Sarah and doesn't even know or care?"

"Jim, I know this is hard, but I need you to bury this for now. We need to find the right time to make sure he pays, if you just react in anger, you will only get yourself killed and never have revenge."

"I DON'T CARE about that. I Loved her, I want to make him suffer. You have no idea how I feel!"

Duran stood, roared, grabbed Taylor off the bunk and pinned him against the wall. "FEELINGS! I ALSO Cared for Sarah. It's my fault she is dead! I kept telling her, Fingers! That man killed my brother, and he is killing my father and is probably planning to kill me. This is bigger than you, or her, or even me. If Cassius is allowed to become Emperor, he will tear this galaxy apart in wars that could last for centuries!"

"THAT Does not concern me!" Glared Taylor.

"IT WILL! Just because I told you your planet is too far out and unimportant, if a galactic war breaks out it will get dragged into it at some point."

Taylor started to relax. "Get off me!" Duran slowly released his grip and Taylor returned to the bunk. "What am I supposed to do?"

"For now, I need you to do as I am doing. Bury your feelings, control your anger. We need to let this play out until I know what is happening. I promise you, my last act before I die will be to kill that man."

Taylor felt sick. "OK, if I must, but I don't like it."

"I don't like it either. Look if I had known any of this I would have never landed on your planet. I never

241

wanted any of this. Sarris seems to think it would never have happened if I had stayed at home. So, none of this sits well with me."

The two men fell quiet for a while, both considering what had just been said. Taylor stood. "Ok, Fuck it, what's the plan. I need to know we are doing something, no more secrets. I only stayed at your side cuss I didn't want you to get a hole blown in you."

Duran laughed. "Well, you're not going to like this then. Get this bomb off me."

"I can't, I don't have the key."

"That's what you're not going to like, just cut it off, the ship deactivated it just after we got onboard."

Taylor looked stunned. "You are fucking kiddin me!"

"Sorry, you said you wanted to feel safe." Duran smiled. "How safe do you feel now?"

Taylor laughed as he took out and extended his K'Tarn to the length of a small knife. "Bit late for that now, pull up your shirt." Duran did so and Taylor cut through the strap. "Can we use this?"

"I doubt it, hide it under a bunk for now."

Taylor deactivated his blade and clipped it back onto his belt. "Any more surprises?"

"Only the ones that will happen the next time that door opens. As for a plan, that's hard until I have more information. Give me your side arm." Taylor removed the weapon and handed it over. "I am going to unlock this and give you full control of it. When I hand it back, hold it by the grip in front of your face and say 'Weapon, give me full control, my authorisation only.' got it?"

"Got it!" Replied Taylor.

Duran held the gun in front of his face. "Weapon, full unlock, give full authorisation to next user." The gun bleeped twice, and he handed it back.

Taylor took the grip and held it up. "Weapon, give me full control, my authorisation only." Again, the gun bleeped twice.

"Remember, try not to go over level three, they start to make one hell of a mess if you do."

"Understood!"

"I will try and make sure we stay together, if we do get split up, just bide your time for a few days. Remember to look out for my crest, Cassius's is similar but has a few differences. So be careful who you talk to, maybe try and find Sarris or my sister. If all else fails the ship will try and get in contact with you, if it does, do whatever it tells you and it will try and get you home."

"Pretty shitty plan so far."

Duran laughed. "Often the best ones are. Look, there are loads of ways I can see this going. One, we get there, we are taken to my father, he is getting better, and this all get sorted out. Two, my father is dead, I become emperor, and I get this all sorted out. Three, we find my father is still ill….."

"Yada yada, look you have no idea, what is the worst case, and how do we plan for that?"

Duran thought. "You're right, I have no idea. If this is a power play by my uncle to become emperor, then he will need to do something to make him look the good guy, or this could end up in a civil war between the two houses."

"So, for that to happen, you either need to have an accident or look like the bad guy?"

"I don't think they will be able to arrange another accident, not so soon."

"Looks like you have to be the bad guy, or they will bide their time." Suggested Taylor.

"They can't wait too long, or I will just undo all the changes they have made. Unless they have a way to blame me for all of this. When I talked through all the facts with my ship it joked, I was the one who benefited most, so maybe they have a way to make everyone else think like that."

Taylor stood and started to pace. "The fact is we won't know anything until it happens. Will we still be able to communicate?"

"I can't be sure of that. In the past some areas of the palace have had blockers in place. We won't know till be get there."

"So back to plan shit then!" Taylor returned to the bunk and led back. "I'm going to have a nap."

Duran went to the bunk opposite. "That sounds like a good plan."

Chapter 11: Solantra.

The door slid open, and one of Kai's men entered. "We are entering orbit with Solantra. Please follow me; I will take you to a surface transport."

The two men shook themselves awake and stood. The man exited the room turning to the right. As they followed another man was waiting and two more fell in behind them.

'*Not sure I'm feeling like much of a guest.*' Projected Taylor.

'*Whatever happens, just remain calm.*'

The group walked through several different corridors until they eventually came to an airlock with a transport docked to it. Duran looked around the empty cabin as they went in and took a seat. "Kai isn't joining us?"

"My lord as already gone down to the palace. We have been instructed to escort you there and wait for the emperor's command."

The doors closed and the transport detached from the ship, swiftly descending to the planet. As they got closer to the palace Taylor could see it nestled on the shores of a lake with huge snowcapped mountains behind. The architecture, colours, design, and size were like nothing he had ever seen before. "So, that's your dads place?"

Duran scoffed. "Yeah, try not to get lost."

The transport landed and they all moved out to be met by more guards. "My Lord, we have been instructed to escort you to rooms. Please follow us." Said one of the men.

Kai entered his father's rooms to find him seated in front of a large open fireplace, his gaze fixed intently on the dancing flames as he sipped from a cut glass goblet.

"Father, Duran will be landing shortly. I have ordered him taken to the successor's rooms as you instructed." Reported Kai.

"Good! You have done well my son."

"Father, he is not alone."

Cassius placed his glass on a side table and stood to face his son. "Who is with him?"

"I don't know. He wears the crest of Durans house, but I have never seen him before. I had him scanned; we know the area of space Duran was coming from and it looks like he may have picked up the man on the planet Terra. He is also carrying a type of weapon not used in thousands of years."

Cassius pondered on this information. "That is one of the banishment worlds," he remarked with a slight smile. "A world where travel is not permitted. A world where removing someone who has been banished is a crime."

"Yes father."

"Oh, this could play out nicely. What is this weapon you mentioned."

"It is a projectile hand weapon that uses a chemical propellant. Much like some of those in your collection."

Cassius turned, looking over to one of the walls where a large collection of handguns was displayed. He smiled broadly. "Oh, this just gets better and better. He brings me the means to destroy him and a trophy to mark the occasion."

"What would you have me do now father?"

"Let them get settled in rooms. Send in servants with food and drink, make sure they tend to any needs they may have. Get one of the guards to tell Duran his father is undergoing treatment, and he can see him in an hour. Make sure everyone shows the correct etiquette to the emperor's son and heir."

"Yes father, I will see it is done."

"Kai, make sure the neural comms suppressors are on throughout the palace. Oh, also have Clio and Nova sent in, I have a job for them."

"Yes father." Kai turned and left to carry out his father's orders.

The guards threw open the large ornate doors to the rooms and stood aside to let Duran enter.

Duran looked uneasy as he walked in. "These are Milo's rooms."

"They were my Lord, these are the successors rooms, so they have been made ready for you." One of the men informed him.

Duran walked in slowly with Taylor following him. Looking around Duran felt uneasy, he had been here a few times, but without his brother's presence it all looked so different. This started to make it all feel so real and it unnerved him.

"My Lord, I have been instructed to tell you your father is with his healers and will see you in about an hour. Please make yourself comfortable, servants will be in shortly with refreshments and will get anything else you need." Duran nodded to the man and he left closing the doors behind him.

Taylor stood and turned in a full circle. "Wow, I've been in a few posh places in my time, but this beats the hell out of anything I've seen."

Duran slumped into one of the chairs. "This is what the wealth of two hundred systems can buy you. This one set of rooms has six bedrooms, two receptions, dining, and a terrace."

Taylor could see this wasn't being easy for Duran. He considered a few comforting things to say but changed his mind. "Duran, is this what you expected?"

It wasn't. He stood and started to mess with his gauntlet, waving his arm around, scanning the room. "No, it's not. But now I am here they have to play nice. Too many people have seen me." He stopped scanning. "I think we are safe to talk. I want you to keep your armour on for now. I am going to see what clothes I can change into, staying in armour in the palace would not look right for me."

"OK, but I could do with a piss."

Duran pointed. "Take that room over there, you will find what you need."

As Taylor went into the room, he heard a knock at the door. Turning he could see several people walking in with trays of food and drink. "My Lord Duran. My name is Jarren. I have been assigned as your personal valet. Would you like these refreshments in the dining room or on the terrace? I must say it is a lovely day outside."

"Yes, the terrace will be fine." Called out Duran.

"Would you like any of my staff to stay and serve you and your guest?"

"No, we will be fine, just leave it on the table."

The man clapped his hand and ushered his staff to the terrace to lay out the food. They all quickly did this and then rapidly left again. "My Lord, if there is anything else you should need, please press a call button. As I say my name is Jarren."

"I will Jarren, now leave us!"

Suitably relieved Taylor went out onto the terrace to see what had been left for them. Jarren was right, it was a beautiful day with a warm soft breeze. His eyes were caught by the amazing views of the mountains and then the gardens that seemed to stretch off for miles. He could see people tending the grounds, also guards patrolling in pairs. It struck Taylor that the few days Duran had insisted they train was in no way enough for all of this. Duran came out to join him now wearing a much more regal outfit. Taylor could not contain how impressed he was with everything. "Wow, look at you and Wow. Look at all this and, have I said WOW enough."

Duran laughed and gazed out over the land. "It must be nearly a year since I stood here last. Enough with the Wow's, you need to conduct yourself more like a warrior."

"I was just thinking you didn't give us enough training."

"You weren't supposed to see this or be here. You were all supposed to be halfway home by now. None of you were meant to be dead!" Duran turned to the table and sat down. "Sit, eat, you need to keep your strength up." He grabbed a few different items and put them on to his plate.

Taylor sat across from Duran and looked over the array of food. "I have no idea what any of this is, or if it is safe for me to eat."

"Here let me." Duran stood and with a spoon put some items on Taylors plate. "You'll be fine with those and that is water in the glass jug, keep your head clear. I'll drink the wine; I think I may need it."

Taylor tentatively started to try the items he had been given. "Humm, not bad."

"Yeah, we just have to hope none of it has been poisoned!"

Taylor panicked. "WHAT!"

Duran burst out laughing. "Don't worry, they would never try a cheap move like that."

Taylor slowly started to eat again. "You can be an arse you know." Duran smiled and nodded. "Look, I don't blame you for Sarah. You warned us and you taught us. You did all you could."

"Thank you. I just wish I could forgive myself. For now, I am going to put it all out of my mind. I must deal with the matters at hand. We have a grand hall in the palace. When this is done, I will put her name on it, alongside many other great warriors."

There was a loud knock on the door and one of the guards entered. "My Lord Duran, I have been instructed to escort you to your father when you are ready." Duran stood and started to walk towards the man, Taylor followed. "My Lord, I have been instructed to only take you."

Duran stopped and glared at the man. "Wait outside!" He snapped.

The man turned and did as he was told. Duran looked at Taylor. "Well, here we go I guess. Just wait here, eat, relax, enjoy the view. I should not be too long and hopefully I will get some answers."

Taylor looked concerned. "What if someone comes here?"

Duran puffed and shrugged. "No one should. If they do, be polite, try not to give anything away and if all else fails shoot them." Taylor just held his arms out to the side and looked dumbfounded as Duran left the room.

The guard that had been waiting for him bowed slightly. "Please follow me My Lord."

"I grew up in the palace, I do know my way to my father's rooms."

"Yes My Lord. I have been told to take you to Cassius. He wishes to talk with you before you see your father."

Duran was not happy about this, but he would let it play out. Instinctively his hand went to his belt. He had his sword, maybe seeing Cassius he could just end all this with one stroke.

Going back to the terrace Taylor sat down to do just as Duran had suggested. There was a knock on the door, as Taylor turned, two very attractive young ladies entered, they were dressed in beautiful long silk gowns that left nothing to the imagination. Ok, he thought, this wasn't what he had expected.

"Helloooo.." Called out one of the girls. "Oh, there you are. My name is Clio, and this is Nova. We have been told to keep you company while Lord Duran is with his father."

Wolves in sheep's clothing immediately jumped into Taylors head. "Told by who? My Lord Duran told me to wait here." Still, he had never seen more attractive wolves.

"Well, I was told by Jarren. I'm sure he was told by someone else. In the palace you learn to do as you are told, it saves being punished."

"I am sure it does." Taylor was still wary, this all seemed very convenient.

Nova walked up to Taylor and took his hand. "What should we call you, they didn't know your name."

Taylor looked confused, unsure what to say. "Come on, have you forgotten how to speak." Said Nova with a cheeky grin.

"No. Erm Taylor, please call me Taylor."

Nova looked at Taylor with a big, dreamy smile. "Taaylooor, I have never heard that name before. It's cute, just like you."

Clio noticed the food on the terrace. "Oh, I'm Starving. Do you mind?" She said as she skipped up to the table.

"Be my guest." Gestured Taylor.

"Come Join us." Nova led Taylor by the hand, seating him, then pulling her chair up close to his side. "Oooo, Grapes I Looove grapes, could you pass me some." Taylor reached over and picked up the plate passing it to her. She just sat with her mouth open. He pulled one off and placed it in her open mouth. She bit down just catching his fingers. "Hummm, Sooo sweet, have you tried them?" she pulled one off and went to put it into Taylors mouth. As interrogations went this was one of the better ones he had endured. Taylor opened his mouth; she popped it in slowly running her finger across his lips.

Taylor started to chew. "Yes, these are delicious."

Both girls giggled. "Taylor what system are you from?" Said Clio. "I was born on Solantra. Nova is from Cellus."

"I've just come from Cellus, but I am originally from Earth." Taylor replied, he assumed they would already know this much.

Nova looked cutely confused. "Earth, I have never heard of that system. Still, I don't need to understand such things. I don't remember anything of Cellus, I was very young when I left there." She picked up one of a decanters and started to pour wine for each of them.

"I am told my planet is very far out in the galaxy and not well known. We just came from Cellus. I wasn't there long so I don't know anything about it. And this is my first visit here." Taylor was trying to stay with, 'be polite', and stay with facts he was sure they already knew. Shooting them seemed a little over the top at the moment.

"Hummm, this wine is divine. Have you tried it?" Clio's face matched her feelings.

"No, my master has told me I need to keep a clear head."

"Oh, that's so boring, you must, just take a sip, we hate to drink alone." Nova gave him her big puppy dog eyes.

Taylor took the glass and sipped from it. "Yes, this is also very nice."

Clio jumped to her feet. "Have you seen the gardens? You must see the gardens if it is your first time here."

"I can see them just fine from here, and I have been told not to leave the rooms." Taylor was starting to get the urge to shoot.

Nova got up and started to pull on Taylors arm. "Don't be silly, its only just down these steps. You can see the terrace if Lord Duran comes back."

As Taylor allowed Nova and Clio to lead him down the steps into the gardens, his uneasiness grew. He felt he should be ok as long as he could see his way back. Despite his instincts telling him to be cautious, he couldn't help but feel drawn to the enchanting atmosphere and the company of the two beautiful women. The scent of flowers wafted through the air, and the soft glow of the late afternoon sun cast a magical aura over the surroundings.

As they strolled through the meticulously manicured pathways, Taylor couldn't shake the feeling of being watched. He scanned the surroundings, trying to discern any signs of danger, but everything appeared serene and peaceful. Nova and Clio chattered animatedly, seemingly oblivious to Taylor's apprehension. They pointed out various features of the garden, from exotic plants to hidden alcoves, their laughter echoing on the breeze.

Taylor couldn't help but wonder about their true intentions. Were they simply keeping him company as they claimed, or was there something more sinister at play? He couldn't afford to let his guard down, especially in unfamiliar territory.

"Nova, look, a star fruit tree." They joyfully skipped over to a nearby tree. "Taylor, you have to try one of these they are my favourite." Clio picked some of the fruit and handed them out.

Taylor took it cautiously. "These aren't some sort of forbidden thing that I can be put to death for eating, are they?"

Nova bit into hers. "Don't be silly, all the forbidden fruits are over there." Both girls started to giggle. Taylor hoped they were messing with him. He bit into his own, it was, impossible to describe. May be this was how ambrosia tasted. He could not help taking another bite. Grabbing his arm Nova started to pull Taylor to one side. "Ooooo, you have to see the statue of Duran. It is just round here." She skipped off leaving Clio to pull Taylor along by his arm.

Rounding the corner Taylor was met with the view of a very impressive statue. It was at least ten meters tall and looked to be made from gold and silver. Apart from the sword it held out to the front, that was pitted and rusty. It looked to be made from steel. Taylor looked intently at the face. "It doesn't look much like Duran."

Both the girls giggled once more. "Don't be silly." Nova took his hand. "This Duran is the founder of the Tar dynasty, not your master."

"Sorry, I'm new to all of this." Taylor was starting to feel slightly lightheaded.

"But you must know the story of Tar Duran?" Asked Clio.

"Yes, I have been told how he defeated his enemies."

"Only told. Oh, you must see the frescoes, they are exquisite." Once more the girls skipped along pulling Taylor as they went. This was it, his patience was starting to ware, ten more minutes of being polite and he would head back to the rooms. No, I am sure it is fine he thought. He was finding it hard to concentrate for some reason. There was a real feeling of euphoria slowly washing over him.

Duran was shown into Cassius's rooms. "My Lord Duran." Cassius bowed ever so slightly. "It has been too long. I trust you are well, and your rooms are satisfactory."

"Yes Uncle, everything is fine." Duran was still very unsure of the situation.

"May I get you a drink or anything?"

"No, I have had my fill for now. Forgive me for being blunt, but I really should see my father."

"Yes, yes my lord. I just wanted to see you first and apologise for the death of your brother."

Apologise, why would he need to do that. "I thought my brother's death was an accident?"

"Yes, it was, a very tragic one. But I feel responsible as one of my men caused it."

Durans mind started to race. Why would he admit to this. "I am sorry uncle; I don't understand why you would say this?"

Cassius turned away to a side table and poured himself a drink. "The man, well boy, was young and had never done a hunt before. He was tasked to lay a trail to attract in a bull. We don't really know, but he did something wrong. He got pheromone on some of the horses, or used to much and then the coward ran."

"Where is he now, I would like to talk to him?"

"Dammed fool could not even do that right. He died from his injuries not long after he got back to the palace."

Lies within truths, truth within lies. Should Duran believe this or what Sarris had told him. "I guess we will never know the full truth, Uncle."

"I must also apologise for my son. When I ordered him to send the fleet out to find you, I think he read too much urgency into it and overreacted slightly."

"Yes, I did find his actions strange." Duran was finding the same about this conversation.

"Forgive me my lord. With your father ill, your brother, and the fact we were unable to contact you, it all had me very worried."

"I am sure it did. Well, I am here now, I think I should see my father." Duran was starting to get impatient.

"Of course, forgive me, I will take you to him now. I must warn you he keeps drifting in and out of consciousness and none of the healers have been able to work out what is wrong with him."

Duran looked intently at Cassius, he wanted to see his reaction. "I have asked Sarris to join me here. I would like him to bring in some, other healers."

"I was informed just before you came in that your sisters ship had landed. I instructed the guard to take them to your rooms and wait for you there. But I assure you I have done all I can. I have brought in many different healers from other systems. None of them can find out what is wrong with your father."

Cassius seemed to be one step ahead all the time. This wasn't helping Duran come to any conclusions. "I would still like Sarris to try. Now please. My father."

"Of course, My Lord." Cassius turned and walked to the corridor Duran knew joined to his father's rooms. Duran took some comfort seeing royal guard along the corridor and when they entered his rooms two more were stood either side of his bed. So far most of the palace guard he had seen had Cassius's crest. At least these wore the crest of his father. There were also two women attendants sat either side of the bed. They both immediately dropped to first position, one thing the royal guard never had to do.

"Stand!" Commanded Duran. He walked to the foot of the bed. "How is my father?"

They both stood, one took a step forward. "My Lord, your father is resting comfortably."

Looking down at his father he looked nothing more than if he were just sleeping. Duran walked around to one side of the bed and sat down. He took his father's hand and squeezed it gently. "Father. It is Duran, can you hear me?" His hand felt cold and there was no reaction.

The woman spoke again. "I'm sorry my lord. The times he wakes are becoming less and less. When he does, he is confused. He keeps asking for the late queen."

"If he wakes again, you are to send for me immediately."

"Yes my lord. I will make sure everyone knows."

Duran lent forward and kissed his father on the forehead. He then stood. "I am going to my rooms. I will return as soon as I have spoken with Sarris."

Everyone in the room bowed slightly as Duran walked away. "My Lord, I will wait in my rooms." Called out Cassius. "If there is anything you need just send for me." As he said this he reached up and pressed down on a small pendant around his neck.

The girls were right, they were beautiful frescoes. They had been explaining each one to Taylor, guiding him through the story of Durans rise to power. To be honest Taylor was starting to get very bored with it all and the lightheaded feeling he had was making it hard to concentrate. But, wow, these girls were even more beautiful. Suddenly they stopped talking and felt the pendants around their necks.

"Oooo, the weapons collection." Said Nova. "We must show you that. Any warrior like yourself would die to see it." She giggled. "Excuse the pun." They both giggled some more.

Taylors mind was screaming at him to return to Durans rooms. "I'm Sorry ladies, I really think I should go back, Duran maybe waiting for me."

Clio grabbed his arm. "Don't be silly, he will be ages, talking all that royal stuff. Come on, ten minutes, then we will take you straight back." She went back to puppy eyes. "Please, we would get punished if we had not shown you a good time."

"Ok, if you promise." Something was clouding his better judgement. Ten more minutes can't hurt.

"We promise." Said both the girls as they each took an arm and started to lead him along a corridor. Approaching a large set of ornate doors Taylor was surprised at how the guards just turned, opened, and stood to one side to allow them to pass. The girls led, almost pulled Taylor into the room, with the guards closing the door behind them.

Taylor felt the fog in his brain was starting to clear a little. But wait, where had the girls gone? Why are they on the floor? Is that first position? He dropped; he was confused but it seemed like the best thing to do.

"I am sorry My Lord. We didn't know you were in here." Said Clio.

"That's Ok my child, stand, stand. Who is this you have with you." Cassius, was of course, not surprised in the least.

"This is Taylor my lord. Taylor, this is Lord Cassius, our Lord Chancelor."

"Taylor? Aww, you must be Durans friend. Please stand, let me get a look at you."

Taylor got to his feet. This could not be good; he felt sure he had been led into an ambush. "Thank you My Lord. It is a pleasure to meet you."

"I understand you are a long way from home. A planet called Earth I believe, out on one of the spiral arms if I am not mistaken?"

"I'm sorry my lord, I will have to take your word for it. I am not very good on these things."

"Hummm, so how did you end up getting Duran to bring you so far from your home?"

Taylor felt more and more like he was being ambushed. "He errr. He got into a bit of trouble on my planet. I helped him out and he said he would take me for a drink to say thanks, then we got brought here. He was going to take me straight back. To be honest it is all very confusing, I'm ready to go home if anyone would like to point me in the right direction."

"A drink. Well, I am sure we can arrange to get you home. Unfortunately, Duran may be a little busy, his father is very ill and needs him at his side."

"Yes, Duran told me he was unwell."

Nova took a step forward "My Lord, we are sorry for the intrusion, we just wanted to show Taylor your collection." She said sheepishly.

Cassius turned to look at his collection on the wall. "My collection, of course." He said enthusiastically.

"Taylor come over here. You two may leave. I will make sure he gets back to Duran." The girls bowed, turned, and left. "My father left these to me; I have continued to collect ever since. I am fascinated with how the hand weapon has developed over time and on different planets and cultures. Look here, this is a prototype for an early laser pistol." Cassius chuckled. "Damned thing would blow up more times than it worked."

Taylor laughed nervously. "It is all very impressive."

"There are weapons here from over one hundred systems." Cassius looked intently over the collection. "I don't believe I have one from earth." He paused and looked at Taylor. "I am told you are carrying a weapon from your world. Is that correct?"

Taylor was feeling even more nervous. "Errrm, yes, I do. I hope that isn't a problem, Duran said it would be ok?"

Cassius laughed. "No, of course not." He then took a sterner expression. "Well, it maybe if you don't let me take a look at it." He then gave Taylor a wry smile.

Taylor reached around to his back and pulled out the pistol. "Yeah, sure, hold on." He ejected the magazine then slid the action to the rear and lock it to make sure it was clear. "Here. It's called a Glock 17. It's safe."

Cassius took the pistol and started to look over it admiringly. He felt the weight in his hand and slid his fingers over it feeling its form and design. "I must say, this is a piece of art." He pressed the button on the side to release the action. Holding the gun at arm's length he sighted along it and pulled the trigger. Pulling the action back he locked it. "This is really well made. And what you have in your hand contains the bullets?"

"Yes, it does. The magazine can hold seventeen rounds."

"Seventeen. Very limited compared to our energy-based weapons. May I see?"

Taylor reluctantly held out the magazine. "Sure, here."

Once again Cassius made a show of looking over and studying all its details. Suddenly he slid the magazine into the handle and released the action.

Taylor was shocked. "Woah, Wooah! Take it easy. It's now loaded and ready to fire. It doesn't have a safety, so keep your finger away from the trigger."

Cassius smiled. He expertly ejected the magazine, slid back the action ejecting the round. Catching it and putting it back in the magazine. "Don't worry Taylor, my collection has taught me how to handle these things." He then slid the magazine back in. "Perfectly safe, yes?"

"Yes it is, but I…"

Cassius calmly butted in. "Do you know, this would look very nice in my collection?"

"I am sure it would. I would be more than happy to have one sent.."

Again, Cassius cut him off. "I know you already have the favour of the future Emperor. It could never hurt to also have the favour of his Lord Chancelor." Smiled Cassius.

Taylors mind scrambled. He still had his other weapons. He didn't feel totally threatened. "Yes, it would My Lord. Consider it a gift. The first of many from my world, I'm sure."

"Excellent! It is very much appreciated. I have never been to your Earth, maybe one day you could give me a tour." Cassius patted Taylor on the shoulder like they had just sealed some sort of intergalactic deal. Turning, a loud clunk could be heard as Cassius seemed to place the gun on a side table.

"It would be an honour to do that for you, but I really must be getting back to Duran. He did tell me I should wait for him in his rooms."

"Why yes, I am sorry. We can talk more of guns and visits later. Come with me, I will escort you. We will go this way; he may well still be with his father."

Duran entered his rooms to find Sarris and Alana waiting for him.

"Duran, I was starting to worry." Said Sarris.

"I wasn't, if he were dead the same would have happened to us." Scoffed Alana.

"Alana, always the optimist." Duran walked over and hugged his sister.

"What news of father?" She asked.

"He is sleeping." Duran stopped and looked around. "Where is Taylor?"

"The rooms were empty when we came in. Alana and I were not told anyone else was here."

Duran hurriedly walked to the main doors and opened them. "Guard, what happened to the man I came here with?"

"I'm sorry My Lord, I have just been assigned this post. I was unaware of anyone else in the room, no one has come through these doors since I have been here."

Closing the door Duran went back into the room. "This can't be good, I told him to wait here."

Alana walked up to the terrace. "Maybe he went to walk around the gardens." She called back.

Duran followed and they scanned the gardens below. "I doubt it. I made it clear to wait."

"OK, he should be waiting, but he's not." Alana had little patience. "Sarris, could anyone have taken him."

"Who knows. This is a dangerous game. I saw very few of a palace guard with your father's crest when we were brought in. I would go ask, but I suspect my words carry little weight these days."

"I noticed that too. All the royal guard I've seen so far have our crest." Duran considered this for a moment. "Sarris, maybe you could find someone in the royal guard to speak with. I'm not sure we can trust anyone in the palace guard."

Approaching the doors to the emperor's rooms, the guards dutifully open them to allow Cassius and Taylor to enter, closing them again once they had gone through. Cassius made his way up to Borrel's bedroom; the two nurses immediately went to first position as he entered.

"Where is Duran?" Commanded Cassius.

"He went back to his rooms a few minutes ago my lord." Said one of the women.

In a blur of speed and strength, that totally took Taylor by surprise, Cassius pushed him to one side. He reached into his cloak pulling out Taylors gun that he had hidden inside, cocking it has he did. As Taylor fell to the ground he could only look on as with amazing speed and accuracy Cassius put a round between the eyes of both of the guards and then the two women cowering on the floor. Taking aim at Borrel he fired five rounds into his body. Turning he levelled the gun at Taylor before he could stand.

"Stay there, earth man. Duran couldn't have made this easier for me."

Cassius swapped the gun into his left hand. "Duran was supposed to be lost to the depths of space; my ungrateful half-brother could then just fade away leaving the empire to me. But, well this will make it so much easier for the people to believe. A renegade son hires a hit man to do his dirty work."

Turning the gun into himself he fired through his right side. "And this will just add to the sympathy of the people. Injured while trying to defend the emperor."

Cassius tossed the gun to Taylor who instinctively caught it. In the same moment he activated a shield from his belt that covered his entire body. Taylor got to his feet and half-heartedly held the gun towards Cassius. "Seven bullets left I believe, but they will do you no good. When I call out the guard will swarm this room in seconds." He pointed. "If you go down that corridor you may make it back to Duran for protection before they find you. If the guard find you first, they

271

will end you where you stand." He smiled as he fought with the pain. "Run Earth Man…. GUAAAARD!"

Fight or Flight! This was definitely a flight time. Taylor turned and ran down the corridor as fast as he could. In his mind there was little doubt Cassius wasn't lying. He wanted him to be with Duran and he was playing right into that. He also knew his chances of survival were zero without his help. Bursting through the doors he saw Duran, Sarris, and Alana. Quickly turning he closed the doors behind him. "Shit! Shit! Shit! We are so screwed!"

"Taylor, where the hell have you been and what are you on about?" Duran said as he marched over to Taylor.

Taylor was panting and trying to calm himself. "I know what Cassius's plan is, but it's too late. He's screwed us over big time!"

"Spit it out then, so I can figure out what to do?"

Taylor stood and looked Duran straight in the eyes. "The emperor is Dead, Cassius killed him. Two young women lured me to his rooms, I think they drugged me. He tricked me into giving him my gun." Looking down he noticed it was still in his hand. "He then shot the guard, the nurses, your father, then himself. He's going to pin it on me and say you arranged it."

Sarris looked stunned. "No, surely not. Not even Cassius would be that bold?"

272

This enraged Taylor. "Look! I'm telling you; it happened right in front of me. There are five dead bodies down that hall with bullets from this gun in them." Everyone was silent. "What the fuck! Come on guys, we need to get out of here or do something."

"Yes!" Said Alana in a low tone. "We fight! We dig out that coward and rat of a son, we kill them and anyone else that stands in our way."

"Don't be stupid." Sarris was not having this. "There are hundreds of palace guard all loyal to Cassius. You would not stand a chance."

"Better that, than dying at the hands of an executioner." Scoffed Alana.

"STOP!" Duran needed to take control. "It is too late to run and would serve no purpose. The fact the guard has not already kicked in the doors tells me Cassius has either more to his plan, or he wants us to try and make a break for it."

"Well, I am not going to just sit here and wait to be slaughtered like a lamb." Alana already had her sword in her hand.

"I am now the head of this family and this house! You will do as you are told. Put that away!" Alana reluctantly clipped her sword back to her belt. Duran knew he needed to take charge if they were to have any hope.

"You are also now the emperor." Sarris reminded him.

"Yes, I am sure that is something Cassius has every intention of disputing."

"Duran is correct. We need to let Cassius make the next move and reveal his plans." Sarris knew this was a complex situation and Duran needed support and council. "Taylor, that weapon of yours. Make it safe and place it on the table over there." Taylor did as he was told.

Alana started to pace in frustration. "So, we just wait!"

She didn't have to wait long. Men from the palace guard started to enter from all the doors and terrace surrounding the group. This made Alana uneasy, she clutched at her weapons but did not draw them. The men stood ready around them, but they also did not draw their weapons. What seemed like an age passed until Cassius was pushed in on a hoverchair.

As he looked around the room, he gave the smug impression of a man who had everything on his side. "My Lord Duran. I am here to charge your man Taylor with the assassination of your father the emperor. I am also charging you with conspiracy in the commission and aid of the assassination."

"That's all a pack of lies!" Taylor yelled. "You shot the emperor using my gun!"

"Taylor, be silent!" Ordered Duran.

"Yes Duran, control your man. I would hate for anything, unpleasant to happen. You should have hired a better assassin. It was a mistake leaving me alive to bear witness to your foul scheme."

Duran took a few paces towards Cassius making his guard uneasy. "Cassius, if you end this madness now, I will allow you to retire with your family to a planet of your choosing."

Cassius smiled. "I thought this might happen. I assume you wish to deny all the charges."

"Yes, I do. The only conspiracy here is the one you have orchestrated."

"Indeed." Cassius paused as if considering his options. "Then we will need to hold an inquisition. I have already contacted the council of barons and told them to send in five members for this. They will be here in the morning and the inquisition will start as soon as they arrive."

This incensed Sarris. "And how do we know if these barons will be impartial?"

"Hold your tongue old man. Be thankful you are also not under charge. I have made the request for their attendance. They do not know why, and I have selected no one." Cassius looked too smug for this to be true. "You will remain in these rooms under guard until you are called. You will also relinquish all weapons to the guard immediately."

Duran sigh. "Do as he says." The guard moved among them collecting whatever they could find.

Cassius watched intently. "Make sure you search the rooms as well. Where is the weapon the assassin used?" Taylor pointed to the table where he had left it. A guard moved over and placed it into a bag.

"Could I request that Jovan is contacted and asked to come here as soon as possible?" Duran asked with all the politeness he could manage.

Cassius looked confused. "Jovan? I can put in a request to the council of clerics, but there is no guarantee he will be here in time."

"The request will be good enough."

Cassius was unsure about this turn. "And why would you want to drag your brothers good name into your mess. Is he part of this plot?"

Duran was glad he no longer had his sword. "No, I have not spoken to him in over two years. I wish him to represent me at the inquisition. He may also like to show his respects to his father. I don't even know if he has been told Milo is dead."

"You!" Cassius pointed at one of the guards. "Send a request to the council of clerics, ask that Tar Jovan attend to his brother at the palace immediately."

"Yes My Lord." The man turned and left.

"There, request made. But the inquisition will start as soon as the barons are ready. There will be no delays." Cassius could see the guard had finished searching. "I think we are done here. I want four men on each door until the accused are called for in the morning." He signalled to the man who had pushed him in. "I suggest you get some sleep." The man pulled Cassius from the room and the rest of the guards left closing the doors as they did so.

Silence fell over the group.

"I need a drink." Alana marched out to the terrace to see if anything was left.

Taylor was still in shock from all that had happened. "So, how screwed are we?" There were no answers. "Come on, with all this amazing technology you guys have, there has to be some way to prove I didn't do this?"

"Cassius has played this well. Or more to the point, I handed him everything he needed." Duran turned and despondently followed his sister to the terrace. He sat and poured himself some of the wine.

Sarris and Taylor followed. "So, you think drinking can solve our problems?" Asked Sarris.

Taylor poured himself a drink. "Well, it can't hurt." He took a large mouthful. "That is good. Can we get some more, I think I am going to need it?"

"There is no time for self-pity! We need clear heads. We need to come up with a way out of this." Sarris was clearly trying to take charge.

Taylor drank deeply. "Seeing as I have no idea what the hell is going on, you lot keep your heads clear, and I will take care of the wine." He drank some more. "Hey! I don't suppose the punishment for this crime will be banishment to, oh I dunno, a planet called Earth?"

Sarris laughed. "Regicide, you would be beheaded, your body fed to pigs and your head put on a spike for the birds."

"Didn't think it would be that easy. No surprises there, all very medieval for a culture as advanced as yours." Taylor continued to drink.

"Some things, need no improvements." Smiled Sarris. Taylor raised his glass to the old man.

Taylor suddenly realised he didn't know what happened with his team after they were captured. "Alana, Sarris. Do you know what happened with my team?"

"They should be safe and on their way home." Said Alana. "That slimy toad Aldon took us all back to Durans ship. I told it to take them all home and we came here in my ship."

Taylor was afraid to ask. "What about Sarah, is she definitely dead?"

"They took her to the medical bay, but it was too late. I know the ship did all it could, but too much time had passed for it to do anything for her." Alana put her hand on Taylors arm. "Was she a close friend?"

Taylor stared blankly. "She was a lot more than a friend!"

Silence again fell over the group.

With a loud knock on the main door, a figure entered in hooded purple robes. He walked towards the group.

"Jovan! Is that you?" Asked Duran in amazement.

Still walking the figure took off his hood. "Yes brother."

"But how, we have only just sent word for you to come here?"

Jovan joined the group on the terrace. "I have received no message from you. I am here because about a week ago I was told of Milos accident, I came as soon as I could to pay my respects. But as soon as I entered the palace, I got a very uneasy feeling. Seeing you all here I can tell there is more going on than I know."

"And then some, sit down, grab a drink, you are going to need it." Taylor was starting to notice just how strong the wine was.

Duran stood and embraced Jovan. "Excuse my friend Taylor, he is drunk, in shock and new to all of this. Brother it is so good to see you, it has been too long, and we really need your help."

Jovan turned to Alana. "And how is my favourite sister?" She stood and the two embraced.

"Wishing I was drunk and new to all of this. It is so good to see you." She took her seat again.

Holding out his hand Jovan turned to Sarris. "Have you forgiven me yet my old master?"

Sarris knocked his hand to one side. "NEVER!" he roared and gave Jovan the biggest hug.

"Okaay! That's confusing!" Slurred Taylor.

"And you are Taylor, who I believe has had enough wine for now." Jovan reached over and took Taylors glass away from him. "So brother, maybe you can tell me why you are all here and why the palace feels so full of fear?"

Jovan sat and they all started to tell him how they got to this night. Durans quest and capture on earth. The bargain he had made, how it had ended with Taylor in Borrel's rooms, Cassius taking his gun and shooting the emperor in his bed. Jovan questioned them on every detail as the conversation went back and forth. The initial loathing he had for Taylor started to fade as he understood how this all came about.

"So, can we go back to my original question. How screwed are we?" Taylor asked again.

"Very!" Was Jovans simple answer.

"I thought you were some sort of all knowing mystic type guru?"

Jovan didn't much like Taylors attitude. "Even when you know all the answers, there isn't always one to fit the question."

Taylor scoffed. "That's it, that's all you have?"

Jovan turned to Duran. "The inquisitors will have very little choice whoever they are. As Lord Chancellor, Cassius will be seen in the highest regard. You my brother, should also be seen in the same way. The problem will be Taylor. A man from a banishment planet, no family or heritage, anything he says will be treated with contempt."

Taylor sat bolt upright. "Woah, I don't like the sound of where this is going!"

Jovan ignored him. "As I see it there are only two options. Taylor admits to the charges, and we hope we can convince the inquisition you had no part in it."

"This isn't an option I like!" Said Taylor.

"OR! We have Taylor call out Cassius as a liar and do it in such a way that questioning his honour demands a challenge."

Duran thought for a moment. "Cassius would never fall for such an obvious move. He will be confident he has won and has nothing to gain by a challenge." Duran looked at Taylor. "Also, I don't think I can betray an innocent man."

"Even if Cassius does get mad enough to issue a challenge, you know full well he will just get Kai to fight for him. Just because Taylor beat you, do you think he can beat him?"

Duran scoffed. "No! Taylor beat me in an unfair fight. Kai would never make that mistake."

This was another comment Taylor didn't like. "HEY! How was it unfair, I still took you down."

"Ten to one and I was a fool. You would not last five minutes in the pit with him."

"As you know, if Kai can fight for Cassius, then you could fight for Taylor." Jovan reminded him.

Duran considered this for a moment. "If I could get to the sword I may have a chance."

"Are you mad!" Exclaimed Sarris. "You maybe one of the best fighters I have ever trained, but that monster would pound you into the ground before you got as far as the sword."

"When you say the sword, do you mean a K'Tarn?" Taylor was trying to understand. "I know how good you are with that."

"No, tactics are similar, but it's with a traditional steel sword along the same designs." Explained Duran. "But that doesn't matter. I am faster, more nimble. I just need to keep him at bay for the first two rounds, then I could take him with any form of sword."

Taylor had to jump in. "Hey, don't forget being a fool. I saw a TV show once, the fast nimble guy was winning, but because he was a fool he got cocky, and ended up getting his head crushed by the bare hands of the bigger guy."

"TV show? Taylor, your advice is not helpful." Jovan was starting to find Taylor annoying again. "I don't think having Taylor admit to killing our father will work. We have to assume Cassius has the inquisitors on his side and the admission would reflect badly on Duran. Cassius maybe hoping you will force a challenge fully expecting Kai to kill you both, ending the situation with no questions."

Taylor was looking confused. "Could someone explain to me how this challenge thing works? Also, why can't we just challenge him for lying outright?"

"Normally we could, but Cassius has too much power in the palace. Now he has taken it to an inquisition we must be seen to follow it, or Cassius could claim anything he liked. As to the challenge, these can come in several forms." Explained Jovan. "From a simple on the spot, to a more complex traditional challenge. This would take the form of the latter. The traditional challenge takes its form in showing the development of fighting styles over the years; it is conducted over four rounds. The first is hand to hand and lasts five minutes. In the second the fighters are allowed sticks or a staff and again is five minutes. Next is the sword, again five minutes. Finally, if both fighters are still standing, the fourth round is anything goes until one of the fighters is triumphant."

"And by this, I assume you mean the other guy is dead?" Taylor needed to clear this up.

"Yes, dead!" confirmed Jovan. "And anyone else who is party to the challenge."

"Does this mean there is a referee to make sure the fighters follow the rules."

Jovan laughed. "In a way yes. The referees as you call them were replaced by three sentinel robots. Many referees were killed in the pit by the fighters or could not be trusted, so these sentinels are now used. If a sentinel deems a fighter is not being honourable it will fire a stun blast. These blasts will increase in power each time they are used."

Taylor liked the sound of this. "Can I assume Kai will find fighting honourably difficult and get blasted?"

"Kai is used to having things go his way. He is also not used to controlling his anger. So yes, it's a good chance this will happen."

Taylor felt a little more optimistic. "So, all I need to do is goad Cassius into challenging me for questioning his honour, and get Kai to break the rules?"

Jovan's reply was a little sarcastic. "Yes, that is all you need to do, but it is unlikely to be easy. Cassius is not a fool, if he thinks the inquisition is siding with him, he may simply ignore you."

"I guess I will have to make sure he doesn't. If Sarah were here, she would tell you I can be pretty damn annoying, and for her sake, I will make sure of it."

"So, we are decided." Jovan announced. "I doubt anyone will get much sleep, but it would be a good idea to retire to rooms and rest, tomorrow will be a long day. Taylor, you need to get out of that armour and into something more respectful for the inquisition."

Alana got to her feet. "I'll help him with that. He will have no idea what would be respectful here."

Duran laughed. "Alana, please remember he is in mourning and rest is needed."

She glared back at him. "This is for the family brother! If we are still alive this time tomorrow, then I may see things differently."

In Taylors room Alana went to one of the wardrobes and started messing with the control unit. "Get that armour off so I can get a better look at you."

285

Taylor could not help smiling. "Not something I ever expected to hear from the lips of a beautiful woman."

"Your Sarah never said this to you?"

Taylor thought. "I don't think so. On earth we never used armour like this. She told me to get my clothes off enough times."

"So, you were a couple?"

"Yes, but not officially. Our job didn't really allow it."

"You fought in many battles together?"

"Yeah, quite a few. Saved each other's asses many times. It was her quick thinking that allowed me to capture your brother."

Alana giggled. "I cannot wait to rub that in his face. His pride would be shattered."

"Don't be mean, your brother is a nice guy. I like him."

"He is, and look where it got him." Alana punched the wall. "Running around doing stupid things, getting captured, making stupid deals, bringing you here, getting your friend killed!"

Taylor walked over to Alana and spun her round; he could see tears in her eyes. He hated it when women were like this, all he knew was to hold them close. "Hey, take it easy. We got this."

Alana gently pushed him away. "Did Duran tell you of our birth and up bringing?"

Taylor tried to sound understanding. "I've heard bits and pieces. Didn't sound like the best of starts."

"Sarris and his wife did the best they could when our father wanted nothing to do with us. And as a girl I was of even less value to him or the family. If you manage to get this challenge, do you know what happens to the loser's lands and property?"

"I guess the winner will get them?"

Alana tried hard to control her emotions. "YES! And that includes me! I would be absorbed into Cassius's house and as such have to do as he commands. At best he will marry me off to some back water prince. At worse, well neither will happen, I will die first!"

"In That case, I need to do this for both you and Sarah." Taylor took Alana's hand. "Look, it doesn't matter what happened or how we got here. There is only one way we can make it right, so let's just focus on that for now."

Alana took a deep breath and squeezed Taylors hand. "Thank you, I just hate the feeling of not being in control."

Taylor smiled. "I can tell, you remind me of Sarah, she would be the same."

"Ok, look, put this on in the morning." She slid open the door. "I think we should try and get some rest. I'll see you in the morning." Alana turned and hurriedly left the room.

Taylor looked at the outfit. "Pretty sharp!" he said to himself.

Chapter 12: Inquisition.

Taylor was woken by loud knocking on the main doors. He got up, grabbed a robe, and slowly walked towards the main room. It surprised him to see several servants marching in with trays of food and drinks that they placed in the dining room. For a moment, in his semi awake state, he was confused as to what was going on. That was soon snapped back into reality.

The man he recognised as Jarren saw him. "I have been ordered to bring you refreshments and inform you the inquisitors have started to arrive. You will be called in one hour to stand before them in the throne room."

"And a very good morning to you Jarren." Taylor thought it may help to be cheery. "I don't suppose there's any coffee among all that?" Jarren didn't answer he just turned and followed the rest of the servants out of the room. No guessing who's side he was on.

Taylor walked over to the dining room. Looking over what had been left he could see some jugs. Sniffing each one, he recognised the first few as juices and then his day was made. If this wasn't coffee it smelled good enough to him. He poured a cup, drank, and sighed in relief. Gradually, everyone else started to join him. "Morning all! Did you all hear what Jarren said?"

"Yes I did." Said Jovan, filling a plate with fruits. "Make sure you eat your fill. It may be some time before we get another chance."

"Or at all if I force Cassius to a challenge?" Asked Taylor.

"Correct, in this case, such a challenge would be held immediately."

Duran was not going to stand for talk like this. "Enough of that talk! Tonight, we will celibate, a banquet, to my victory and crowning as the new emperor!"

"Here, Here!" Sarris replied. "Taylor, a true warrior never talks of defeat!"

"I'm not! I'm just a little out of my depth here, I'm just being practical."

Jovan turned to Taylor. "I understand this is difficult for you. You have been thrust into a world that is very alien to your own. We have all been thrown into a situation we never expected. I need you to remain calm. You must control your anger and any other feelings you may have until the time is right."

"And when will that time be?" Taylor asked.

"I wish I could answer that for you. But when it is, you must still remain calm. As any warrior knowns, if you lose your head in battle, you will most likely end up losing your head."

Taylor laughed. "I actually get that, thanks."

"One of the best warriors I have ever trained and look at you now." Scoffed Sarris.

Taylor got curious. "You said something last night that I didn't understand. What is the deal with you two."

Sarris laughed. "He betrayed me!"

"I didn't betray you Sarris." Started Jovan. "As part of our training we spend time with different masters. As the heir to the throne, it was always assumed I would become a warrior, but when I started training with the clerics, I found a deeper, more spiritual calling that I could not shake. So, in the end I joined them, and Sarris has never forgiven me."

"You would have made a great emperor; it drove your father mad when you renounced your titles. I just wish he could have seen you altogether in better circumstances." This clearly meant a great deal to Sarris. "But, before this day is over, Duran will be emperor and you must all stand strong at his side."

"You too my old master. Unless you feel I will not make a great emperor." Said Duran. "I will need your help to clean up this mess."

Taylor jumped in. "While you are all making plans, if, sorry, WHEN we get out of this, can someone please just get me home."

"Seeing as how our fate rest with you Taylor, WHEN you get us out of this, I am sure I can let you borrow my ship." Said Alana.

"Come on." Jovan was impatient. "We need to be ready. The last thing we need to do now is keep the inquisition waiting."

They each quickly finished eating and retired to their rooms. Taylor had the feeling the clothes Alana had chosen may have been respectful, but also practical. Black knee length boots, loose-fitting pants, a tight-fitting top and three-quarter length black jacket with Durans crest on the upper arms. With the jacket gone it would give him great mobility in a fight. As he looked at himself in a full-length mirror Alana walked in.

"I knew that would look good on you." She walked over and ran her hand over the shirt. "You look the part, just don't let any of this intimidate you too much."

Taylor shrugged and puffed. "That's easy for you to say. I am bricking myself. This is the second fight I have had to go into recently and been expendable."

Alana lightly kissed him on the lips. "You're not expendable to me."

Taylor was slightly shocked; he had always been drawn to strong women and she was definitely intoxicating. He went to answer but was cut short by three slow bangs on the main doors. They were opened and once again Jarren entered the room. He spoke in a loud commanding voice. "You are all hereby commanded, without delay, to attend the throne room and face your inquisition!" He stood, almost to attention. Seeming he had gone from a simple valet to someone of importance, or at least that was how he felt.

They all gathered; Taylor noticed Duran was dressed similarly to him apart from his jacket. Duran's jacket was strikingly ornate, adorned with intricate gold and silver embroidery, along with what appeared to be precious stones studding its surface. It was evident that this choice of attire was intended to send a clear message, showing who was the most important person in the room.

"Please follow me." Jarren turned and started to walk towards the throne room. As the group followed, guards fell in behind them. Entering, they could see many people were already seated and talking amongst themselves. They formed a semi-circle in front of a slightly raised platform with five impressive chairs on it. In front and to the left were two chairs and to the right Cassius was already seated in his hover chair, behind him sat Kai. Jarren stopped and turned. "Lord Duran, Taylor. Please take the seats to the left. Your guests can be seated with the rest of the people."

Taylor a Duran walked over and took their seats while Alana, Jovan and Sarris walked to the front of the onlookers. Looking, Alana could see all the seat were taken, she walked up to the people on the left end of the front row. "Do you know who I am?" She asked in a very stern tone. The people looked shocked but obviously did. "Then find somewhere else to sit!" Three people quickly got up and moved away as she took one of the now empty seats.

Jovan looked down at her disapprovingly. "Sister, it may be better if people were on our side!"

There was a slight commotion to one side of the room as a door opened and five impressively dressed figures entered the room. They walked onto the raised platform and took their seats. The chattering from the people in the room slowly died down.

"My name is Quinton of the house faber." Spoke the man sat in the middle chair. "To my right is Miles from the house Albani and Anothony from the house Gallus. To my left is Vincent from the house Maiorana and Ariana from the house Tremellius. We have been called here to make judgement on a very severe matter raised by Lord Cassius. I hereby call this inquisition to order. Lord Cassius, please stand and state your business."

Cassius spoke, trying to sound weak and feeble. "My lords, I mean this inquisition no disrespect, but may I be permitted to stay seated. I sustain quite a severe injury in the attack."

Quinton nervously adjusted his position in his seat. "Under the circumstances this will be acceptable."

"Thank you, I appreciate this concession." It was obvious to Duran Cassius was playing on his injury.

Cassius started. "The man seated next to Duran, Taylor, came to my rooms yesterday appearing to be lost. I tried to be polite to Durans guest and we got into a conversation about my weapons collection. He proceeded to show me a weapon he had from his home planet and then started to get agitated. He told me he was supposed to meet with Duran in his father's rooms and could I show him the way. When we entered the emperor's rooms, he took out the weapon, shot the guards, the nurses, myself and then slayed the emperor in his bed." The were gasps from the crowd. "The coward then ran back to his master like a pet hound to receive his reward."

Taylor jumped to his feet. "That's a lie! Your harpies took me to you. You had the gun; you did all the shooting." The crowd was once again shocked.

Quinton was enraged. "DURAN! Quiet your man or I will order him gagged!"

Duran stood, grabbing Taylors arm he pulled him back to his seat. "Now is not the time. What happened to remain calm?" He whispered.

Taylor was not so quiet. "I will not have my honour insulted by a liar who has none!"

Kai stood and took a few paces towards Taylor clutching at his sword. Cassius quickly waved at him to return to his seat. Taylor could see the anger on

Cassius's face, but Jovan was right, he was not going to be easily provoked.

Quinton rose from his chair. "Silence!" he ordered. The crowd started to settle with Quinton re-taking his seat. "Lord Cassius, please continue."

"Thank you. Scans have found the man Taylor, is an inhabitant of the banishment planet Terra, located in the Orion Spur. As you know my lords, unauthorised landings on a banishment world are forbidden, and removal of anyone is a capital crime. I can only conclude Duran went there to find a gullible simpleton to do his bidding, killing his father and making him the emperor. For all we know he also ordered the death of his brother." There were more gasps and muttering from the crowd. "I respectfully request this inquisition find them both guilty and sentence them to death!"

Quinton spoke. "Silence, if the audience cannot control itself, I will have the room cleared." He paused, waiting for quiet. "Thank you Lord Cassius. Lord Duran, you may now answer the charge."

Duran stood and cleared his throat. "Thank you my Lord. I admit to the charge of landing on Terra. In doing so my only intent was to try to locate a journal made by Bede of the house Eachus. It was intended as a dowery gift for Claudia of Eachus. Unfortunately, while locating the journal I was captured by Taylor and his men. I struck a deal, in exchange for my freedom I had to provide them with data they could use to advance their technology. We were on Cellus doing this when we were detained and brought here by Kai." Duran paused, he needed to remain calm and keep his voice clear with no emotion. "While I have no first-hand knowledge, I believe Taylor when he tells me he was tricked into going to Cassius's rooms, I told him to wait in my rooms and not to meet me anywhere. I also believe him when he says he was tricked into giving Cassius his gun, the gun that took the life from my father by Cassius's hand. I have only known Taylor a few days, in that time I have found him to be an honourable man, so I have no reason to believe he is lying. As most of you know, I have never sought the throne, that should have been Jovan or Milo. I was happy to be the third spare son and just get on with my life. The only thing I did to hurt my father, was seek to marry a woman he didn't approve of." Duran turned and took his seat.

The room fell completely silent, for a moment it felt as if everyone were lost in Durans words. Quinton seemed cautious to break the silence. "Thank you Lord Duran." He adjusted his posture and cleared his throat. "Taylor, you may now speak, but I warn you I will not tolerate any outbursts!"

Nervously, Taylor rose to his feet. He wished he had better prepared himself for this. "Urrmm, thank you, err, My Lords. Um, until a few days ago, I didn't know any of this, of you, existed. On my planet, we thought there had to be life out in the universe, but we could not be sure. Um, Duran is right in what he said. When we first met, we had one hell of a fight. It took ten of us to take him down. And at first, we didn't believe he had come all the way to our home, just for a diary. Like he said, it was only after we came out here, we found out he had problems at home. He was going to send us all home with his sister, but, well then, we got split up and I ended up here. I was tricked into going to Cassius's rooms. He did trick me into giving him my gun. He told me it would make a nice addition to his collection. He then used it to kill the emperor and everyone else in that room, including shooting himself. He even told me this was his plan as he threw the gun back to me. YES! I panicked; I ran back to Duran; he was the only person I could trust. Look, all I want to do is get back home. I didn't kill the emperor; Cassius is the one you want!"

People in the room gasped and started to mutter with each other. They all knew insulting such a powerful man in this way was a dangerous game to play. As Taylor returned to his seat, he looked at Cassius from the corner of his eye. He could see from his body language he wasn't happy. Kai on the other hand looked as if he were about to explode.

"Is there anyone else who feels they have the right to speak on this matter?" Quinton scanned the room as people looked around expecting someone to speak up. "In that case the inquisition will retire to consider the matter." The five barons stood and walked out the door they had come in.

Kai went to his father's side and whispered. "Father, why do you let this man insult you so openly. Let me split him in two for you."

Cassius smiled. "Patience my son. They cannot prove anything. The barons will have no choice but to find in my favour, then the executioner can take their heads and I can rule with you at my side."

Jovan walked over to Duran and Taylor. "How are we doing?" Asked Taylor.

"As well as expected, badly." Was Jovans simple answer. "Cassius is no fool. He knows we have no way to prove your innocence in the matter."

"You know, on earth, our justice system works on the basis of innocent until proven guilty."

Jovan smiled. "It does here too, well mostly. But this is an extreme case that must be resolved quickly and decisively. I agree it is not perfect, but with two differing points of view, no evidence for either side, their choice will be limited. The decision usually goes to the one who brought the allegation."

"Look at him sat over there all happy and smug." Taylor sneered in Cassius direction.

Duran placed his hand on Taylors shoulder. "I am sorry I got you into this my friend. When the barons return, it is highly likely that they will find against us and sentence us to death. I just hope you can face this with honour and dignity."

Taylor shrugged. "Dignity I can do, not sure there is much honour in any of this. I don't blame you; you warned us, and you were right, we are not prepared to be out here." The side door opened, and the barons returned to the room. Taylor felt worried. "Wow, that was quick, can't be good for us."

As the barons returned to their seats so did the rest of the people. Quinton waited until everyone had settled. "Would all parties in this matter please stand." Duran stood followed by Taylor taking his cue from him. "Lord Cassius, if you could please also stand." Cassius's expression became that of a man who was intensely annoyed. He signalled Kai to help him.

Quiton stood, pausing for a moment to collect his thoughts. "We have been asked here to consider and assign judgement for this inquisition. Due to the lack of testimony and evidence it has been very difficult. We can only make judgement on the facts we have to hand. Cassius has been a man of honour, good standing and Lord chancellor for the last ten years. Duran although also a man of good standing has admitted to several wrong doings that cannot be ignored. Finally, Taylor, a man we know very little about. He is from a banishment world, probably descended from a traitor and therefor a traitor himself. With these facts alone we must rule in favour of Lord Cassius and condemn Duran and Taylor." Gasps and muttering came from the assembled crowd.

Cassius looked visibly pleased; he had got what he was expecting. He squeezed Kai's arm tightly. "You see my son. Once they are dead there is nothing to stop us!"

Quinton paused again waiting for the crowd to settle. "It is the decision of the inquisition that Taylor be sentenced to death, sentence to be carried out without delay." More gasps came from the crowd while Cassius's smile grew even larger. "As the inquisition can show no direct involvement by Duran in the death of his father, he is to be exiled to the planet Terra for the rest of his life. This is the final judgement of this inquisition, and it is now closed!" Quinton sat back in his chair.

The crowd became more excited, some not believing in the judgement, others desperate for more blood. Cassius lost his smile. This wasn't what he needed.

"My Lords." Cassius blurted out. "No Direct involvement? He brought the assassin here!"

"We were told your son brought him here. Would you like us to reconsider the verdict?" Quinton was not happy about being questioned.

"No my lord, my apologies." Cassius returned to his hover chair, suddenly a man who didn't look in that much pain.

Kai clumsily tried to help him. "Father, what is wrong you got what you wanted."

301

Cassius sat, seething. "No, I needed them both dead, so I never have to worry about Duran again."

More and more of the people in the room returned to their chairs, all except Taylor. He could see Cassius was angry, Maybe now was the time, maybe this was his moment. Honour and dignity. He took a few paces towards the seated lords. "My Lords, may I be permitted to speak?"

Quinton looked down on him. "You may, but the verdict cannot be changed, and I will not tolerate any outbursts!"

"Thank you." Taylor turned and faced the crowd. "If I must go to my death I can do so with honour and dignity." He turned to face Cassius. "You may try to convince yourself, and those around you, that you are a man of honour, but you're not. When I die, I will go to my death knowing I have told the truth and so will the people close to me. You will spend the rest of your life knowing you are a liar. You will always have that looking over your shoulder and wonder, who else sees through your lies."

In his chair Cassius' blood started to boil. Everything he had wanted, planned for, was within his grasp. He desperately tried to process the anger he had. There was very little chance that Duran would ever come back to challenge him, but that was too great of a chance. He needed him dead, not in days or years, he needed to see his dead body at his feet now. Could he be sure if he threw down a challenge

Duran would step in. He had to, he knew Duran would have no choice, his honour would force him to protect a weaker man who was by his side. He stood, once again trying to make a show of his wounds. "HOW DARE YOU!" He yelled. "You, a condemned man, who continues to insult me. You are nothing! I will not allow you the quick easy death given by the executioner. I would have you suffer in your last minutes and regret ever opening your mouth."

A hush fell over the room.

Taylor took a pace towards Cassius. "You have nothing that can scare me! All you are good for is shooting unarmed women and old men in their beds. All I see is a coward."

Kai could no longer take it, jumping to his feet and charging towards Taylor roaring in anger. Taylor calmly stood his ground. Waiting until the last second, he skilfully moved to one side, tripping the big man, sending him crashing to the floor. Duran rushed to Taylor side ready to defend him.

"STOOOOOOOP!" Roar Quinton. "GUARDS! Draw your weapons and stun anyone that does not stand fast." The guards surrounded the group pointing their weapons. "All of you, return to your seats before I lose patience!" The guards motioned with their guns and order was restored, each man returning to his seat.

Duran turned to Taylor. "Once again you surprise me. Maybe there is a small chance we will not die today."

Taylor scoffed. "Just another bad plan. I guess it's all down to you now."

Quinton stood. "Never have I had to witness such dishonourable conduct. Lord Cassius, do you wish to forgo the verdict of this inquisition and challenge Taylor?"

Cassius stared at Taylor like a mad dog. "Yes! Yes I do My Lord. Due to my injury my son will fight to prove my honour."

Quinton turned to Taylor. "Taylor, You have been challenged. You have no choice but to accept or be struck down."

Taylor stood, but before he could speak Duran pushed past him. "My Lords, by Taylors own admission he knows nothing of our ways. As we were charged together, I am responsible for him. I will undertake the challenge in his place."

"Taylor, do you understand that your lives are now bound?" Asked Quinton. "If Duran stands in your place and loses, your life is also forfeit."

Taylor considered this for a moment. "I understand. If my life were to be bound to anyone, I would want it to be this man."

Quinton shouted. "GUARDS! Prepare the challenge pit!"

The room was filled with the sound of mechanical clanking and grinding, men started to file in from all directions, moving the crowd back, bringing in stands and placing weapons on them. Slowly the floor in the middle of the room started to sink. It formed a circle about ten meters in diameter and one meter deep. Two sets of steps formed on either side followed by three sentinel bots equally spaced, rising from the floor. By the side of each set of steps, what looked to be large hour glasses also rose from the floor.

Duran removed his jacket and shirt and started to stretch. He looked at Taylor. "When you get back home, if they ask you to catch another alien, what will you tell your boss?"

Taylor burst out laughing. "No problem! Where is it!"

Duran laughed. "What would your Richards say if he were here right now."

Taylor thought. "Jim My Boy! Give um hell."

Alana, Jovan, and Sarris came over to them. "Duran, remember all I taught you, and keep out of his grasp. He will most likely charge and try and grab you, so be ready." Sarris was always the teacher.

"I will my master." Duran held out his arm to shake with Sarris. "You taught me well."

Alana embraced Duran as hard as she could. "Woah, go easy." He said. "I don't need broken ribs before I start."

She pulled away, holding him at arm's length, looking deep into his eyes. "Kill Him! Kill them Both!"

Duran smiled softly. "Anything for you sister."

Jovan took Durans hand. He closed his eyes for a moment, as if he were in prayer. He opened his eyes and smiled. "Be like water."

"Wait... What.." Taylor looked astonished. "Did you just quote.. No, forget it. Just don't get cocky and get your head crushed." Holding up his hands he turned away.

Duran and Jovan smiled in amusement. Turning, Duran walked to the top of the steps his side of the pit still stretching. Looking across he could see Kai was already waiting, teeth gritted, breathing deeply, full of rage. Duran closed his eyes and relaxed his body.

A guard struck a large gong and the room fell silent. Quinton stood. "The challenge will now commence. Fighters, enter the pit."

Both Duran and Kai walked down into the pit. Duran, calm, not even opening his eyes. Kai roared, throwing his arms in the air to the on lookers. He then stood, panting like a caged animal waiting to be set free.

"Fighters, you will obey the rules of the old ways and fight with honour. May the just prevail." Quinton sat, then nodded to the guard by the gong. The guard struck the gong, followed by the sentinel bots sounding a horn, the hour glasses rotating with the sand in them starting to flow.

Kai roared and started to charge across the pit towards Duran. In his mind, Duran could picture the approach. He could hear as each massive foot hit the ground. He counted down, waiting, waiting for the exact moment. Just as he was about to be swallowed in the oncoming grasp, Duran sat and rolled onto his back. He extended his legs, collecting Kai perfectly in the guts and pitching him high, the momentum sending him crashing into the steps behind Duran. Kai roared with frustration and pain. As he recovered to his feet, blood poured from a deep gash in his head. Duran quickly sprung to his feet and walked to the opposite side of the pit.

Kai was dazed and groggy, bringing up his fists to stagger towards Duran. Duran again waited, he brought up his fists and allowed the big man to approach. With a quick sidestep, he landed a good jab to the wound on Kai's head. This sent him reeling back to the wall of the pit. Kai lifted his arm higher to protect his head, leaving his mid-section open. Duran was quick to exploit this, stepping in to deliver a good double punch to the gut.

Taylor could not control himself as he let out a loud "YES!" He was confident Duran had this in the bag.

Duran stayed steady, taking a few steps back to the middle of the pit. The best way to kill Kai was with the sword. He just needed to pace himself till then. Kai recovered himself and glared at Duran. Pushing himself away from the wall, he approached Duran more cautiously this time with his guard up. The two men circled each other, looking for an opening. Kai swung, Duran ducked and got another shot into the mid-section. They circled again, again Kai swung, and Duran sent another blow into his ribs. Kai was ready for him; he spun and landed the back of his arm across Duran's head. The force of the blow sent him reeling across the pit. Kai chased after Duran, who quickly did a tuck and roll across the floor to keep his distance.

"FIGHT Me You coward!" Roared Kai.

Duran glanced over at one of the hourglasses. It felt like an hour had passed, not a few minutes. Moving more to the centre of the pit, Duran again lifted his guard, waiting for Kai to approach. The big man started to lay in a combination of punches and jabs. Duran held his ground, blocking, dodging, or deflecting each blow. He was waiting for a mistake; sure enough, Kai shifted his weight from the front foot. Duran quickly took advantage; he swept the foot back, causing Kai to lose balance and fall forward. As the man's entire weight came towards Duran, he skilfully raised his knee to connect with Kai's face. Such a blow would have knocked out most men, but Kai staggered to his feet once again.

Duran moved in feeling he had the upper hand. He threw a hard punch to the side of Kai's head but this time he was ready. He grabbed Durans arm and spun him at the same time, wrapping his other arm around Durans neck. As Duran felt the massive arm clamp down on him, he tried to break free. But Kai quickly brought his other arm round to complete the head lock, so it was too late. Struggle as he may Kai was just too strong. Duran tried to pound his elbows into the big man's ribs with little effect. Glancing over at the hourglass he could see he only had to hang on for a few more seconds and stopped his struggle to conserve his remaining breath. Sensing this Kai moved his hand to the side of Durans head in an attempt to break Durans neck. Instinctively, Duran forced his hand between Kai's lock to prevent this. Duran felt consciousness slowly slipping away from him as he saw the last few grains of sand drain from the top of the hourglass.

The horn sounded from the sentinel bots to signal the end of the round, but it didn't. Instead of releasing his grip Kai squeezed harder than before. One of the sentinel's fired a stun blast into Kai. He convulsed from the shock, dropping to the ground releasing his hold. Duran started to crawl back to the steps on his side of the pit, gasping for air as he went. Standing, Kai started to move towards Duran then noticed the sentinels tracking him and thought better of it.

Crawling up the steps Duran was relieved to see Sarris waiting for him with a flask of water. "Here, drink." Duran downed a mouthful then washed out his mouth and spat to one side. He took the rest of the flask and poured it over his head. "You cannot let him get his hands on you. He is too strong." Said his teacher.

Duran, still panting, looked at Sarris. "I think you know I know that! Get me the sticks."

"Are you sure?" Questioned Sarris. "You know he will go for the staff."

"Sticks!" Duran was sure of his choice. Sarris took the sticks from the rack and passed them to him. Duran stood and started to breathe deeply to get his oxygen levels back up. Sarris was right, of course. Kai had gone straight to his rack and taken a staff. Duran was again hoping his speed with the sticks could overcome the power and reach of the staff.

Both men took their position in the pit. Kai still seething that victory had been taken from him, Duran still trying to catch his breath. The horn sounded from the sentinels and the fight restarted.

Kai jerked his staff into the air. Grabbing one end with both hands he started to slowly whirl it around his head. His arms and the length of the staff far out reaching that of Duran.

Duran took a deep breath and twirled the sticks in a display of agility. He waited, watching, again he was in no rush. Kai started to walk towards Duran, slowly closing the gap between them. Duran stepped back again waiting for Kai to give away his move. He did, changing his stance Kai swung the staff hard towards Durans head. Duran was ready, he dropped using the sticks to deflect the staff up, then spinning forward on his knees under the swing, he struck hard connecting with Kai's right knee.

Kai roared with pain, stagging to the wall for support. With a quick tuck and roll Duran was back on his feet on the other side of the pit. Turning, Kai faced Duran, grasping his staff in a more traditional stance. He swung and lunged with the staff each time finding his thrusts blocked by Duran. Kai spun round bring the staff up high and then striking down for Durans head. Raising his sticks, Duran crossing them to catch the blow, quickly adjusting to put a heavy blow of his own into Kai's right side. Staggering back, Kai quickly regained his composure, trying not to show the pain he was in. Duran glanced over at one of the hour glasses, he just had to keep him at bay for a few more minutes.

Kai came at Duran again. He swung the staff for all he was worth. Each swing met by another block or deflection. His anger getting greater and greater. Starting to fight more with power than any form of skill was getting him nowhere. With a roar Kai charged at Duran using the staff more as a lance. Duran dodged and caught one of the passing legs with a stick. Kai, crashing into the wall slumped to the ground looking exhausted. Panting heavily, he got back to his feet ready for his next attack only to hear the horn sound and end the round.

The two men fixed their eyes across the pit as they slowly returned to their sides. Kai broke his gaze first, but he had no intention of giving in that easy. Duran let down his guard and turned away. Kai quickly glanced back, seeing Duran walking away he turned and swung the staff at full stretch connecting with Durans upper arm so hard you could hear the bones shatter across the room. Large gasps came from the on lookers and one of the sentinel robots blasted Kai, sending him reeling across the floor.

Taylor and Sarris jumped to their feet and rushed down to Duran. "Duran! How bad are you injured?" Asked Sarris.

Durans mangled arm and shoulder said it all. "Arrgggg! Bad, that dishonourable piece of shit!"

Sarris gently felt around the arm. "Collar bone, shoulder, upper arm, all broken. You can't fight like this."

"I have no choice! Get me up, strap it as best you can." Duran struggle to stand.

Taylor stood. He looked over as Kai slowly crawled back to his steps, he started to walk over.

"TAYLOR!" Boomed Quinton. "What do you think you are doing."

"This man is a coward and a cheat! I thought you had rules, I thought this fight was conducted with honour. I have seen none of this from him. He has shattered Durans arm, there is no way he can fight now."

"Kai has been punished for his actions under the rules. Duran has no choice; he must move on to the next round or forfeit."

Taylor was incensed. "Punished! He will recover from that stun in minutes. This is bullshit! Duran won't have a chance."

Quinton was starting to lose patience. "This is the way of the challenge. If you don't like it, you should never have accepted."

"Wait!" Taylor didn't like what he was thinking. "I accepted the challenge. Duran stepped in for me, Can I not step in for Duran?"

The barons started to whisper between each other before Quinton finally spoke. "This is an unusual request, but not unheard of. For that reason, we can see no reason why you can't." Quinton began to chuckle. "You're going to lose your head either way."

"Don't be so sure of that!" Taylor ran back over to Duran. He threw off his jacket and shirt and grabbed a sword from the rack. "Duran. Can I take him?"

Through the pain Duran smiled. "Yes!"

Taylor marched down the steps into the pit, he could see Kai was still slumped on the steps his side, so he started to warm up with some Kenjutsu movements.

Sarris was concerned. "Is this wise, does he have any idea what he is doing?"

"He is better than he knows." Said Duran. "Still, he has more of a chance than I do."

Sarris was not so sure. "I hope you are right."

Taylor was getting impatient waiting and started to taunt Kai. "Come on you piece of shit. Get off your fat arse, get a sword in your hand and prepare to die. I ent gunna cheat like you, I'm just gunna kill ya!"

Cassius walked over to the stand and took a sword. He went over to Kai's side and handed him the blade. "Look at that puny excuse for a man. I'm surprised he even knows how to hold a sword let alone use it. Now be a good son, go and carve the flesh from his bones for me."

"I will father. Then I will remove Durans head and place it at your feet."

The two men grinned at each other. Kai stood, then moved down into the pit. He glared across at Taylor, he was going to enjoy this. Taylor stopped what he was doing, he turned, taking up a stance, blade extended in both hands ready to fight. Kai just stood, his blade extended in one hand, he had no respect for Taylor in the slightest.

The horn sounded from the sentinels and both men just stood there. "I thought you were in a hurry for me to end you." Scoffed Kai. Taylor said nothing, he slid back his right foot and turned his sword slowly down and behind him. He wanted Kai to commit to the first move.

Kai let out a slight laugh then lunged towards Taylor. In a flash, Taylor brought up his blade to defect the lunge then quickly to one side slashing under Kai's extended arm. Looking down at the wound, blood dripping on to the floor, Kai no longer had a smile on his face. Taylor stepped back, left foot in front of right in a wide stance, the sword hilt up to his face, the back of the blade resting on his left arm. His eyes, fixed along its length at the now worried man.

Kai paced like a caged animal; a cage built in his own mind. He had never learnt the lesson of not underestimating his opponents, he had never needed to. As Kai paced, Taylor slowly kept the point of his blade fix on its target. Kai started to slash his sword from side to side through the air, Taylor knew this was a distraction and stayed in his stance. Quickly changing position, Kai swung his blade to come down on Taylors head. Swiftly blocking it, Taylor swept the blow to one side then thrashed back across Kai's upper leg making a deep cut.

315

There was a large gasp from the crowd. Even Sarris was starting to be impressed. "Your right, he does seem to have an unusual set of skills." He said to Duran.

Stepping back, Taylor stood, holding the sword against his chest with both hands. Kai's eyes were now those of a man filled with rage, and fear. With a roar he charged at Taylor, wildly swinging his blade with all the power he had. Blocking every swing, Taylor danced around the pit and his opponent. Kai broke off, screaming in anger.

"I will kill you! I WILL KILL HIM!" Roared Kai, glaring at Duran.

Taylor slowly circled around Kai keeping his distance, eyes fixed on his every move. For the first time Taylor noticed the wounds he had inflicted on Kai had nearly stopped bleeding, 'Bloody nanites' he thought to himself.

Kai tried to compose himself. He took up a traditional stance with the sword held forward in both hands. Taylor mimicked him, his blade tip next to Kai's. Taylor rocked forward with a small slow step; Kai retreated. He moved again, Taylor was hoping to bait him into attacking, Kai held fast.

Taylor could see a smile starting to form on Kai's face. "I am going to make you beg for mercy." Kai taunted, then lunged.

That was all Taylor needed, his body just took over. Pushing Kai's thrust to one side he took a step forward then spinning, his blade going to its full reach in his right hand, he could feel the resistance as the blade passed through Kai's neck.

"Fuck your mercy!" Taylor turned and fell to his knees his body drained. The empty eyes of Kai's severed head staring back at him. Gasps came from the onlookers, some moving around to get a better look, others turning away in horror.

Cassius screamed. "NOOOOO!" Then dropped to all fours at the side of the pit. He looked down at his son in total disbelief.

Staggering to his feet Taylor turned to find the faces of his friends. They looked down on him from the top of the pit with obvious expressions of relief and joy. Slowly, the same feelings started to wash over Taylor. He had done it, he had saved not only himself, but so much more. He closed his eyes and pictured Sarahs face smiling at him. 'I'm sorry' he said to himself. 'Now I know you can rest in peace.'

Quinton stood and pointed at Cassius, "Guard!" He shouted. A group of the guard quickly moved to Cassius. Grabbing him, they dragged then threw him down the steps to land in a heap at Taylors feet. "Taylor," Continued Quinton. "You have been shown to be just. It is now your right to complete this by taking the head of your accuser, Cassius."

Taylor looked down at the cowering man in front of him, then he turned to look at Duran. He felt conflicted on what to do. "My Lord, I am sorry I cannot take the life of a man in cold blood."

Quinton turned to Duran. "Lord Duran, as the second in this challenge the honour must fall to you."

Duran considered this for a moment. "Thank you my lord. I accept this man's life. First, with respect, can you confirm that I will now be emperor?"

"Why yes my lord. By right, and by blood. You will be crowned emperor at the earliest opportunity." Quinton dropped to first position. One by one everyone else in the room followed suit, it took a poke from Sarris for Alana to show the same respect.

Duran looked down at Cassius who was still on his hands and knees. He spoke in a firm tone. "Cassius!" Looking up to see Duran glaring down at him, Cassius slowly and painfully adjusted his position.

Duran surveyed the room around him. "I, Duran of the house Tar, hear by claim the position and title of emperor by right of blood. I also claim dominion over all lands and people held by the previous emperor my father Borrell. I hereby command that the following preparations should be made. Three days from now at dawn, we will hold a funeral to lay my father and brother to rest, and at noon my coronation. Please stand." The people started to rise to their feet. "NOT YOU Cassius!" Duran wanted to make sure he knew his place. "I am naming my brother, Jovan, as Lord Chancelor." There were gasps from the crowd. "I know this breaks from tradition, but under my rule, there will be many changes. I also name my sister, Alana, as head of the Imperial Guard, Sarris you will mentor her for a year."

Sarris bowed deeply. "Your Majesty, you honour me."

Duran laughed. "I hope you can still say that in a few months."

Alana smiled. "Brother, what are you insinuating? Don't worry, I won't let you down. This will be fun."

"I will need my family close by my side. I will need people I can trust to sort out this mess, undo all the changes made by Cassius without the empire falling apart." Duran knew there was a lot of work to be done. "Taylor, you should also be rewarded, I need to find a way to show this."

Taylor noticed he was still holding the blooded sword and threw it to one side. "Look Duran, all I want to do is go home. I have had enough excitement for one lifetime."

Duran chuckled. "I expect you have. Alana said she would loan you her ship so that isn't a problem. You will also have my eternal gratitude and I will have your planet removed from the list of banishment worlds. Maybe with your newfound knowledge your people will venture out and join us."

319

Taylor laughed. "More likely to blow the crap out of each other first, But I hope so. Be nice to catch up when things have calmed down."

"That we will my friend." Duran turned to look down on Cassius. "Cassius, for your betrayal to my father and the empire, everything that was yours is now mine by right. Your life is also forfeit and belongs to me. I will however not take it today. I want you to see me crowned emperor before you die. GUARDS! Take Cassius to the cells, search him and place him in chains. He is to be shown no privileges." The guards moved in to drag Cassius away.

Sarris moved over to Duran and whispered. "Is this wise? He should be put to death immediately."

"You are probably right. But I want him to suffer, and I want to be the one that does it. Besides, it will be hard to swing a sword until my arm heals." Duran turned. "Alana, make sure he is well guarded, with men from our house."

Alana bowed. "Yes, Your Majesty! Oh, I like this."

"So, Taylor. We have a lot of work to do. Let's start by getting you on your way home. Alana, tell your ship to prepare and take us to it."

Taylor climbed out from the pit, he grabbed his shirt and put it back on. Following Alana out to her ship not much was said. Each in their own way coming to terms with all they had just been through.

At the ramp Alana stopped. "I have told the ship to take you home. If you go straight into stasis, at hyper speed you should arrive home just a few days after the rest of your friends."

"Thanks, I appreciate it."

Alana embraced Taylor and gave him a long slow passionate kiss. "Maybe the next time we meet we can get to know each other a little better."

"I think I would enjoy that." Smiled Taylor.

Duran held his unbroken arm out to Taylor which he grasped. "Taylor, I will miss your company!"

"Likewise! Hey, if there is ever a next time, let's make it a little less exciting."

"Indeed! Now be on your way and have a safe journey. We have an empire to rebuild."

Taylor turned and walked up the ramp. The ramp and door closed as the ships lift engines slowly started to push it away from the ground. Entering the command deck he sat in the first seat he saw with a huge sigh. "Ship, you know what you are doing?"

"Yes, I do. Best speed to Earth. Please prepare for stasis."

Taylor settled back in his chair and closed his eyes. A big smile came over his face, Richards was going to get one hell of a debrief.

Duran's Next Adventure.

DURAN
The Improbable Child

James Kilbraith

What if an AI could care.
Death would not always be the end of the journey.

Scan for more information.

This is a work of fiction. Names, characters, events, and incidents are the
products of the author's imagination. Any resemblance to actual persons,
living or dead, or actual events are purely coincidental. It contains
descriptions of violence and some offensive language.
www.jameskilbraith.co.uk

Printed in Great Britain
by Amazon

53829722R00178